TERMINATOR
SALVATION
TRIAL BY FIRE

Also available from Titan Books:

TERMINATOR SALVATION
From the Ashes
By Timothy Zahn

TERMINATOR SALVATION

The official movie novel
By Alan Dean Foster

TERMINATOR SALVATION

Cold War
By Greg Cox

TERMINATOR SALVATION
TRIAL BY FIRE

TIMOTHY ZAHN

TITAN BOOKS

Terminator: Trial by Fire
ISBN: 9781848560888

Published by
Titan Books
A division of
Titan Publishing Group Ltd
144 Southwark St
London
SE1 0UP

First edition July 2010
10 9 8 7 6 5 4 3 2 1

Visit our website:
www.titanbooks.com

Did you enjoy this book? We love to hear from our readers. Please email us at readerfeedback@titanemail.com or write to us at Reader Feedback at the above address.

To receive advance information, news, competitions, and exclusive Titan offers online, please register as a member by clicking the "sign up" button on our website: www.titanbooks.com

For James Middleton,
who brought me into the Resistance and guided
those first tentative steps.

CHAPTER ONE

His name was Jik.

That wasn't the name his mother had given him, back in those quiet, peaceful times before the horror of Judgment Day. But it was the name everyone had always called him, ever since his first week in school. It was what his classmates had called him, and his teachers, his friends, and eventually even his college professors. Everyone called him Jik.

Even the thing that was stalking him through the tangled woods of the eastern Sierra Nevada mountains called him Jik.

The thing that was trying to kill him.

"Jik?" the gruff voice called through the fading light of evening. "Jik? Come on, friend, this is ridiculous. I'm not going to rob you—I promise. All I want is to talk."

You're not my friend! Jik wanted to shout back. But he knew better. Making any noise, giving any hint of where he was, would be suicide. Besides, his throat still hurt from that branch he'd run into two days ago. Pressing his back a little harder into the thick bole of the tree behind him, he tried to think.

There really wasn't much thinking left for him to do.

There were just the two of them out here in the forest. The thing back there wanted to kill Jik. Jik didn't want to die. All very simple, all very cut and dried.

Jik swallowed hard around his sore throat as he resettled his grip around the big handgun that was all that stood between him and death. This particular section of mountains hadn't suffered much from the missiles of Judgment Day, and the trees and shrubs were thick enough to give him plenty of cover.

Unfortunately, plenty of cover for him also meant plenty of cover for his stalker.

"Jik?"

Jik hunched his shoulders, wondering for the thousandth time what the hell kind of Terminator that was back there. It wasn't a T-600—that much he was sure of. The rubber-skinned T-600s barely had faces, let alone voices. It wasn't a T-700, either, the nightmarish dark-metal skeletons that Skynet used these days as their basic ground troops. This was something new.

"Jik?"

Jik peered up through the canopy of matted tree branches above him. The cloud cover was a mottled gray-white, and had gotten visibly darker over the past half-hour as the sun continued its slide behind the mountains toward the distant Pacific Ocean. In other circumstances, darkness would be a friend, giving him a chance to slip away.

But darkness wouldn't help against a Terminator. Darkness would just be one more enemy.

Which meant Jik had to have this out right now.

He lowered his eyes, focusing once more on the gun pointed toward the sky in front of him. It was a Smith & Wesson Model 29, an eight-inch barrel wrapped around a .44 magnum cartridge. More like a small cannon than a regular gun, really, a copy of the weapon Clint Eastwood had carried in *Dirty Harry* and which had been the pride of his father's collection. A single round could probably take down a small buffalo, if there were any buffalo nearby that needed taking down. Hopefully, a single round could also take down a Terminator.

If it couldn't, he was in trouble, because he only had three rounds left.

"Jik?"

Jik grimaced. From the direction of the voice, it sounded like the Terminator had moved to the base of the small defile that Jik himself had climbed earlier, a deep crease in the earth's surface that led up to the tree Jik was currently hiding behind. On both sides of the gap were trees and thick stands of bushes, impossible to get through without making a lot of noise. If the Terminator back there was smart—and so far it definitely seemed smarter than the T-600s Jik had tangled with back in Los Angeles—it would probably move up the pass instead of trying to climb the bank.

But not until it was sure Jik was up there.

"Jik?"

Taking a deep breath, keeping as quiet as he could, Jik worked his way back up from his crouch into a standing position. Getting to the next large tree should make enough noise to attract the Terminator's attention, while still leaving Jik able to cover the top of the defile. He stepped away from the tree.

And suddenly a figure burst into view, charging up the defile toward him, its feet scattering dirt and rock. Spinning around, Jik squeezed the trigger.

The blast hammered across his ears, the recoil of the gun jamming his arm back into his shoulder. The

Terminator's charge stopped in mid step with the impact as the big bullet slammed into its chest.

It was as Jik fired his second round that his eyes caught up with his brain, and he saw that his pursuer wasn't a Terminator at all.

It was just a simple, normal man.

But the horrifying realization had come an eternity too late. The slug slammed into the wide-eyed human, boring through the hole the first round had blown in his chest and pitching him backward down the defile. He slid halfway down and then ground to a halt, the tips of his scuffed shoes still visible.

Jik stared at the man's unmoving feet, his breath coming in little gasps of relief and bitter shame. His knees fluttered and gave way, and he dropped into a crouch amid the soft matting of dirt and pine needles, his stomach churning and wanting to be sick.

He'd just killed a man.

Minutes passed. Jik never knew afterward how many. Enough that his knees hurt when he finally straightened up again.

He'd killed a man. Not deliberately, really. Certainly in the belief that he was acting in self-defense. But the fact was that a human being was now dead, and Jik had done it, and there was nothing he could do to change that.

All he could do now was give the man a decent burial. That was what made men different, a Resistance fighter in LA had once told him. Terminators left their fallen on the streets. Human beings buried theirs.

Sliding the .44 back into its holster, he walked tiredly over to the dead man. The human had landed flat on his back, his arms flung over his head as if he was trying to surrender. His chest was soaked with blood, and Jik could see the ends of a couple of broken ribs sticking out.

If the man's chest was a nightmare, his face was even more so. There was a long jagged scar trailing out from beneath his right eye, and the entire left side of his face was a splotchy, sickly white, as if he'd been burned by acid.

Maybe he'd absorbed a massive dose of radiation during the hell of Judgment Day, though how he could be walking around after a jolt like that was a mystery. Still, radiation poisoning might explain the insanity of his trying to chase down and kill a perfect stranger.

And then, Jik spotted a glint of metal protruding from the gaping wound.

He leaned closer, his heart suddenly starting to pound again. He hadn't imagined it: the broken rib ends weren't made of bone. They were made of metal.

What the *hell*?

He snatched out the Smith & Wesson again, pointing it at the body as he knelt beside it. Gingerly, he pulled back the layer of skin and peered into the wound.

There was a heart in there, all right, or at least there had been before the .44 slug had torn through it. He could see a pair of lungs, part of a stomach, and what seemed to be a somewhat truncated circulatory system. There were blood vessels going upward from the heart, which implied there was a human brain tucked into the skull behind those staring eyes.

Or maybe not. The T-600s got along just fine with computer chips for brains, and there was no reason he knew of why this thing couldn't do so as well. The skin seemed real, too.

But between the skin and the organs, everything else was metal. Metal ribs, metal plating behind the ribs, metal spine, metal shoulder blades.

Jik had been right the first time. The thing chasing him through the mountains had indeed been a Terminator. Some chilling hybrid of man and machine, straight from the back porch of hell.

He looked up at the darkening sky. He was still a couple of days out from the little mountainside town of Baker's Hollow that was his goal, the town where his uncle had once lived and where Jik had spent a couple of weeks each summer when he was a boy. If the town still existed—if Skynet hadn't already found it and destroyed it—maybe someone would remember him and let him stay.

He looked at his watch, then slid off his backpack and pulled out the precious radio he'd lugged all the way from Los Angeles. It was nearly time for John Connor's nightly broadcast to the world, and there was no way that Jik was going to miss that.

The message tonight was brief.

"This is John Connor, speaking for the Resistance. We've won a major battle, struck a vital blow for humanity against the machines. I can report now that Skynet Central, the enemy's big San Francisco hub, has been utterly destroyed, as have large numbers of Terminators.

"But this victory has come at a horrendous cost. Now, more than ever, we need you. Come to us—look for our symbol—and join us. Humanity will win. I promise you that. All of you who are listening to my voice, you are part of us. You are the Resistance. Stay safe, keep fighting, and survive.

"This is John Connor, for the Resistance, signing off."

Jik waited a moment, then shut off the radio and stowed it away in his pack, his eyes drifting once again to the abomination lying in the leaves and twigs beside him.

The difference between humanity and the Terminators, the words whispered through his mind, *is that humans bury their dead.*

Ten minutes later he was on the move again, picking his way through the growing darkness, hoping to find someplace hidden or at least a little more defensible where he could spend the night. The body he left covered by a thin layer of dirt, stones, and leaves.

Maybe the saying was right. But the dead man back there wasn't one of theirs.

Not anymore.

CHAPTER TWO

The T-600 was in bad shape.

Really bad shape. One leg was completely gone, the other had been twisted and then mashed flat, and the minigun still gripped in its hand was long since empty and useless. Its eyes still glowed their malevolent red, but there was nothing to speak of behind the glow, not since the Skynet Central command structure that had once controlled it had been reduced to slag. The T-600 was more pitiful now than actually dangerous.

Barnes shot it anyway.

He watched with grim satisfaction as the light in the machine's eyes faded to darkness.

"For my brother," he muttered.

Not that the T-600 cared. Or would have even if it had been functional.

We bury our dead, the old defiant Resistance claim ran accusingly through Barnes's mind. *We bury our dead*.

There was a burst of gunfire to his left, and Barnes looked up from the empty Terminator eyes. Kyle Reese was over there, and even at this distance Barnes could see the grim set to the kid's jaw as he blew away another of the crippled Terminators. As Barnes watched, Reese stepped over to another twitching machine and fired a half-dozen rounds into it.

Shaking his head, Barnes swung the barrel of his SIG 542 assault rifle up onto his shoulder. Glancing around at the rest of the clean-up team scattered across the half-slagged debris field, he headed toward Reese.

The kid had just unloaded another third of a magazine when Barnes reached him.

"Hey! Reese!" he called.

Reese paused in his work. "Yes?"

Barnes gestured down at the twisted mass of metal at the kid's feet.

"You think that's the one who got Connor?" he asked.

"What?"

"Or that one?" Barnes asked, pointing back at the last Terminator Reese had blown apart. "Or that one over there?"

"No, of course not," Reese said, a wave of anger and pain flickering across his face.

"Then stop taking this personally," Barnes said firmly. "Stop taking *them* personally. They're machines, nothing more. Skynet's your enemy the way a thunderstorm or earthquake is your enemy. *It* isn't taking this personally. You can't, either."

For a moment Reese just glared up at him. Then, reluctantly, he lowered his eyes.

"I know," he said.

"Then act like it," Barnes growled. He pointed again at the Terminator at Reese's feet. "One or two rounds into the skull is all you need. More than that and you're just wasting ammo."

Reese nodded. "Yeah," he said. "Sorry."

"It's okay," Barnes said, feeling a small tugging at his

heart as he gazed at the kid's solemn face. How many times, he wondered, had he had to hear that same speech from Connor? Enough times, obviously, that he now had the whole thing memorized.

Distantly, he wondered how many times his brother Caleb had had to hear it.

"Just go easy," he told Reese. "You'll get the hang of it." He pointed to the gun in the kid's hands. "Just remember that if it takes three or four rounds to do the job, go ahead and spend those three or four rounds. Saving ammo is just as stupid as wasting it if saving it gets someone killed. Especially if that someone is you."

For a second he saw something else flick across Reese's face, and waited for the obvious retort: that maybe Reese's own life wasn't worth saving anymore. That maybe it would be better for everyone if he *did* just let himself get killed. God knew Barnes felt that way himself a couple of times a month.

But to his surprise the kid didn't go that direction.

"Okay," he said instead. "Sorry. This whole thing is still…" He trailed off.

"Kind of new," Barnes finished for him, impressed in spite of himself. Maybe Reese was actually smart enough not to base his ideas and future plans on how his emotions were churning at the moment. Barnes had known plenty of people who'd never learned that lesson.

Or maybe it was just that the kid didn't have the guts to say something that self-pitying to someone who'd lived through more of Skynet's indifferent savagery than he had.

"But you've got lots of good teachers here," Barnes went on, waving around at the other men and women moving across the field and blowing away damaged

Terminators. "Listen and learn."

Behind them a high-pitched whistle sounded, the noise cutting cleanly through the scattered gunfire. Barnes turned to see a Chinook transport chopper settling to the ground.

"Shift change," he grumbled to Reese, promising himself once again that he was going to find whoever had come up with this stupid whistle code and kick his butt. "Come on—a little food and sleep and you'll feel better."

"Okay," the kid said, his voice neutral.

Barnes grimaced as he headed toward the chopper and the squad spreading out from it, come to continue the clean-up work. That last had been a lie, and he and Reese both knew it. All the food and sleep in the world wouldn't ease the kid's pain. Not yet. Only time would soften the loss of his friend Marcus Wright, and his memories of how that hybrid Terminator had risked his life for Reese and his young friend Star, and then had sacrificed himself to save John Connor.

Just as only time would help Barnes's own memories of his brother. The memories of Caleb's last encouraging smile as he climbed aboard the chopper with Connor and the others for that ill-fated mission to Skynet's big desert lab.

But maybe there was a way to help that process along a little.

The main camp was a fifteen-minute chopper ride away. Barnes waited until his team had turned over their heavy weapons to the armorers for inspection and cleaning, then sent them over to the mess tent for a meal.

And once they were settled, he headed to the medical recovery tent to talk to John Connor.

"Barnes," Connor said in greeting when Barnes was finally allowed through by the door guards and entered the intensive-care recovery room. As usual, Connor's wife Kate was sitting at his side, a clipboard full of reports and logistics requests propped up on the edge of the bed between them. "How's the clean-up going?"

"It's going okay," Barnes said, wincing a little as he eyed the bewildering collection of tubes and monitor wires sprouting from Connor's arms and chest. Barnes had seen plenty of people die, most of them violently, but there was something about medical stuff that still made him a little squeamish. Probably the feeling that all patients who looked like this were dying by degrees, the way it had happened to his and Caleb's own mother.

"Don't worry, it's not as bad as it looks," Kate soothed.

Guiltily, angrily, Barnes wrenched his attention away from the tubes and bottles. He'd sort of gotten used to Connor reading his mind that way, but he hated it when Kate did, too.

"Yeah," he said. "I have a request."

Connor nodded. "Go ahead."

"You told me that Caleb was on the surface when Skynet blew its research lab," Barnes said. "That means he wasn't underground with the others." He braced himself. "I want to go and bury him."

Kate stirred but didn't speak. "Are you sure?" Connor asked. "It's been a couple of weeks, you know."

"It's a desert," Barnes growled. "He'll still be... You know that thing Kowlowski used to say? That Skynet leaves its fallen lying on the streets?"

"But that we bury ours," Connor finished, a flicker of something crossing his face. Maybe he was thinking about Marcus Wright, too.

"The clean-up's going fine," Barnes said. "It looks like the outer sentry line were the only Terminators that survived the blast, and most of them are pretty smashed. You've got more than enough people to clear them out—"

"All right," Connor said. "You can go."

Barnes stopped, the other four points he'd been planning to make fading away unsaid. He hadn't expected talking Connor into this would be that easy.

"You'll need a pilot," Connor continued. "I'll have Blair Williams check out a helicopter for the two of you."

A knife seemed to twist in Barnes's gut. *Williams?*

"Can I have someone else instead?" he asked.

Connor shook his head. "You two have been avoiding each other ever since San Francisco," he said. "It's time you cleared the air."

Barnes clenched his teeth.

"All due respect, this isn't the right time to do that," he said.

"Let me put it another way," Connor said. "You go with Williams, or you don't go at all."

If the man hadn't been hooked up to a hundred tubes and wires, Barnes reflected blackly, he would have considered hitting him. Not that he actually *would* have hit him, but he would definitely have considered it. As it was, he couldn't even have that minor satisfaction.

We bury our dead.

There was no point in stalling. Connor had him, and they both knew it.

"Fine," he bit out. "*If* she's willing. Otherwise, I get someone else."

"She will be," Connor promised. "I'll make sure of that. Go eat and then get some sleep. You can leave in the morning."

Barnes nodded, not trusting himself to say anything else, and stomped out of the room.

He should have known it wouldn't be *that* easy.

CHAPTER THREE

The eight-point buck was nibbling on the ends of some tree branches when it suddenly froze.

Hope Preston felt her cheek twitch. So the animal had heard them. She'd been afraid it would. Hope herself was more than capable of silent stalking, but this was the first time out for Hope's new hunting partner Susan Valentine, and the older woman simply wasn't experienced at moving through the twigs and dead leaves that matted the forest floor beneath their feet.

But it was too late now. The deer had been alerted to their presence. One more suspicious sound or movement and it would be out of here, escaping from the clearing into the deeply forested mountain slopes behind it.

Keeping her head motionless, Hope looked at Susan out the corner of her eye. There was an intent, grimly earnest expression on the woman's face, and Hope had no doubt she was going to try her hardest.

But willpower alone wasn't enough to send an arrow to its target. Susan's bow was less than rock-steady in her left hand, and the taut bowstring was wavering visibly as she held the fletching close beside her right cheek. Already she'd held position longer than should have been necessary to aim, and there was no indication even now that she was preparing to release.

It wasn't hard to guess why. That wasn't a simple softwood target out there, like the ones Hope had spent all those hours training Susan to shoot at. It was a living, feeling creature, something that would gush blood, go limp, and die. Some people simply couldn't handle that.

Hope, born and bred out here in the mountains, had a different take on the ethics of the situation. That buck out there was dinner. For the whole town.

And she was *not* going to let it get away.

Her own arrow was already nocked into her bowstring. Measuring the distance with her eyes, keeping her arrow pointed at the ground in front of her, she drew back the string as far as she could without being obvious about it. If Susan was going to stay in Baker's Hollow, she was going to have to learn how to do this. Hope could take the shot, and she would if she had to. But she would rather give Susan every reasonable chance to do it herself.

Maybe Susan sensed that. Maybe she'd come to the same conclusion about this being her make-or-break moment. A small whimper escaped her lips, and with an odd sort of abruptness she released her arrow. It flashed between the small branches of their blind and buried itself in the animal's side.

Too far back. The buck jerked with the impact, but instead of falling dead it twisted around and leaped for the pathway that led out of the clearing.

It was crouching into its second leap when Hope's arrow drove into its side, dropping it with a thud onto the ground.

Susan's bow arm sagged. "Sorry," she said.

"It's okay," Hope replied, lowering her own bow and

pulling out her whistle. "Watch your ears," she warned, and gave her personal signal: one long, four short. "Come on—let's make sure it's dead." She stepped out from behind the bushes and headed across the clearing. With only a little hesitation, Susan followed.

The buck was indeed dead.

"Good shooting," Hope said, drawing her knife and starting to dig out the arrows.

"You're very kind," Susan said, an edge of weary bitterness in her voice. "But we both know better. I missed, pure and simple."

"It's not easy to hit the heart," Hope responded diplomatically. "Especially your first time out."

Susan exhaled a quiet, shuddering sigh.

"This is my last chance, Hope," she said. "I can't sew, I can't tan, I can't cook worth anything. I barely know which end of a hammer is which. If I can't learn to hunt, there's nothing left."

"You'll get the hang of it," Hope soothed her, barely noticing the oddness of a fifteen-year-old mountain girl comforting a forty-year-old former world-class scientist. Maybe because it wasn't girl to scientist anymore, or even teacher to student. Maybe because it was now friend to friend. "Or else you'll find something else you're good at," she added. "Maybe something you don't even know about yet."

Susan sighed. "I just hope I can find this mystery talent before your father throws me out of town."

"He won't do that," Hope said firmly.

But that was a lie, and she was pretty sure Susan knew it too. Hope's father Daniel was the mayor of the small, tight-knit community that had built up in Baker's Hollow through the dark years following Judgment Day. From the very beginning one of his jobs had been to make sure that everyone who ate their food pulled their weight.

And right now, Susan was the only one who wasn't doing that. Nathan Oxley had been a molecular biologist, and his general medical training was also augmented by a leather-working hobby. Remy Lajard had been a computer programmer, but he'd also dabbled in microbrew beers in his spare time, a skill he'd brought with him to Baker's Hollow. That had made him very popular among the residents, even more popular than Oxley.

But Susan had nothing. She'd been a metallurgist, dealing with high-tech alloys and materials that were miles beyond the iron, copper, and steel that were the best anyone here had or would ever hope to have. Up to now, she'd demonstrated no other skills except the ability to put an arrow into a piece of soft wood fifty yards away. If she could parlay that into the ability to hunt, great. If she couldn't, it would be useless.

Hope's father wouldn't want to send Susan away. But he wouldn't have a choice. Duke Halverson would insist that she be expelled, and Halverson had enough clout to get his way on things like that.

Hope had seen him do it at least once before, five years ago, when that clothing store manager had stumbled half-dead into town. Three months later, having exhausted every attempt to make him useful, he'd been taken to the edge of town and ordered to leave. Halverson had seen to it personally.

Three months was Halverson's rule of thumb… and Susan's three months were nearly up.

It wouldn't be just Halverson who would insist, either. There were still fair numbers of deer and elk out there, but the wolves, coyotes, and cougars had also been coming back and were starting to seriously compete with the humans for those precious resources. Hope's hunting party had had to travel nearly seven miles from town to find this buck, and that was going to translate into a long and wearying trek back home.

A trek the town's best hunters were getting royally tired of. From the bits and pieces of her father's conversations that Hope had overheard, some of the hunters were starting to talk about abandoning Baker's Hollow and striking out on their own. Their argument was that a group of five or ten experts could survive far better alone than they were doing right now.

Which was undoubtedly true. Unfortunately, while that plan might work fine for them, it would devastate the town. Baker's Hollow only had about fifteen good-to-excellent hunters, with another ten who Hope could charitably call competent. Skimming off ten or even five of the best would leave everyone else in serious trouble. The remaining woodsmen would have to scramble like mad to bring the competent hunters up to speed, and they would absolutely have to add new people to the rolls as quickly as possible. And they would have to immediately dump anyone and anything that constituted a drain on the town's resources.

One way or another, Susan's time was running out.

Hope had finished cutting the second arrow out of the deer when she heard footsteps in the undergrowth behind them. Not the quiet and stealthy movements of fellow hunters, but the casual strides of men and women on their way to collect a kill.

"Hope?" Ned Greeley's deep voice called.

"Over here," Hope called back, standing up and waving her bow.

A minute later the big man stepped through the trees and joined them.

"Nice," he said, looking approvingly at the dead buck. "How'd she do?"

Hope suppressed a grimace. Ned was one of the expert hunters, as well as being a decent blacksmith. But if you weren't one of his inner circle he had a bad habit of talking about you as if you weren't there, even if you were standing three feet away. If Halverson ever decided it was time for the top hunters to strike out on their own, odds were that Ned would be the man right behind him when they hit the trail.

"Susan did fine," she said.

"Um," Ned rumbled, tilting his head and gazing pointedly at the marks of two retrieved arrows in the deer's side. "Good save, anyway. Signal the others again, will you? It's pretty thick there to the west, and Pepper may have drifted off target."

Hope nodded and reached for her whistle.

Everyone had a talent, her father always said. That meant Susan had one, too. All they had to do was figure out what it was.

Hopefully before she was sent back out into the forest and the mountains to die.

CHAPTER FOUR

They'd been flying for nearly three hours, and Blair Williams had watched the landscape sliding beneath the Blackhawk helicopter gradually change from forest to sparse grassland and finally to desert. Above her, the sky was mottled with a mixture of feathery white cirrus clouds and long dirty gray stratus ones, interspersed with occasional patches of blue sky. All around her the air was filled with the hum of the Blackhawk's engines and the rhythmic throbbing of its rotors.

Beside her, scowling in the copilot's seat, was Barnes.

Blair sighed to herself. She hadn't wanted to take on this mission, and it had been abundantly clear that Barnes hadn't wanted her along, either. But Connor had insisted, and John Connor wasn't the sort of person you said no to.

Especially when the only reason Connor's dark eyes were even alive to gaze at, into, and through you was because Marcus Wright had given his life to save him.

Marcus Wright. The man who in a few short days Blair had learned to love.

Not the man, a bitter-edged corner of her mind corrected mockingly in Barnes's voice. *The* machine *you learned to love.*

Blair shook her head sharply. *Stop that!* she ordered herself. Yes, Marcus had been mostly machine by the time Blair met him, a hybrid of man and Terminator that was far beyond even Skynet's usual blasphemies. And yes, he'd been created for the express purpose of luring Connor into Skynet Central to die.

But buried somewhere beneath all that machinery had been a man. A man with a living heart, a determined mind, and an unquenchable spirit.

There was no way to know if he'd still had a soul. Blair hoped that he had.

"There!" Barnes's voice growled into her headphones.

Blair blinked away the bittersweet reverie. Ahead on the horizon she could see the still smoldering remains of the massive Skynet dish array and hidden underground lab that the Resistance had hit over two weeks ago.

And in doing so had walked squarely into a devastating, multilayered trap.

Blair still winced whenever she thought about how close they'd come that day to losing everything. The self-destruct explosion that had taken out the lab and killed the entire assault team—except Connor—had been the first, most obvious trap. The data download that the techs had managed to transmit before they died had been the far more subtle, far more dangerous one. Buried inside that data had been a radio kill code that had promised a way for the Resistance to simultaneously shut down Skynet's vast armies of Terminators, T-1 tanks, and H-K Hunter-Killers.

But the promise had been a lie. The code had worked perfectly in Connor's small-scale tests, perfectly enough that Command had given the order for a massive, simultaneous transmission to be followed by a scorched-earth attack on Skynet's huge San Francisco hub.

But when the multiple signals were sent out, the supposed kill code morphed into a homing signal, allowing Skynet to pinpoint and destroy most of the Resistance cells worldwide.

Of all the leaders only Connor had smelled a rat in time, and had shut down his team's transmitter before it could join the party. Only Connor's group and the ones who had heeded his plea for more time were still alive and functioning.

And only Connor's group was back there in the remains of San Francisco, cleaning up the remnants of Skynet's once massive forces.

So far, the clean-up had been relatively easy. A duck shoot, even, at least the mopping-up part that Barnes had been engaged in. Nearly all the surviving T-600s and T-700s were hopelessly crippled, and their demolition was giving some good firearms practice to the new recruits who'd joined up from among the civilians Connor's pilots had rescued before the balloon went up.

But the duck shoot wasn't going to last much longer. Blair had heard rumors that there was some kind of prophecy wrapped around Connor, that he was destined to lead the Resistance to victory over the Terminators. She didn't put a lot of stock in such things, and she couldn't imagine Connor himself taking it very seriously either.

But considering the time and resources Skynet had poured into luring the man into his own private corner of the trap, it was clear that the big computer wasn't ready to dismiss Connor or this so-called prophecy nearly so quickly.

And *that* meant Skynet wouldn't simply write off western North America as a loss and content itself with trying to dominate and wipe out the rest of the world's population. It would be moving resources here, as many as it could, as quickly as it could.

They'd won a major battle. But the war was far from over.

"Well?"

For the second time in ten minutes, Blair found herself jolted out of private thoughts. "Well what?" she asked.

"You going to take us down?" Barnes demanded. "Or you just going to circle around up here looking at the pretty scenery?"

Blair felt her cheeks warm. She had indeed been flying with her brain on autopilot, running them in a lazy circle around the western periphery of the remains.

"I was trying to find a spot that wasn't actually still on fire," she countered, hoping the excuse didn't sound as pathetic to him as it did to her. The big pit in the ground where the team had rappelled down to the lab... okay, there it was. Connor had told them Barnes's brother Caleb had been on the western side when Skynet blew the lab.

She frowned as something caught her eye. It was a small, slender hump in the ground, like a tree root that had been forced aboveground by some obstruction beneath it.

Only there weren't any trees nearby. Not for miles around.

"There," Barnes said sharply, pointing toward the edge of the pit. "I see some bodies. Take us down."

"Okay," Blair said, feeling a shiver run through her. This was not going to be pleasant.

It wasn't. The bodies were in bad shape, burned and mangled by the massive explosion that had taken out the lab. What was left had had two weeks' to begin decaying, though the dry desert air had alleviated the effects somewhat. The human remains were scattered amid tangled debris from the antenna array and the metal skulls, torsos, and limbs of the Terminators that had been defending it.

There were a lot of those pieces, too, along with plenty of T-600 miniguns and the big G11 caseless-round submachineguns that Skynet was arming its T-700s with these days. A lot of the weapons were useless, though a few of the miniguns looked in decent shape and some even had ammo belts still attached. Clearly, Skynet had thrown a huge number of resources into this battle, and Blair found herself wondering how much of a role that desperate-looking defense had played in persuading Command that they were genuinely onto something.

Slowly, methodically, Blair and Barnes continued their grisly task. Each face had to be looked at closely, with the body often first having to be turned over. Here and there Blair spotted someone she recognized, either one of the people from Connor's original team or someone she'd gotten to know in the months since they'd been pulled out of Los Angeles and put under General Olsen's overall command. Each time, she felt a tug at her heart, and a small diminishing of herself. Some poet, she remembered vaguely, had once written about such things.

Caleb wasn't in the first group she and Barnes checked out. Nor was he in the second, or the third, or the fourth. Midway through the fifth Blair's aching heart and churning stomach finally got the better of her, and she had to move away for a few minutes to settle both of them.

Barnes, predictably, didn't seem to notice her distress. He certainly didn't say anything as Blair stood a dozen paces away, breathing shallowly through her mouth. He continued on, as emotionless and machinelike as any Terminator, checking each broken body before moving on to the next.

He was so silent and straightforwardly determined in his quest, in fact, that he had unhooked his entrenching tool from his pack and started digging before Blair even realized that he'd found his brother.

Gingerly, feeling like she was setting off across a minefield, she walked over to him.

"May I help?" she asked.

"No," he said flatly, not looking at her.

For a minute Blair watched him jabbing the tool into the loose sand and throwing it to the side, wondering if she should just take him at his word and go wait in the Blackhawk. Then, moving a few feet away from him, she started to dig.

She half expected him to order her away. But he didn't. Maybe he realized that she'd been Caleb's friend, too, and deserved the chance to help him to his final rest.

Maybe he just didn't consider her worth the trouble of yelling at.

The sun was dipping close to the western mountains by the time they finished the grave. Again, Blair expected Barnes to order her away as he picked up his brother's body and laid it gently in the hole. But again, he simply ignored her as she stood quietly by. He spoke over the grave for a few minutes, his voice too low for Blair to catch more than a few words of the farewell. Then, straightening up, he threw his brother a final salute. Blair did the same, holding the salute for probably half a minute until Barnes finally lowered his arm to his side and again picked up his entrenching tool.

Ten minutes later, it was done. While Blair waited by the grave, Barnes constructed a cross out of his brother's rifle and a slightly warped Terminator leg strut. He dug the cross into the sand, and for another minute stood gazing at the grave and the marker. He took a deep breath, and for the first time in probably an hour he looked at Blair.

"Okay," he said. "Let's go."

"All right," Blair said, her mind flicking to the hundreds of bodies still lying out beneath the open sky. But there was no way she and Barnes could deal with so many. All she could do was put them out of her mind as best she could. "Before we go, I'd like to check out something I spotted on our way in."

He eyed her suspiciously. "What was it?"

"I don't know," she said. "Don't worry, it won't take long."

He glowered, but gave a reluctant nod. "Where?"

Blair turned around, mentally superimposing the image from the sky on top of the landscape stretched out in front of her.

"About a hundred meters that way," she said, pointing northwest. "You want me to go and get the helo?"

With a snort, he strode past her and headed off in the direction she'd indicated.

Blair grimaced. Easy for him to say. *He* hadn't gotten shot during her attempt to free Marcus from the prison Connor had put him in.

Fortunately, the wound hadn't been as serious as she'd first thought. It had probably been a ricochet, and though it had hurt like hell at the time and half paralyzed her leg, it had done a good job of healing in the week and a half since then.

It still wasn't completely well, though, and too much exertion was bad for it. Barnes probably knew that.

And he obviously didn't care.

With a sigh, Blair hurried to catch up to him.

The mysterious hump Blair had seen had been reasonably visible from the air. From the ground, with the western sun exaggerating every shadow, it was even more obvious.

It wasn't a root that had been forced up out of the ground. Instead, it was a root-sized cable.

"Coaxial type," she commented, pointing to the central core and surrounding shielding where Barnes had sliced through it with his trench knife. "Outer shielding pretty sturdy."

"Okay," Barnes said, restlessly turning his knife over and over in his hand. "So?"

"So it was obviously designed to be at least semi-permanent," Blair said, trying to think it through. "And yet it was buried barely thirty centimeters under the sand."

"Okay," Barnes said again. "So?"

"So I'm guessing it was an add-on," Blair concluded, squinting northwest across the glare of the sunlight reflecting off the sand. "Something Skynet laid down after the main lab was set up." She gestured down. "And the fact that this is a data cable and not a power cable tells us it was sending information."

"Maybe it was going over the mountains to San Francisco," Barnes said. "Can we get out of here now?"

"That's an awfully long way to string a cable," Blair pointed out, the annoyance she'd been sitting on ever since leaving Connor's camp starting to bubble up into anger. Was Barnes really too stupid to see what that could mean? Or was he playing dumb just to irritate her? "Especially when they had a dish array right here that could probably punch a signal anywhere on the planet."

"Fine," Barnes growled. "You're the smart one. What do *you* think it was?"

"Well, let's see," she said, for once making no effort to suppress her sarcasm. "You think maybe Skynet might have set up an outlying satellite base out in the mountains? A backup facility in case—oh, I don't know—we managed to take out *this* one?"

"If there's something out there, what's it been doing since then?" Barnes shot back. "Didn't make a peep while we were blowing up San Francisco." He pointed toward the mountains. "Or maybe there's a whole bunch of H-Ks heading toward us from the place right now. You see a bunch of H-Ks heading toward us?"

Blair ground her teeth. "Of course not," she said. "But I still think it's worth checking out."

"So write it up," Barnes growled. "Connor loves getting stuff like that."

"*Or* we could just check it out ourselves," Blair said. "See if there really *is* something out there before we bother him with it."

For another moment Barnes glowered at her. Then, reluctantly, he shifted his glower toward the mountains. Whatever the man thought about Blair, he was hound-dog loyal to Connor, and even in his current grouchy state of mind he couldn't help but see the logic of not burdening his commander with extra stuff during the man's recovery. Especially if, as he obviously thought, there turned out to be nothing out there at all. "Fine," he agreed at last. "A quick check, and then we go."

"Thanks." Blair braced herself. "But we'll have to wait until tomorrow."

Barnes twisted his head back around to look at her. "*Tomorrow?*"

"We need to be able to see the loops where the explosion forced the cable to the surface," Blair explained hurriedly. "I know there are more of them—I saw at least three on our way in. But we'll need the shadows from an early-morning sun to see them. At night, we'll lose the trail completely."

Barnes snorted. "This is ridiculous. It probably just

connects to one of the perimeter sensors."

"Maybe," Blair conceded. "But we won't know unless we check it out." She waved a hand. "Look, it isn't that big a deal. We take off as soon as the sun is up, follow the cable, turn the Blackhawk's machineguns loose on whatever's at the other end, and go home." She cocked her head slightly. "Caleb would have wanted to make sure."

The instant the words were out of her mouth she knew she'd crossed the line. But it was too late. Barnes's expression went rigid, and for that first frozen second Blair felt she was staring death squarely in the face.

"Don't do that," he said, the utter lack of emotion in his voice more terrifying than any scream or curse he could have snarled at her. "Don't ever use my brother's name that way again. Ever."

"You're right," Blair said, her mouth suddenly dry. "I'm sorry."

For another moment she faced into the bitter iciness of Barnes's gaze. Then, he exhaled quietly, and the moment had passed.

"I'll be sleeping on the right-hand side of the chopper," he said gruffly. "Shoot anything that comes near that isn't me." Turning, he stalked back toward the distant Blackhawk.

"Right," Blair called a bit timidly after him. "I'll take the first watch, then?"

Barnes didn't bother to reply.

Blair gave the new grave a final look. Then she set off after him.

She had the first watch, all right. And given that it would be her job to wake him up for his turn, chances were very good that she was going to have the *only* watch.

She sighed. It was shaping up to be a long, lonely, chilly night.

CHAPTER FIVE

Jik had just settled for the night into his chosen tree when he heard the faint whining sound in the distance.

He froze, his ears straining, his eyes trying to pierce the canopy of branches and leaves above him to the glimpses of starry night sky beyond. The sound was growing louder, and for a minute he wondered if it might be a Resistance jet or helo heading across the mountains on some mission.

But no. As the noise grew louder, it resolved itself into the distinctive hum of Hunter-Killer turbofans.

He bared his teeth in a scowl, his hands pressed against the rough tree bark. During the long walk from Los Angeles he'd spent his nights off the ground whenever he could, both as a defense against predators and also because he hated the sensation of ants and other ground insects crawling over him.

But he was only safe from ground-based dangers like wolves and coyotes. Against flying threats like H-Ks, setting himself above the bushes and other ground cover was not only useless but decidedly counterproductive.

He peered beneath him, trying to recall the details of the terrain. There was a large section of dead log about ten meters away, he remembered, surrounded by a group of thorn bushes. If the log was hollow, he might be able to squeeze himself inside. Surely the infrared signature of a man inside a log would be significantly different from that of a human out in the open?

But did he dare risk the movement required to climb down the tree? And once he was down, what about the coyotes and wolves he'd heard prowling around earlier?

The H-K was getting closer. Abruptly, Jik made up his mind. The leaf canopy was no defense if the H-K was hunting humans tonight, and wolves he would at least have a fighting chance against. Better to go with the log.

He was adjusting his grip on the branches around him, preparing to swing out of his perch, when a new sound came to him across the breeze. Like the H-K's engines, this one was instantly recognizable: the heavy, steady cadence of large metallic feet.

The H-K wasn't alone. It had brought some Terminators with it.

Jik froze, the bitter irony of it drying his throat. All the way from Los Angeles... and now, with Baker's Hollow practically in sight, the Terminators had finally caught up with him.

And pinned between earth and sky, with nowhere to go and no time to get there anyway, Jik literally had no other option but to trust in luck to get him through the next few minutes. Tucking his arms against his chest, he pressed up against the tree bole and tried to look as much like a bear as he could.

The footsteps swishing through the leaves and thudding against the ground grew louder, and a minute later he caught a glimpse of glowing red eyes through the vegetation to the south, heading northeastward more or less parallel to Jik's own route. A glint of starlight on dark metal showed that it was a T-700, not one of the rubber-skinned T-600s. A few meters behind it was a second T-700, which was followed by a third and then a fourth. All of them walking in the same path, Jik noted, probably to disguise their numbers should anyone happen across their trail.

He tensed, waiting for the moment when they spotted him and turned to the kill. But they didn't. They continued on their stolid, mechanical way, their footsteps fading away into the night. As the normal forest sounds began to reassert themselves, Jik heard the distant hum of the H-K's turbofans also fade away.

The Terminators had been hunting him, all right. But his luck had held.

Or had it?

He looked around again, this time with new eyes. His estimate when he'd first settled down for the night had been that he was about ten miles from Slate River, with just another half a mile until he reached Baker's Hollow itself. Slate River was only about fifteen feet wide, but it was relatively deep and as fast and rock-filled as any other mountain stream. Back when he'd spent summers here, he'd been warned repeatedly not to go anywhere near it.

But warnings like that never stopped ten-year-old boys. He and one of the local kids, Danny Preston, had routinely crossed the river at the spot everyone else used, a somewhat wider section where the slightly slower current had built up a mass of stones that made the water shallow enough to safely wade through. That ford was the spot Jik was currently heading for, and up until now he'd assumed he was more or less on course.

Now, though, he wasn't so sure. If Skynet was still

trying to nail him—and the presence of T-700s in the middle of the forest was pretty good evidence that it was—its best strategy at this point would be to try to pin him against the river. If one of the machines could reach and hold the ford ahead of him, the others could then sweep in from the west, north, and south, beating the bushes until they ran him down. Simple, straightforward, and an almost guaranteed success.

He smiled tightly into the darkness. Or maybe not so guaranteed... because what Skynet didn't know was that forty years ago Jik and Danny had built themselves a private bridge about a mile north of the ford. If it was still there, he might be able to get across the river and to the relative safety of Baker's Hollow before Skynet even knew the fish had slipped the net.

His smile turned into a grimace. *If* the bridge was still there, and that was a mighty big *if*. He and Danny had built the thing pretty solidly, but forty years was a long time to expect something made of rope and wooden planks to survive mountain winters. Even if Danny still lived in Baker's Hollow, he must surely have found better things to do with his time than maintain an old childhood plaything.

But with the next nearest practical crossing over twenty miles downstream, Jik had no choice but to try it.

Luck hadn't failed him yet. He could only hope it would stay with him a little while longer.

Slipping off his branch, he slid down the tree as quietly as he could. There was a cabin of sorts, he remembered, just a little ways this side of the bridge. No more than a shack, really, but if it was still there it might provide him with a place where he would at least be out of direct sight.

And being out of direct sight suddenly seemed like a good thing to strive for.

For a moment he stood at the foot of the tree, straining his ears. But the first line of Terminators had long since passed, and if there was another line coming up behind them they weren't close enough to be audible.

It was now or never.

Taking a deep breath, he headed off into the night.

The figure standing among the trees on the far side of the river was so silent and still that most people would never notice it in the dim starlight. Even if someone did, he would most likely dismiss it as a trick of the light on some misshapen tree bole.

But Daniel Preston wasn't most people. He'd lived in Baker's Hollow all his life, and he knew every tree and bush for ten miles around. The thing standing across the river was no trick of tired or nervous eyes.

He was pretty sure he knew what it was. But it never hurt to get a second opinion.

"Nate?" he murmured, just loudly enough to be heard over the sound of the rushing water.

Beside him, Dr. Nathan Oxley lowered his binoculars.

"It's a Terminator, all right," he murmured back grimly. "T-700, probably. It's not bulky enough to be a T-500, and it seems to be reflecting more starlight than a T-600 would."

"Alive, I assume?"

"You mean active?" Oxley shrugged. "Probably. It's facing the other way, so I can't see its eyes. But it would be rather too much to hope for that a T-700 would get all the way out here in the forest and then just happen to break down half a mile from town."

Preston grunted. "Probably also too much to hope that the river's going to stop it."

"Well, it's not going to rust, if that's what you're thinking." Oxley shook his head. "Beats me why you never put a bridge there."

"Before Judgment Day everything over there was private property," Preston said, eyeing the Terminator. "The owner didn't want us walking on his land and absolutely wouldn't allow anything like a bridge. Afterward, we kind of liked the idea of having a barrier between us and any predators that might want to wander this direction. So the water won't hurt it at all?"

"Not at all," Oxley confirmed. "There's a ferrous component to their construction—that's why they can pull their limbs back together if they get blown apart. But—"

"Wait a second," Preston interrupted. "They can put themselves back *together*?"

"Of course." Oxley waved a hand. "Sorry. I forget sometimes that you never worked with the damn things staring over your shoulder. Yeah, they can pull themselves back together. They can also stand up to anything but big-caliber, high-power bullets, and keep going pretty near forever."

Preston squeezed his left hand into a fist. *Terrific.*

"So what's it waiting for? I assume it's not afraid of the dark."

"No, of course not," Oxley said thoughtfully. "And you're right, that's the part that doesn't make any sense. I mean, aside from the question of what the hell it's doing out here in the first place."

"Any thoughts? On either point?"

Oxley shrugged. "You'll recall I said I couldn't tell if it was active because it's not facing this direction. Not facing this direction may imply that it's not interested in Baker's Hollow, but is waiting for something to happen over on *that* side of the river."

"Like what?" Preston asked.

"How should I know?" Oxley growled. "You want to go ask it, be my guest. But it's definitely not standing there because it's afraid of the river. Even if it was worried about the depth or the current, the ford's right there in front of it."

Belatedly it struck him. *Of course.* "It's not waiting for something," Preston said. "It's waiting for some*one*. Someone who's trying to get to Baker's Hollow."

"Someone trying to get *here*?"

"Why else guard the ford?" Preston replied.

"But who in the world would want to come here?" Oxley protested. "Who out there even knows Baker's Hollow still exists?"

"I don't know." Preston nodded toward the Terminator. "And from the looks of things, odds are we never will."

Oxley sighed. "You're probably right. Poor devil."

Preston nodded. *Poor devil indeed.*

But right now, he had more urgent things on his mind than some random migrant who might be wandering this way.

"Let's assume for a minute it gets whoever it's here for," he said. "Will it just leave? Or would it decide to take out the town as long as it's here anyway?"

"For starters, T-700s don't *decide* anything," Oxley said. "They're wholly controlled by Skynet, and I have no idea what that means now that the lab is gone."

Despite the seriousness of the situation, Preston had to smile at that. *Gone.* Like the massive explosion that had rattled buildings in Baker's Hollow and lit up the entire sky to the southeast qualified as just being *gone.* Sometimes Oxley showed an awesome flair for understatement.

"Where would the next nearest Skynet center be?"

"San Francisco was the nearest command hub," Oxley said. "But if Connor was right about that one being gone, I don't know what's left. There might be another hub in Missouri, or there might not be anything until the east coast."

"Could something that distance away even get a signal this far?"

"Oh, sure," Oxley said. "Shortwave would do just fine. Never fear—Skynet's in complete control of any Terminators it's got left out here." He grimaced. "And will continue that control straight through a massacre of Baker's Hollow, should it decide to go that route."

"So what do we do?" Preston asked.

Oxley shrugged. "We wait."

Preston peered out into the darkness.

"And meanwhile let whoever's out there walk into a trap?"

"I know," Oxley said heavily. "But the only other option is to try to take out the T-700 ourselves. That's not easy to do."

"So I'm told," Preston said, eyeing the unmoving machine. So it had finally come. The confrontation he'd been afraid of ever since the fires of Judgment Day died away and the first rumors of killing machines began to drift up to their little refuge in the mountains.

Their town's isolation had protected it for a long time. But the reprieve was over. Skynet had found them, and every man, woman, and child in his care was now in deadly danger.

Including his own daughter.

"You haven't asked the obvious question," Oxley said carefully.

"You mean whether or not you and your friends might be the reason for this visit?" Preston suggested.

"That's the one." Oxley hesitated. "Do you want us to leave?"

"Depends," Preston said with a shrug. "You think your presence in town would hurt us, or help us?"

Oxley snorted. "Even asking such a question presupposes we were more than just cogs in Skynet's giant machine. Unfortunately, we weren't. As a matter of fact, if Skynet thinks of us at all it's probably as deserters. Or whatever term it uses for humans who drop off its grid."

"Most likely the same term it uses for all the rest of us," Preston said grimly. "Dead men walking."

Oxley sighed. "Sounds about right."

Preston nodded, watching the other out of the corner of his eye. Oxley had always been vague as to what exactly he and the other two scientists had been doing down in that big underground lab. Lajard and Valentine had been even more tight-lipped than Oxley, saying only that they had been part of Skynet's vast contingent of human labor.

But that had never rung exactly true to Preston. All three of them had the kind of high-class scientific credentials that should have lifted them well above the general mass of humanity they had described as being down there. Had Skynet put them to work doing something else? Some job they were too afraid or too ashamed to admit to?

Or maybe Skynet simply didn't care about high-class scientific credentials. Maybe to it, all human slave labor was created equal.

"Well, whatever we end up doing, we're not doing it tonight," Preston decided. "Let's go sleep on it. Maybe by morning we'll have thought up some better options."

"Maybe," Oxley said. "You might want to post a guard here, though. Just in case."

"I already have," Preston said. Though what a lone guard could do against a T-700 he couldn't guess. Probably little more than be the first of them to die. "Let's get back to town."

It was after midnight, and Blair was trudging her sixth weary and leg-aching walk around the perimeter of their camp when she heard a sound that chilled her even more than the cold desert air.

The sound of a distant Hunter-Killer.

She froze in her tracks, her right hand dropping to the grip of her holstered Desert Eagle, her head turning slowly back and forth as she tried to locate the noise. *Somewhere to the northeast*, she decided.

She was staring in that direction, trying to figure out whether it was coming closer, when something grabbed her ankle.

Reflexively, she tried to jerk away. But the grip was too solid. Snatching out her gun, she looked down.

To find that one of the broken pieces of a T-700—a crushed skull, partial torso, and one arm—had inexplicably come back to life. The skull was half turned upward toward her, its red eyes glowing angrily, the bent fingers tightening around her ankle.

"Damn," she snarled. Lining up the muzzle on the damaged skull, she squeezed the trigger.

The big gun bucked in her hand, the thunder of the shot slamming across her face and ears. The Terminator ignored the attack, its cold hand continuing to tighten its grip. Clenching her teeth, Blair fired two more rounds into the skull. This time, the machine's grip slackened, and the glowing eyes faded once again to emptiness. Quickly, she worked her ankle free, then looked up again.

And caught her breath.

All around her, the desert was in motion. The scattered fragments of Terminators were on the move, crawling and clawing and hunching themselves across the sand like grotesque metal caterpillars. Their eyes, which had been blank and dead all afternoon, were once again spots of glowing red. As the echoes of her shots faded away, she could hear the faint clink of metal on metal as other scattered pieces began to magnetically reassemble themselves into some semblance of the once proud killing machines.

And all of those broken, deadly, grotesque things were heading straight for her.

CHAPTER SIX

Blair filled her lungs.

"Barnes!" she yelled.

His response was exactly what she expected: no startled words, no useless questions, just a pair of bursts from one of the Blackhawk's two door-mounted M240 machine guns. The two Terminator segments nearest the helo blew into shards that went flying across the sand.

"*Move* it, Williams!" he shouted.

Another broken T-700 had crawled nearly to grabbing range. Blair considered shooting it, decided she had better things to do with her time and ammo, and took off instead in a dead run toward Barnes and the Blackhawk.

She damn near didn't make it. There were a half dozen more Terminators between her and the helo, none of which had betrayed its functionality by moving, all of which now lunged up and tried to grab her as she raced past. One of them had managed to collect a pair of broken leg segments along with an arm and was able to rise to something resembling a kneeling position and actually throw itself toward her.

A shot from Blair's gun staggered it back. Before it could regain its balance another burst from Barnes's M240 blew it to pieces.

Ten seconds later, Blair was inside the Blackhawk.

"Strap in!" she snapped, ignoring her throbbing leg as she dropped into the pilot's seat and keyed for quick-start.

"Just get us in the air," Barnes snapped back, firing two more bursts. "I think I heard an H-K before all this hell broke loose."

"You did, and it's headed this way," Blair confirmed, running her eyes over the gauges. To her left, a misshapen Terminator hand suddenly appeared, clawing for a grip on the edge of the door opening as a pair of glowing eyes lifted into sight. Snatching out her gun, Blair gave a quick cross-body shot that knocked the machine back into the sand. "Here we go," she said, dropping the gun onto her lap and grabbing the stick and throttle as the rotors began to turn. "Strap in—I don't want you falling out."

"Forget that!" Barnes shouted. He fired another burst, then leaned in toward Blair and pointed out the windshield's right-hand section. "That way—a hundred fifty meters. Go!"

"What?" Blair asked, frowning as she peered out the windshield. There was nothing anywhere in that direction but more desert and more crawling Terminator segments. "Why?"

But Barnes was already back at the door, firing more bursts at the metallic bodies still trying to overrun them.

"Barnes, we have to run," Blair shouted over the noise. "I'm not sure we can get away as it is."

"A hundred fifty meters," Barnes insisted. "*Do* it."

Swearing under her breath, Blair fed power to the engines and leaped the helo into the air. Swiveling its nose, she headed in the direction Barnes had indicated.

"Behind you!"

Blair spun around. Another T-700 segment was

hanging off the helo's portside door-jamb with one hand while it other clawed for purchase on the deck itself with the other. Blair snatched up her gun, but before she could bring it to bear Barnes took a couple of rapid steps across the cabin and kicked hard at the arm gripping the door. The impact dislodged its grip, and the Terminator disappeared into the night.

"There," Barnes called over the engine noise, pointing out the windshield. "Another twenty meters, then put 'er down."

Blair nodded and threw a quick look to her left. She could see a faint red glow in the distance now, the telltale lights of a rapidly approaching H-K.

"Barnes—"

"That little mound," he cut her off, pointing again. "Put us down next to it."

Blair grimaced. The H-K was coming in fast, and even in the air the Blackhawk would be a painfully easy target. On the ground, it would be a sitting duck.

But it was already too late for them to get a real head start. Whatever Barnes had up his sleeve, Blair could only hope it was good. Braking beside the mound, she dropped the helo onto the ground.

It hit with a crunch of metal from beneath the wheels that made her wince. Barnes was already moving, dropping out the side door and disappearing to the helo's rear. A few seconds later he reappeared and climbed back inside.

With a Terminator minigun cradled in his arms, the ammo belt triple looped over his arm and disappearing out the door behind him.

"Go!" he ordered, dumping the gun onto the deck and yanking hard on the ammo belt's trailing end. It came

free, and Barnes grabbed for the safety harness by the
M240. *"Go!"*

Blair pulled on the throttle and once again took the
Blackhawk into the air. She should have known Barnes
would have taken note of where all the abandoned
miniguns and other weapons were while the two of them
were out searching for his brother.

But even with their newly acquired firepower, this
was going to be seriously problematic. Fleetingly, Blair
wished she was back in her preferred A-10 fighter, or that
the Blackhawk at least had a couple of pylon-mounted
Hydra 70 missile clusters.

But she wasn't, and it didn't, and they would have to
make do with what they had. Climbing as fast as the
Blackhawk could manage, she looked back toward the
incoming H-K.

Only to find that it wasn't there.

"Where'd it go?" she shouted, looking frantically
around. It couldn't have overflown them already—it
hadn't been *that* close. "Barnes?"

"There—left," he shouted back.

Blair looked out the portside door. There it was, all
right, speeding toward them with its searchlights off
and its turbofans angled for maximum forward velocity.
It must have swung around to that side while the helo
was on the ground and she was distracted by Barnes's
weapons hunt.

Only that didn't make any tactical sense. Why waste
time circling around to a new vector when it could have
maintained its course and charged straight down the
Blackhawk's throat?

Unless one of the broken Terminators down there had
spotted Barnes loading his new minigun into the helo's

starboard door and Skynet had brought the H-K around to keep it away from that side.

If so, the time the H-K had lost in that maneuver might just be the breathing space they needed. Blair twisted the stick around, sending the Blackhawk into a tight turn. If she could get Barnes and his minigun into range before the H-K could line up a clear shot...

The helo had barely started into its turn when a burst from the H-K's Gatling guns disintegrated the windshield in front of her.

She twisted her face away from the flurry of flying glass, reflexively twisting the stick to spin the cockpit away from the incoming fire. She heard a shout from beside her, but with the wind suddenly roaring in her ears she couldn't tell whether it was a shout of pain, anger, or encouragement. She blinked something out of her eyes— sweat or blood, she wasn't sure which—and kicked the engines to full speed.

The enemy had gotten in the first punch, and her job now was to get away, get out of its crosshairs, and buy herself enough time to regroup. At least this was one of the older H-K models, still packing Gatling guns instead of the new plasma weapons some of the Skynet Central defenders had been armed with. *Small favors*.

Abruptly, the Blackhawk bucked, dropping like a rock, as if Blair had suddenly flown it into a downdraft. She fought the controls, trying to get the aircraft back in hand.

It was only then that she noticed that the wind was not only blowing *in* at her through the disintegrated windshield but was blowing *down* on her as well.

She looked up, squinting against the blast. The H-K had taken position directly above them, flying with its underside bare meters from the Blackhawk's main rotor.

Instead of simply blasting them out of the air, like H-Ks usually did, the damn thing was trying to force them down.

Twisting the stick, Blair tried jinking to the left. But at these speeds the Blackhawk wasn't nearly as responsive as an A-10 would have been, and the H-K easily matched the maneuver. She jinked the other direction, dropping her nose a few degrees to give herself some extra speed. Once again, the H-K stayed right there with her.

"Barnes!" she shouted.

"I see it," he called back, and out of the corner of her eye Blair saw him pop his restraint harness. "Drop and dust."

Blair made a face. *Drop and dust*—put the Blackhawk on the ground, or close to it, and immediately head up again. A standard enough tactic, but in this case it might prove fatal. If the H-K matched the move, she would end up virtually pinned to the ground, with nowhere to go and no maneuvering room at all.

But continuing to play Skynet's game would be to lose by default.

"On three," she called. "One, two, *three*."

Slamming the stick forward, she dropped the Blackhawk to the ground. The wheels hit hard, bounced her a meter back up—

And as Barnes dropped out the starboard side door she angled the helo as far as she could to port and clawed for altitude.

She nearly made it. But at the last second the H-K managed to sidle back into place above her, once again trapping her between earth and metal. With her last bit of maneuvering room she turned the Blackhawk in a tight circle, bringing the pair of them back toward where she had dropped Barnes.

She could feel the buffeting as her rotors' airflow bounced off the ground and up into the Blackhawk's belly when Barnes finally opened up with his minigun.

The H-K's nose took the full brunt of the blast, the smooth metal shattering into scrap. Instantly, it swerved away, abandoning its attack on Blair as it tried to get clear of the deadly stream of lead.

But Barnes was clearly expecting that. Without letting up on the trigger, he shifted his attack from the H-K's nose to its starboard turbofan. Blair skidded the Blackhawk sideways as she heard the turbofan disintegrating, managing to get completely out from under the H-K as its starboard wing suddenly drooped nearly to the ground.

Once again it tried to dodge away.

Once again Barnes shifted his attack, this time back to the machine's nose and the Gatling guns nestled there.

Blair was circling back toward the battle when the H-K was rocked by a massive explosion as the minigun's rounds ignited the machine's ammo supply. Floundering like a beached fish, the H-K swiveled around, making one final attempt to escape.

It had gone fifty meters when Blair brought the Blackhawk's wheels down on top of its spine, forcing the crippled aircraft into a sand-billowing impact with the ground.

"See?" she muttered toward it under her breath. "I can do that, too."

The H-K was bucking weakly, trying to throw off six thousand kilos of dead weight, as Blair crossed to the portside M240, flipped the selector to full auto, and fired a long burst into the remaining turbofan.

The bucking had stopped, and Blair was back in her seat, when Barnes reappeared.

"Dead?" he grunted as he heaved the minigun in through the door and clambered in behind it.

"Close enough," Blair said, frowning as she eyed the weapon. Surely Barnes must have emptied the thing in the past two minutes. "Bringing home souvenirs?"

"'Course not—this is a new one," he said, pulling the rest of the new minigun's ammo belt inside and taking hold of the harness. "We getting out of here, or what?"

Glowering, Blair turned back and fed power to the engines. Seconds later, they were far above the crawling Terminators and burning their way through the night sky.

"Any preferences as to where we go?" she asked, squinting through the cold wind hammering against her face as Barnes dropped into the copilot's seat.

"Yeah. Somewhere else."

Blair nodded, and settled in to the task of flying.

Ten minutes later, she set the helo back onto the ground.

"What are we stopping for?" Barnes asked as she ran the engines back down.

"You wanted to go somewhere else," she reminded him. "This is it."

"Funny," he muttered, leaning forward and giving the area around them a careful look.

"More specifically, we're a long ways from anything that might still be moving back at the lab," Blair continued. "Too far away for anything to get here before daybreak, but not so far that we waste fuel. We may need that tomorrow."

"Or we could just head back to San Francisco right now," Barnes said.

"And give up on that cable we saw?" Blair asked. "After all that?"

"After all what?" he retorted. "So they tried to kill us.

They're Terminators. That's what they do. Doesn't mean there's anything out there worth looking at."

"Then why did that H-K try to force me down instead of just destroying us?" Blair demanded. "And why didn't the T-700s attack until nightfall, which was *after* we'd talked about following the cable to the other end? If they'd just wanted to kill us, they should have tried it during the afternoon, when we wouldn't have had a hope of getting back to the Blackhawk."

Barnes glared out at the desert landscape.

"Yeah, I suppose that's a little strange," he conceded.

"More than just a little," Blair persisted. "Look at the timing. The machines didn't move until after sundown, which is when shortwave transmissions open up again and they can communicate with the eastern hubs. Skynet finds out we're interested in the buried cable, and suddenly all the machines have orders to take us out."

"Yeah," Barnes said. "Maybe."

"Maybe, like hell," Blair growled. "Something's going on here, Barnes. We need to find out what. And it's going to take both of us to do that."

He eyed her suspiciously. "Yeah. Convenient, huh?"

Blair frowned. "Meaning?"

"Meaning this looks a lot like one of Connor's little *trial by fire* learning experiences," he said. "You two set this up together?

Blair shook her head. "I have no idea what you're talking about."

"Sure you don't," Barnes said scornfully. "Connor says we need to clear the air between us, and suddenly here we are in the middle of a firefight. Which he *also* says is the way you forge good combat teams."

Blair stared at him. "Are you suggesting Connor *knew*

all those Terminators were going to come back to life and try to kill us?" she asked. "Hoping that if we lived through it we'd be good friends afterward?"

"Why not?" Barnes asked pointedly. "That's how it worked with you and Marcus Wright, isn't it?"

A jolt of jagged-edge pain stabbed into Blair's gut.

"That's not fair."

"Isn't it?" Barnes countered. "It sure as hell wasn't the guy's native charm."

"No, it was his humanity and his loyalty," Blair bit out. "Sorry if those qualities are too old-fashioned for you."

"Hey, *I'm* not the one with the team loyalty problem," Barnes retorted. "You want to see that, go look in a mirror."

Blair stared at him, her anger and pain abruptly vanishing. Suddenly, a crack had opened in the barrier he had kept between them ever since San Francisco.

"What do you mean?" she asked carefully.

Apparently not carefully enough. Even as Barnes turned away, she could sense the barrier slamming shut again.

"Doesn't matter," he muttered. "You want to track that cable? Fine. You're the pilot. But we go home the minute we find the other end."

"Sure," Blair promised. "Barnes, look. We really need to talk about—"

"Get some sleep," he cut her off. Standing up, he went to the door and dropped to the ground. "I'll take watch."

"Come on, Barnes, don't do this," Blair said, trying one last time. "Barnes, stop."

"You want to stop me?" Barnes demanded, throwing his arms out to both sides.

Blair caught her breath, her pain and anger suddenly flaring up again. Barnes's pose was an exact, deliberate

parody of the way Marcus had been secured above the
empty missile silo back at Connor's base.

"You want to stop me?" Barnes repeated. "Shoot me."
He held the pose for another second, probably just to
make sure she'd gotten the message. Then, dropping
his arms again he picked up his rifle and stalked back
toward the helo's rear.

Blair ground her teeth, forcing her anger back down as
unwanted tears suddenly began to flow. The man was,
without a doubt and without serious competition, the
biggest pain in the butt she'd ever known.

But he was one of Connor's people. That meant he
was also one of her people. And she was not going to let
him spend the rest of his life brooding and hurting and
avoiding her. Or worse, lashing out at her.

One way or another, she was going to crack that shell
and find out what was bothering him. If only to prove to
him that she was as loyal to Connor's people as he was.

And also because her butt was on the line here too.
Brooding, self-absorbed soldiers tended to get themselves
and their teams killed.

Sniffing back the tears, she wiped her sleeve across her
wet cheeks. Then, trying to ignore the pains in her injured
leg and her aching soul, she folded her arms across her
chest and settled down to sleep.

Kyle was sleeping soundly under the gently rippling
barracks canopy when a sudden grip on his wrist snapped
him fully awake.

He opened his eyes, squinting a little in the diffuse glow
from the distant searchlights. Nine-year-old Star was
sitting up beside him, her hand still gripping his wrist, her
back unnaturally straight as she gazed out into the night.

There was no mistaking that look. Not from someone who'd lived as long with Star as Kyle had.

The Terminators were coming.

Quickly but gently twisting his arm free of her grip he half turned and reached for the rifle laying beside his sleeping mat. He got a grip on it—

"Easy," a voice murmured in his ear.

Startled, Kyle craned his neck to look behind him. Joel Vincennes, one of Connor's original Resistance team members, was crouched at his side, gazing out in the same direction that Star was.

"Terminators," Kyle murmured urgently.

"I know." Vincennes pointed past Star's shoulder. "Eight T-700s, with a T-600 armed with a minigun at point."

Kyle squinted into the darkness. He could see nothing out there but twisted metal and concrete, all of it covered by a layer of hazy smoke.

"You can *see* them?" he asked.

"No, but I can see *that*," Vincennes said, pointing thirty degrees to the side.

Kyle frowned. Then he spotted it: a faint, hooded light pointed back toward them, flickering rapidly on and off.

"Morse code," Vincennes identified it. "One of the things you'll be learning later. There—between those two broken towers. There they are."

Kyle nodded. He could see the line of Terminators now, metal skeletons striding toward the camp, their weapons held ready.

"Shouldn't we be doing something?" he whispered, his hand tightening on his rifle.

"We are," Vincennes said calmly. "Wait for it..."

And abruptly, the night erupted with the shattering noise and stuttering light show of the Resistance counterattack.

From an arc around the approaching machines a dozen guns opened up, some of the flashes coming from small bunkers, others from behind piles of wreckage, still others from places where Kyle wouldn't have thought a human being could actually lie concealed from view.

For perhaps half a second the Terminators staggered in the flood of lead slamming into them. Then they opened up with their own weapons, and the fury of the machineguns was punctuated by the shouts and cries of wounded men and women. From a sagging building fifty meters to the right of the battle another set of heavy machineguns joined in, and between bursts Kyle could hear the sound of engines revving up as one or more of the A-10s and Cobra attack helicopters prepared to take off. The Terminators' assault was faltering, the machines stumbling and then collapsing as their limbs, torsos, and heads shattered under the withering fire.

"H-K!" Vincennes snapped, pointing to the left.

Kyle's throat tightened as he spotted the two small red lights centered in the black shadow flying low across the night sky. Was Skynet hoping to slip in the H-K under cover of the battle noise?

If so, it was a futile hope. Even as the H-K snaked back and forth in an attempt to avoid fire, a small missile sputtered up from the ground, matching the incoming aircraft swerve for swerve. The missile's exhaust trail intersected one end of the black shadow—

The exploding turbofan lit up the whole area, briefly illuminating the high clouds overhead. As the crippled aircraft slammed into the ground, Kyle saw the skull of the last of the approaching T-700s explode into metal fragments, and the headless Terminator collapse into the rubble around it. The T-600 held out the longest, standing almost defiantly among the shattered bodies of its companions, firing its minigun until it too finally dropped backward onto the ground.

The gunfire ceased, and the world once again fell silent.

"And that," Vincennes said with grim satisfaction, "is that." He clapped a hand on Kyle's shoulder. "You and Star need to get back to sleep," he added. "Morning comes early, and I believe you, Kyle, are scheduled for first-shift clean-up duty." Straightening up, he headed across the shelter toward his own sleeping pad.

"Right," Kyle murmured, frowning across the ground at the remains of the nine Terminators, the wreckage still visible in the light of the burning H-K. He looked at Star, found her gazing back at him with a troubled expression on her small face. "What do you think?" he asked.

Her hands moved in their private code. *Too easy.*

Kyle nodded. He'd been thinking the same thing.

"Any more of them out there?"

Star considered, then shook her head. *A diversion?* she suggested.

"Maybe," Kyle said, looking around. "Maybe we nailed them faster than Skynet expected. Maybe before they could bring in the real attack."

Star's lips puckered. *Too easy*, she signed again.

"I know." Kyle touched her shoulder. "But whatever it was about, we're not going to figure it out tonight. Go back to sleep. If Skynet's got anything else planned, Connor's people will handle it."

Star still looked troubled. But she nodded and lay back down on her mat.

Reluctantly, Kyle settled down beside her. *Too easy*, the words echoed through his mind. *Too easy.*

Eventually, he fell asleep.

CHAPTER SEVEN

Preston was careful to close the door quietly behind him when he got home. After his daughter's long day hunting in the woods, the last thing he wanted to do was wake her up in the middle of the night.

The caution turned out to be a waste of effort. Hope was already in the living room, wedged into the half-broken recliner that she had always liked, her eyes closed, a blanket wrapped around her and tucked up under her chin.

For a long moment Preston gazed at his daughter, the usual kaleidoscope of thoughts and memories and regrets flashing through his mind. Hope was a child of the post-Judgment Day world, unschooled, uncivilized in the traditional sense of the word. Her knowledge and training were strictly limited to those skills needed for survival here in the wild.

And yet, amidst all that, she'd somehow also managed to develop a maturity far beyond her years. She had knowledge, but she also had wisdom. She had physical and mental toughness, but she also had compassion. She knew woodlore, but she also understood people.

Susan Valentine was a perfect case in point. An older

woman, a brainy ex-scientist on top of that—on paper there was no way she and Hope should ever have been more than polite working companions. But Hope hadn't settled for that. She'd taken Valentine under her wing, helping her work through the bewilderment and fear of her new environment, nurturing her like a mother helping her child through those first confusing and terrifying days at school.

Even more amazingly, Valentine had responded, not with the pride or resentment someone in her position might have gone with, but with gratitude and a deep respect for her young mentor's patience. Somewhere along the way, somewhere in the short span of three months, the two of them had become friends.

Which was going to make it that much harder when Preston was forced to order Valentine to leave Baker's Hollow.

He was taking off his gun belt, wondering if Hope might be sleeping deeply enough for him to carry her back to her room, when her eyes fluttered open.

"Hi," she murmured sleepily.

"Hi," he said. "Your bed just too warm and cozy tonight?"

"I heard you go out," Hope said, pushing down the edge of the blanket and yawning widely. "Right after I heard the H-K pass by to the west. Did you see where it went?"

"Somewhere southeast, I think," her father replied, stepping over to the small hurricane lamp on the table and lighting the wick. "I couldn't tell for sure." He hesitated, wondering if he should let her have one more night of peaceful sleep before he dropped the bombshell on her along with everyone else. But he needed to work through his options, and Hope was the only person whose advice he genuinely trusted.

"We did see something else, though," he continued. "Just across the ford, apparently waiting for someone coming in from the west. Oxley says it's a T-700 Terminator."

In the soft lamplight he saw Hope's face tense. Then, as he'd known she would, she put the shock behind her and nodded.

"Are we going to try to destroy it?" she asked.

Preston snorted. "Do I *look* crazy?" he countered as he sat down on the lumpy couch across from her. "Or do you know something about T-700s that I don't?"

"There's that weak spot on the base of the skull," Hope reminded him, touching the spot on the back of her own head. "Connor talked about that in one of his broadcasts."

"He was talking about T-600s, not T-700s," Preston pointed out. "Skynet may have plugged that design loophole by now. Besides, as I recall, all you get by poking something sharp there is some temporary confusion. We need something that'll actually kill it."

"Okay, but if poking the spot causes trouble, maybe digging in deeper will hit something more vulnerable," Hope suggested. "I was thinking one of Halverson's carbon shafts with a broadhead at point-blank range."

Preston pursed his lips. "No," he said. "We'd want an aluminum shaft. Better electrical conduction."

Hope's face lit up. "So I can try it?"

"Whoa, girl," Preston said, holding up a hand. "That's not Plan A, B, or anywhere else in the alphabet. That's an absolute last resort."

Her face fell. "Oh."

"What I want from *you*," Preston continued, "is your thoughts of where you'd move everyone if we had to abandon the town."

Her eyes were steady on his.

"You think we're going to have to?"

"I don't know," Preston said, his eyes flicking around the room. It was an old house, the house he'd grown up in, and the hard years since Judgment Day hadn't been very kind to it. But it was still weather-tight, and more comfortable than a lot of the other houses in town.

More than that, the house was *his*. His and Hope's. It was their home, their sanctuary, and one of the few things left in their lives that still resonated with the memories of Hope's mother. The thought of abandoning it, even in the face of a Terminator attack, grated more bitterly than anything else that had happened since her death.

"I'd rather not," he said. "But if that Terminator decides to cross the river, we may have to."

"Boy, that's a tough one," Hope murmured, her eyes taking on the faraway look that meant she was thinking hard. "We'd want to settle near one of the old upslope hunting cabins. That would at least give us a place to store whatever supplies we were able to bring."

"But there wouldn't be enough room for anything except supplies in any of the cabins," Preston pointed out. "Especially since the biggest is the Glaumann place, which is a little too close to the river for comfort. At least, for now."

"So we'd need tents," Hope continued, still gazing into space. "Lots of them. And pallets and blankets." Her eyes came back. "We haven't got them," she concluded quietly. "Not for eighty-seven people."

Her father nodded. He'd already run through the same logic on the trip back from the river. "Which means we'd either have to split up the town among the various cabins, putting everyone inside that we could, or else throw together some kind of big group shelter."

"If we'd have time for that," Hope said doubtfully. "And any kind of building project would take people off hunting duty. We can't afford to do that for more than a couple of days."

"Agreed," Preston said. Her conclusions were a vindication of his own thought processes, but that was pretty cold comfort. He would rather that she'd spotted something he'd missed. "Well, at least we know what we're up against," he said, forcing himself out of the couch. "You'd better get back to bed. It's been a long day, and tomorrow will probably be worse."

"Unless the Terminator attacks tonight," Hope said soberly as she gathered her blanket together and levered herself out of the broken chair.

"In which case, we won't have to do any planning at all tomorrow," Preston said grimly. "And pleasant dreams to *you*, too."

"All part of my daughterly duty," Hope said, forcing a smile she clearly didn't feel. "Don't worry, Dad. We'll get through this."

"I know." He wrapped his arms around her in a tight hug. She hugged him back, and for a moment hunger, cold, and even Terminators could almost be forgotten. Then, reluctantly, he let go and kissed her on the cheek. "Now off with you," he said, patting her shoulder.

"Right." She gave him a wry look. "Like I'm going to be able to sleep *now*."

Back outside the demolished lab, Williams had set herself a thirty-meter perimeter while she was on watch. Out in the middle of nowhere, Barnes made his perimeter a full sixty meters. Just to prove he could do it. Also so he wouldn't have to look at her slouched there asleep in the pilot's seat while he plodded through the desert sand.

Because he knew full well what this was all about. She could deny it all she liked, but he knew better. This trip was Connor's way of trying to nudge the two of them into making up.

Right. When hell froze over.

He glowered toward the Blackhawk. Unfortunately, much as he would like to think of Williams as stupid, he knew better. The girl was smart. Sometimes too smart for her own good, but still smart. Even if you had to hold your nose while you did it, she was usually worth listening to.

Especially since in this particular case Barnes knew down deep that she was right. Back at the lab, in the middle of the Terminator attack, it had taken him longer than he'd expected to locate and grab the minigun he'd spotted earlier that afternoon. The H-K had had plenty to time to get the range, and by all rights it should have blown the chopper into scrap.

Only it hadn't. Dodging away from Barnes's firing cone had been a reasonable thing for it to do. Trying to force the chopper down without destroying it hadn't.

He scowled up at the night sky, sending a flood of cold air down the neck of his jacket. Could the H-K have been out of ammo? That might explain it. Maybe Skynet had decided that dropping the big machine on top of the Blackhawk would be the fastest and simplest way to destroy it.

But that didn't make any sense. For one thing, all the H-K would have had to do was nudge its armored nose or flank into the Blackhawk's main rotor hard enough to shatter it. A chopper without a rotor wasn't going anywhere. Alternatively, it could have just dropped straight down on top of the Blackhawk instead of wasting time dancing with it.

And finally, the damn thing *hadn't* been out of ammo. Barnes had proved that himself by blowing up the Gatling guns' ammo canisters.

Had Skynet been trying to take him and Williams alive, then? That idea sent a shiver up Barnes's back that had nothing to do with the night air. Especially after that glimpse of hell he'd had in San Francisco when they were busting Connor out.

But wanting to capture the chopper's crew still didn't explain not wrecking the chopper itself.

Unless it was the *chopper* that Skynet actually wanted.

Barnes chewed at his lip. Even before San Francisco had gone up in Connor's massive explosion Skynet had been running low on resources. Their own experience with the L.A. supply depot had proved that.

But could it really be hurting so badly for aircraft that it would stoop to stealing Blackhawks?

Especially this particular Blackhawk. It was typical of what the Resistance had to work with these days: old, tired, and patched in a dozen places, with engines that had been revamped, rebuilt, and were held together with spit and curses. It was purely through the minor miracles of people like their genius mechanic Wince that aircraft like this were even still flying. The H-K itself had been in far better shape.

Not now, of course. But it had been when it started out. Yet Skynet had apparently been willing to gamble it for the Blackhawk.

And then, abruptly, he got it.

Skynet didn't want just *a* Blackhawk. It wanted a *Resistance* Blackhawk, with all the flaws and patchwork that any genuine Resistance fighter would automatically know to look for.

Skynet was looking for an infiltration vehicle.

Cyberdyne Systems Model 101. Connor had muttered that over and over as Barnes and Wright carried him out of the San Francisco hellhole. When Barnes had asked Kate about it later, she'd told him the 101 was part of a new Terminator series, the T-800s. She'd described them as Skynet's first attempt at a serious infiltrator model, with human flesh covering an updated version of the T-700 endoskeleton.

How she could possibly know things like that Barnes couldn't guess. She'd been pretty vague when he'd asked her about it. Probably something Connor had learned from Command, before Command had gotten itself killed.

Kate had also expressed hope that all the T-800s been destroyed in the explosion. That was one of the reasons, Barnes gathered, why Connor was spending the time and resources to sift through the wreckage. Not just to eliminate any remaining T-600s and T-700s, but also to look for any of the newer models that might have survived.

Maybe one of them had. At least one. And Skynet wanted a genuine Resistance chopper to take it to whatever Resistance group it was planning to infiltrate.

Maybe even Connor's group.

Barnes bared his teeth. Well, the damn computer wasn't going to get *this* chopper, anyway. Not if he had anything to say about it.

Williams didn't even twitch as Barnes climbed carefully back up into the chopper's cockpit. Either the woman was a lot more tired than he was, or else she simply felt safer with Barnes on watch than he did when she was pulling that duty.

Or else the injury to her leg had driven her into a deeper sleep than usual. He glanced at the limb, feeling a brief flicker of guilt. He'd run her harder that afternoon than he'd probably needed to.

The guilt vanished. She still owed him for that crack about his brother. Lying on his back, he hunched up beneath one of the equipment access covers that Wince had put in and popped it open.

Ten minutes later, he closed it again. He didn't know anything about chopper electronics, but he knew a jury-rigged circuit when he saw one, and the power wires to the auxiliary fan Wince had installed in the cockpit to help airflow was easy to spot among the mass of other wires.

And as it so often had, Barnes's pre-Judgment Day expertise in hot-wiring cars had come in handy.

Getting back to his feet, he took one final look at the sleeping Williams. Connor wanted him to forgive her, he knew. Williams probably wanted him to, as well.

But he wouldn't. He couldn't. Not after what she'd done to him.

Not ever.

He climbed back out onto the ground, his boots making little squeaking sounds on the cold sand. He took a moment to give the area around them a careful scan, then headed back out to continue walking his perimeter.

They would follow that cable, just like Williams wanted. Not because she was the pilot and had the final say, but because Skynet was up to something, and there was at least a chance it had to do with the cable.

And when the trail ended, whatever they found at the end of it, he was going to head back to San Francisco to alert Connor about this new T-800 threat. Even if he had to walk.

Even if he had to drag Williams by her sore leg the whole way.

It was a couple of hours before dawn when Jik finally reached the old bridge.

To discover that he was too late. Standing rigidly a meter from the foot of the rickety crossing, its eyes a pair of glowing red embers in the night, was the dark metallic form of a T-700.

For a long minute Jik gazed through the trees at the machine, his mind and heart sinking beneath a bitter wave of defeat. All his hopes and stamina had been focused on this bridge, this frail interweaving of rope and wood. For it to have been so casually snatched away from him was a crushing blow.

Sternly, Jik forced away the emotion. Self-pity was a trap, and he knew better than to let it get hold of him. He'd had more than his share of disappointments and reversals throughout his lifetime, and he'd managed to get over, around, or through every one of them. He'd get around this one, too. All he needed was a little thought, a little planning, and a little ingenuity.

None of which he had at the moment, and none of which he was likely to get until he'd burned some of the fatigue from his mind and body. Taking a final look at the Terminator's positioning, and the big Heckler & Koch G11 submachinegun gripped in its skeletal hand, he carefully backed away from the river gorge and headed into the deep woods.

A quarter mile away, right where he remembered it, he found the old cabin, looking even more dilapidated than it had forty years ago. The door opened about half a foot and then jammed, and it took some serious sweat and leverage to get it open far enough for him to slip through.

The interior was every bit as dreary as the exterior. To one side was an old cot with deep tears in the canvas, partially covered by a thin mattress that smelled heavily of mold and mildew. Hanging over the cot on a set of hooks was an old rifle of a make and model he didn't recognize and a thick coil of weathered and fragile-looking rope. To the other side was the cabin's lone window, broken of course. In the corner between the window and the door was a rusty pot-bellied stove, with a few chunks of firewood lying on the floor nearby.

For a moment Jik looked longingly at the stove and the wood, then turned resolutely away. A roaring fire *would* go a long way toward banishing the cabin's damp and chill.

But from the looks of the stove and kinked chimney, it would be a tossup as to whether he would asphyxiate himself or simply burn the whole place down. Worse, the smoke might attract the attention of the Terminator by the river. If that happened, smoke inhalation and third-degree burns would be the least of his problems.

Unless, of course, Jik wasn't actually here at the time...

He felt a tight grin crease his cheeks. The obvious solution to his problem, and he felt like an idiot for not spotting it sooner.

His first impulse was to grab a couple of chunks of wood and get to work. His second, wiser thought was the reminder that racing through an unfamiliar forest after a tiring hike would be a dangerous and stupid thing to do. Particularly given that he might well end up with the Terminator on his tail. The smoke trick would work just as well in the daylight, after he'd gotten a few hours of sleep.

His first task was to get the sodden mattress off the cot and lug it outside. After that came a quick examination of the rifle on the wall. It seemed to be in decent enough shape, though it was impossible to tell what kind of damage might be lurking in its inner workings. It was a moot point, though, since the weapon wasn't loaded and there was no place in the cabin where a cache of shells might be stored. If push came to shove, he would just have to hope he could make do with the single remaining round in his Smith & Wesson.

Ten minutes later, he was stretched out on the cot, which with all its rips and sags and odors was still the best bed he'd had in a long, long time. He would sleep as long as he could, he decided, then see if a fire in the stove might lure the Terminator away from his post. If it did, he was home free.

If it didn't... well, he would deal with that when the time came.

CHAPTER EIGHT

Before Judgment Day, Baker's Hollow had been a tiny flyspeck community whose main function in life was to act as a jumping-off point for hikers, fishermen, and hunters heading further up into the mountains. At its height, it had boasted fifty houses, many of which were bed-and-breakfasts or vacation rentals, a well-stocked general store, an RV parking area, and three guide services. Nearly two hundred people had lived in town during the tourist season, though many of them packed up and left when the first early snows began to fall.

That had been Baker's Hollow at its height. Now, it was at its depth. Only twenty of the fifty houses remained, the rest having been scavenged for wood and brick to keep the others habitable. The old general store had been turned into a workshop for the metal, cloth, and leather workers. The last remaining guide service office had been converted into a smokehouse for curing deer and elk. The permanent population, including the dribble of people who'd stumbled into town over the years, now sat at eighty-seven.

And better than half of those eighty-seven were waiting outside Preston's door when he emerged from his house just after sunrise.

Apparently, news of the T-700 at the river had already leaked out.

"Morning, everyone," he said, nodding as he swept his eyes over the crowd. "Something I can help you with?"

"We hear we've got a Terminator," Duke Halverson said bluntly. As usual, he'd made sure to take up the most prominent position, right in the center of the group and two steps in front of everyone else. "That true?"

"There's one down by the river, yes," Preston said. There was no point in denying it—chances were good that Halverson had already checked it out for himself. "It's on the far side, by the ford."

"You have a plan for dealing with it?"

"We're working on one," Preston told him. "For the moment, it doesn't seem interested in the town."

"What happens when it *does* get interested in the town?" Halverson persisted. "What then?"

Preston gave the crowd another, more careful look. Eight of them were hunters, Halverson's allies, ready to back anything the big man said or proposed. Twelve of the others were Preston's friends and normally his firm supporters in town disputes. Right now, though, they looked more apprehensive than supportive. The rest were just ordinary citizens of Baker's Hollow who usually avoided town politics and concentrated on basic survival.

All of them, Halverson included, were frightened. As well they should be.

"If the Terminator decides to head this way," Preston said, "I'm thinking the prudent thing might be to move out of town for a while."

"And go where?" Halverson demanded.

"There are a few habitable cabins out there," Preston reminded him, again looking around. No one seemed any happier than Halverson at the prospect of leaving. "We could split up into small groups, each centered around one of them, and wait until the Terminator leaves."

"Those cabins won't hold even a tenth of us," Halverson pointed out. "What about everyone else? We just going to sleep out on the ground with the coyotes and bears?"

"At least bears don't usually attack without a reason," Preston said.

"Yeah." Halverson gestured, a quick flick of his fingers. "We need to talk."

"We *are* talking," Preston said mildly. "But you're right—it's a bit brisk out here." He half turned. "We'd all be more comfortable inside."

"Just you and me," Halverson said, striding toward him.

Preston felt his stomach tighten.

"Halverson—"

"Chris, go get my team together and send them over to Ned's place," Halverson cut him off, motioning to one of the hunters. "The rest of you, go back to work. We'll let you know what we decide."

"Right," Chris said briskly before anyone else could speak up. "Let's go, everyone. Clothes and metalwork don't repair themselves, you know."

A few troubled looks came Preston's way as the group broke up. But no one said anything, and a minute later Preston and Halverson were alone.

"Like you said, it's brisk out here," Halverson said.

Silently, Preston gestured at the door. Halverson strode past him and went inside. Grimacing, Preston followed.

"This isn't right, you know," he warned as Halverson planted himself in the center of the living room and turned to face him. "All decisions are supposed to be run past the council."

"Do I look like I care?" Halverson retorted, the thin mask of politeness he'd been wearing outside now gone completely. "The council is a bunch of fools. None of them would survive a week on their own."

"The work they do is important, too."

Halverson made a face. "Stoves. Clothes. Traps."

"Hey, Chucker's bear traps saved your skin at least once," Preston countered. "And don't forget medical care, vegetable gardening, *and* replacement arrows for you and the rest of the hunters. You can sneer all you want, but you can't deny that life in town is easier for you and Ginny than it would be if you were alone out in the wild."

"I don't deny it," Halverson said with a grunt. "But that's only as long as we're *in* the town. Once we leave it, the gardeners and stove-fixers aren't going to be worth much, are they? Not much point in Ginny and me even hanging around if that happens."

Preston hissed out a sigh. "How many times are you going to do this, Duke?" he asked quietly. "How many times are you going to threaten to take your wife and your friends and walk out if the town doesn't do what you want?"

"You don't like me?" Halverson challenged, just as quietly. "Replace me. Until you do, I've got a right to speak up the same as anyone else."

He leveled a finger at Preston.

"But we're not talking about quotas or crop shares this time. We're talking about survival. There's a Terminator sitting on our doorstep, and we damn well have to do something about it."

"What do you think we've just been talking about?"

"What *you've* been talking about is giving up," Halverson said. "Giving up and running away."

"Only temporarily."

"Yeah, and isn't it funny how easy *temporary* turns into *permanent*," Halverson said with a sniff. "And I'm serious. If we have to give up this town and these buildings, there's no reason for Ginny and me to stay with the group. I can hunt enough just fine for the two of us. *And* have enough spare time left over to make my own arrows."

"And if you go, you'll take Chris and Ned and Trounce with you?"

"Hey, we're all free citizens," Halverson said with a shrug. "I don't speak for anyone except myself."

But whether he spoke for them or not, Preston knew, most of the town's best hunters looked up to Halverson. Many of them would follow the same logic he'd just laid out, and desert Baker's Hollow right alongside him.

Without the hunters, the town was doomed. And when the town died, so would any chance for even a modest degree of civilization here in the mountains.

Preston couldn't let that happen. No matter what it cost.

"So what's *your* idea?" he asked, the words stinging in his throat.

"We take the damn thing out," Halverson said flatly. "Right now."

Preston winced. He'd been afraid that was where he was going.

"We can't do that," he said as calmly as he could. "At the moment it's not coming after us. We attack it, and that'll change."

"Not if we kill it," Halverson said. "Come on, Preston—I've killed full-grown grizzlies. How tough can a Terminator be?"

"For starters, your bear's vitals weren't encased in solid metal," Preston pointed out, striving to maintain his calmness. Arguing with Halverson was an absolutely guaranteed way to solidify the man's position. "Even if you found a way through that, Skynet's not going to just sit back and watch you do it."

"Ah," Halverson said with the self-satisfied air of someone who's been hoping for precisely that question. "It may in fact do exactly that. I talked with Lajard this morning. He says that with the San Francisco hub gone, the nearest Skynet long-range transmitter is on the east coast. If he's right, it can only punch a signal through this far at night."

"Unless Skynet has some kind of relay system between the east coast and here that it can use," Preston warned. "Through smaller stations or even H-Ks."

"It doesn't work that way," Halverson said. "Lajard says multiple relays are too vulnerable to interception and signal something-or-other—signal degradation, I think it was. Anything big, including large downloads or major changes in mission profile, has to come directly from a Skynet hub."

"Interesting theory, anyway," Preston said. And obviously in Lajard's exact words, too. Halverson's vocabulary wasn't nearly that extensive.

"It's more than just a theory," Halverson growled. "The point is that if this Terminator is at the river to catch someone coming in from the west, and we hit it during the day, Skynet won't be able to send any new instructions about fighting back. Not until it's too late."

"Of course, that assumes T-700s don't already come with a built-in set of contingency orders," Preston pointed out. "Something as simple, say, as killing any human it comes across."

"Well, we'll just have to take our chances, won't we?" Halverson said impatiently. "That machine has got to go, and we haven't got time for a long debate. I say we hit it."

"And if I say we don't?" Preston asked, trying one last time.

"Then you'd better hope your daughter feels up to hunting enough to feed sixty or seventy people a day," Halverson said. "I've got Ned going around collecting and checking all the large-caliber rifles in town. You can come with us, or we can do it by ourselves."

Preston shook his head. This was madness. But he was mayor, and if he didn't show up he might as well hand over the last scraps of his authority right now.

"Fine," he said. "I'll meet you at Ned's in fifteen minutes."

"Good," the other said with the grim-edged satisfaction he always showed when he got his way. "Bring plenty of ammo." Striding past Preston, he opened the door and headed back out into the early-morning chill.

Preston waited until he'd closed the door behind him.

"You heard?" he asked.

"Yes," Hope said, stepping into view from the hallway. Her face was pale. "Dad, you can't let him do this. *You* can't do this."

"You feel up to hunting for seventy people?" Preston asked sourly as he headed for the closet where his Ruger 99/44 hunting rifle was stored. "Because unless you do, I don't see anything we can do but go along with him."

"And get everyone in town killed?" Hope countered. "We'd do better to let me take over the hunting."

"Which would just be a slower form of death," Preston said gently. "You're good, Hope, but not *that* good."

Hope wrinkled her nose in frustration.

"You still don't have to go along with him," she insisted. "Maybe if he fell flat on his face a few times people would stop listening to him."

"I'd like nothing better than to watch him eat dirt," Preston said as he pulled out the rifle and the box of shells. "Unfortunately, in this case, if he fails we end up with a Terminator walking through town. I'll try one last time to talk them out of it—" he grimaced "—and if I can't, then we really have no choice but to hit the thing just as hard and as fast as we can."

"I suppose," Hope said, still not sounding convinced. "Let me go get my bow and quiver."

"Yes, do that," Preston said. "But you'll be heading the opposite direction. I want you and Susan to pick one of the clearings near Crescent Rock and start your hunt."

Hope's eyes narrowed. "I thought you just said we need everyone to hit the Terminator."

"Everyone who has a gun," Preston corrected. "Which you don't. More importantly, whatever happens with the machine, some of us will still have to eat tonight."

"Dad—"

"It's not negotiable, Hope," Preston said quietly. "And I've got enough fights on my hands right now. I really can't handle another one."

She sighed, then nodded. "Okay, I just… okay. If that's what you want."

"It is," Preston assured her, giving her a quick hug. "And don't come back to town. If things go all right, someone will come and get you. If no one's there within two hours after the shooting stops, head over to Skink Pond. I'll catch up with you there."

"Okay." Hope took a deep breath. "I love you, Dad."

"Love you, Hope." Releasing her from the hug, he caught her hand and squeezed it. "I'll see you soon. Be careful, and don't worry."

***

The sky was lightening to the east when Blair was startled awake by a slap on her shoulder and a gruff order to get moving. By the time the sun appeared over the horizon, she had the Blackhawk fifty meters above the smoldering Skynet lab, ready to follow the mysterious cable.

At first, it was easy. As she'd already noted, the explosion had sent shock waves through both the ground and the cable, periodically kinking the latter hard enough to shove loops of it to the surface. With the slanting sunlight exaggerating every bump and dip, Blair could usually see five or six of the humps at any given time.

But as the sun rose, and as the distance from the lab increased, the humps grew progressively smaller and less obvious. Finally, somewhere around the twenty-kilometer mark, they disappeared completely.

"Now what?" Barnes asked.

Blair gazed out the window, squinting against the windstorm beating across her face and wishing for the umpteenth time that the Blackhawk's storage lockers had included some goggles. The desert had given way to a sort of tentative grassland, with forested foothills and mountains directly ahead.

"I think we should keep going," she said. "So far, the cable's been running pretty straight along this vector. Let's assume it continues that way, and see what we run into."

Barnes grunted. "Not easy to keep a cable running straight through the middle of a forest."

"True," Blair said. "But if anyone could have done it— or have *wanted* to do it—it would be Skynet."

For a moment Barnes was silent. Blair kept her eyes forward, wincing in anticipation of his inevitable outburst.

She could hardly blame him. He'd kept his side of the bargain she'd forced on him, and had let her drag them out here trying to follow the cable. Now that the trail had petered out, he would be perfectly justified in insisting she drop the whole thing and head back to San Francisco.

And when he did, she was going to have to argue with him. Because the more they'd traveled along the cable's path, and the more she'd seen how much effort Skynet had put into it, the more she was convinced it was something they needed to check out.

But Barnes wouldn't see it that way. He'd already been saddled with her longer than he'd expected, and way more than he'd wanted. He would insist on heading back, and down deep she knew that trying to pull the pilot's trump card on him again would be a dangerous thing to do. He might even put a gun to her head, figuring he could argue his way out of trouble with Connor when they got back—

"We should grab a little more altitude," he said. "In case the cable takes a turn somewhere. Don't want to be too low to see that."

"Yes—good idea," Blair said, fighting to keep the surprise out of her voice as she angled the Blackhawk upward. An actual, rational decision from him, uncolored by his current feelings? Was he finally starting to come back to normal?

She stole a sideways look at him, her small hope fading away. No. He was intrigued by the cable, and smart enough to know how to separate his personal feelings from the job of fighting Skynet. But that single glance was enough to tell her that he still hadn't forgiven her for her brief relationship with Marcus Wright.

That relationship had been real, she knew. So had her feelings, and those feelings hadn't changed with her discovery of the half man, half machine that Skynet had turned him into. She'd done what she'd done, and she had no regrets.

But if her time with Marcus had permanently cost her Barnes's friendship and respect, she might someday have to seriously consider whether it had truly been worth it.

They'd gone another twenty kilometers, and were well up into the mountain forests, when Barnes suddenly pointed ahead and to the left.

"There!" he snapped. "Smoke."

"I see it," Blair confirmed. There were several slender plumes drifting upward from a clearing just east of the river the Blackhawk was currently following. A town or village, far enough out in the middle of nowhere that Skynet had missed it? "Think it's worth checking out?"

"You're the pilot," Barnes said. "You'll just do whatever you want anyway."

Blair sighed inwardly. No, he hadn't forgiven her.

"Okay," she said as she swung the Blackhawk to the right. Whoever was in that town, she didn't want to spook them by landing right in the middle of the place. "Keep an eye out for an open spot where we can set down."

There were half a dozen small clearings within a mile of the smoke plumes, all of them to the east and south. Most were too small for a safe landing, but two looked big enough to accommodate the Blackhawk. Blair picked the larger one and headed down.

The ground was spongy with dead leaves and matted fir needles and a half-buried, decaying log that she almost didn't see in time. She skidded a couple of meters sideways to avoid it, then set the helo down. Taking a careful survey of the area, she shut down the engines.

The roar faded away into silence as she slipped off her headphones.

"You see anything?" she asked Barnes.

"Lots of forest," he replied, already out of his seat. He slung his backpack onto his shoulders, then added his SIG 542 assault rifle and his RAI 300 sniper rifle. "Turn off the cockpit fan on your way out, will you?"

Blair frowned. With the wind whipping freely through the broken windshield, she hadn't even noticed the fan was on.

"You had the *fan* going?" she asked as she thumbed off the switch. "Why?"

"'Cause that's how you start the chopper now," he said calmly. "I hooked the fan into the starter circuit last night while you were asleep."

Blair's first impulse was to ask what the hell he thought he was doing messing with her helo's wiring. Her second was that that was actually a pretty good idea.

"Clever," she said. "We'll probably want—" She broke off, feeling her eyes widening as he heaved the minigun up off the deck. "You're taking *that*?"

"I'm sure as hell not leaving it," he countered with a grunt.

Blair winced, trying to think of a diplomatic way of saying this.

"The people in that town over there may already be leery of strangers," she tried. "If we show up looking like arms dealers—"

"Then they'll know not to mess with us, won't they?" he cut her off. "Grab that shotgun." Without waiting for a response, he hopped out through the side door, landing with a thud.

Blair picked up the Mossberg M500 shotgun and ammo pack and slung them over her shoulder. Checking the Blackhawk's compass one last time to get her bearings, she stepped out into the leaves.

The smoke plumes had been almost directly northwest of their landing site. Barnes was already ten meters that direction, stomping through the undergrowth and forcing his way through the occasional line of close-set bushes. Blair picked the most distant tree she could see in the right direction and set off after him, splitting her attention between the tree and her footing.

She'd closed the gap between her and Barnes to a couple of meters, and the Blackhawk had been lost to sight behind them, when Barnes suddenly slowed.

"Keep going," he murmured. "Straight on, and don't look at the bushes."

Before Blair could ask what that was supposed to mean he was off again, resuming his brisk pace but with his direction now shifted a few degrees to their left.

Frowning, Blair continued forward, casually dropping her hand to her holstered Desert Eagle.

She'd gone another twenty paces when she spotted the glint of metal behind a cluster of bushes to their left. It took her another couple of steps to identify it as an arrowhead, a wide, nasty-looking version that seemed to be made of four angled razor blades. Crouched in the bushes behind the arrow was a shadowy figure holding a compound bow.

And Barnes was heading directly toward him.

CHAPTER NINE

The aircraft suddenly appeared like a roaring predator overhead and Hope's first frantic thought was that it was going to land right in front of her, in the middle of the clearing she and Susan had staked out. But to her relief, it flew past, giving her a glimpse through the trees of a wide greenish-brown body. She listened closely, and a few seconds later heard the roar of the engines change pitch. Half a minute after that, the sound whined down into silence.

"What was it?" Susan asked, her voice hoarse, her face white and pinched. "Did you see it?"

"I saw a little," Hope said, her own voice sounding a little shaky. "It didn't sound like an H-K."

"Who knows what H-Ks sound like these days?" Susan countered, clutching at Hope's arm. "Come on, we have to get out of here."

Hope took a deep breath, sternly ordering the butterflies in her stomach to settle down.

"We first need to find out who or what it is," she told the older woman. "It sounded like it landed in Violet Glen, and there's only one obvious route from there back to town. We'll find a place along the way to hide and see who shows up."

Susan's jaw dropped.

"Hope, those could be *Terminators* back there. Or raiders, or who knows what else."

"They could also be the Resistance," Hope said. "Don't you remember Connor's broadcasts? He promised that if we were out here the Resistance would find us. Maybe they finally have."

"Or maybe they haven't," Susan ground out.

"I'm going to check it out," Hope said firmly. "I want you to head back to town and alert my father."

Susan's eyes narrowed.

"Why? Because I don't know what I'm doing?"

Hope reached down and squeezed her hand.

"Because I don't want you to get hurt," she said gently. "You're important to the town. We need you."

"No, *you* need me, and you need me right here," Susan said firmly. "And anyway your father *must* have heard that thing go roaring past." She gestured. "Show me where you want me."

Five minutes later, they were in position. Hope had found a clump of bushes about ten feet back from the barely visible trail that led from Violet Glen to town. Susan was behind a tree and another group of bushes another ten feet back on the opposite side of the trail.

They were barely in time. Hope had just pulled an arrow from her quiver when she heard someone approaching. Nocking the arrow to the string, she drew about a third back and mentally prepared herself.

Her dad hadn't wanted to let her see what happened if she put a broadhead into the back of a Terminator's head.

Maybe she was going to find out anyway.

It was with a sense of relief, though oddly also with a slight sense of disappointment, that she watched a pair of humans stride into sight. The man was big and black, his face dominated by a fringe of beard and a scowl, the rest of his body dominated by a holstered pistol, two shoulder-slung long guns, and an awesomely scary-looking multi-barreled weapon clutched in his arms. The woman behind him was slimmer and less heavily armed, but no less wary and competent looking.

And both of them were wearing red Resistance armbands.

Or at least, they *looked* like Resistance armbands.

Hope frowned, shifting her attention back to the big gun. She'd heard Susan, Oxley, and Lajard talk about the weapons and equipment carried by the various types of Terminators. That gun with its long ammo belt draped over the man's shoulders looked an awful lot like the way they'd described T-600 miniguns.

She chewed at her lip, suddenly unsure what she should do. If that was a Terminator weapon, then maybe the man and woman weren't Resistance at all. Maybe they were Skynet agents, here to provide support to the T-700 by the river. The T-700 that her father and the others were closing in on at this very moment.

Or maybe the gun looked like a Terminator weapon but wasn't.

Unfortunately, the only person nearby she could ask was hiding behind a tree twenty feet away. Maybe the smart thing to do would be to just let the strangers pass unchallenged, then go grab Susan and find out for sure about the gun.

The woman caught up to the man, who had slowed almost to a halt, and Hope saw his lips move as he said something. The woman nodded, and together they started up again.

Only to Hope's horror, the man was now angling off the path.

Heading straight toward her.

She caught her breath. Had he decided to take a different route across this part of the forest? Had he somehow spotted her back here?

No, she realized suddenly. He hadn't spotted *her*. He'd spotted the arrow.

Her eyes flicked downward to the broadhead, the taste of panic bubbling up into her throat as she saw, too late, the terrible mistake she'd made. Automatically, as she always did when stalking game, she'd eased the tip of the arrow out through the bushes so that it wouldn't get tangled or deflected when she shot.

It never mattered if a deer saw it. Deer couldn't recognize an arrow as a threat. But human beings could.

What should she do? Try to pull the arrow back out of sight, on the slim chance that he hadn't yet spotted it? But if he *hadn't* seen it, any movement now would draw his attention to her in double-quick time.

Should she abandon her position and try to get away? Out of the question. There wasn't enough nearby cover to lose herself in, and she could hardly outrun a bullet.

Should she simply shoot him? Completely and utterly out of the question.

He was still coming toward her. With the suddenness of desperation Hope made up her mind. The gun in his arms was currently pointed up, toward the sky. The second he started swinging it down toward her, or shifted it to one hand and made a grab for one of his other guns, she would shoot the arrow into his hand from her current one-third pull. It wouldn't be going fast enough or hard enough to seriously injure him, but it should be enough to warn him off. By the time he recovered enough to respond, she would hopefully have another arrow nocked and ready.

Almost here. She braced herself, fighting the panicky urge to draw her bowstring all the way back. She wanted to warn him off, not kill him.

She was still watching the gun, waiting for the muzzle to drop toward her, when the man let go of the weapon with his left hand, snapped out his arm like a striking rattlesnake, and grabbed her arrow just behind the arrowhead. Before Hope could even gasp, he turned at the waist and let the big gun swivel and fall onto the top of the bush directly in front of her, crushing down the foliage in a flurry of snapping branches and crunching leaves. Hope flinched back, reflexively blinking as a branch swept past her face.

When she opened her eyes again, her cover was completely gone, the man was looming over her with her arrow in his hand, and his drawn pistol was pointed directly into her face.

"Who are you?" he demanded.

Hope opened her mouth, but her vocal cords seemed suddenly paralyzed.

"Come on—talk," he snarled, twitching the gun for emphasis.

"Back off!" Susan's voice snapped.

Hope turned her head. Susan had emerged from behind her tree and was standing with her bowstring drawn back to her ear, a broadhead arrow glinting in the early-morning light.

"You hear me? I said *back off*."

The man didn't move, but in the sudden brittle silence Hope heard the soft slipping sound of metal on leather as the other woman snatched her own gun from its holster and pointed it at Susan.

And finally, Hope found her voice.

"No—don't shoot," she called, her voice trembling embarrassingly. "Anyone. Please."

For a pair of thudding heartbeats no one moved or spoke. Then the woman stirred.

"Barnes?" she asked.

"She's just a kid," the man said, his voice still growly but maybe a little less brusque. "Yours?"

"Amateur," the woman said.

"Hey!" Susan said, sounding offended.

"It's all right, Susan," Hope called. "Put the bow down. Please."

"You heard her, Susan," the woman seconded. "No one has to get hurt here."

Hope looked over at Susan. The older woman's lips were compressed into a tight line, but she nevertheless lowered the arrow to point at the ground and eased the bowstring back to unpulled position.

"Don't shoot her," she said, nodding toward Hope.

"No one's shooting anyone," the man growled, keeping his gun in hand but raising the muzzle to point over Hope's head. "Not yet, anyway. Let's try again. Who are you?"

"My name's Hope Preston," Hope told him. "That's Susan Valentine."

"I'm Blair," the woman said. She was still holding her gun, but it was also no longer pointing at its original target. "He's Barnes. Are you two from that village over there?"

"Yes," Hope said. "Baker's Hollow. We heard your vehicle, and thought someone should check it out."

Barnes snorted. "And this is the best reception committee we could get?"

"Hardly," Hope's father's voice came unexpectedly from the direction of town. "Both of you, drop your weapons. Now."

"Dad, it's all right," Hope spoke up hastily. "We're

okay. They haven't hurt us."

"Good for them," Preston said grimly. "They can put their guns down anyway."

Hope focused on Barnes. His gun was still pointed away from her, but he had a look on his face that sent a fresh chill up her back.

"It's all right," she told him quietly. "That's my father. He won't hurt you. Please—do what he says."

Barnes hesitated. Then, to Hope's relief, he lowered his pistol and dropped it back into its holster. Behind him, Blair took the cue and also holstered her gun.

Not exactly what Preston had demanded. But it was close enough.

"Their guns are down," she called.

There was a soft swishing of bushes, and six men walked cautiously into sight, rifles held ready.

"Hope?" Preston called.

"I'm here," Hope said, standing up into view. "We're okay. This is Barnes and Blair."

Preston gave Hope a quick, measuring look, then turned back to Barnes.

"What are you doing here?"

"We were following—" Blair began.

"We saw your smoke," Barnes interrupted her. "Thought you might need help."

"You think we need help, yet you land way over here?"

"We didn't want to scare you," Blair said. "I see we didn't have to worry about that."

"So who are you?" Preston asked. "Not your names. I mean *who* are you?"

Hope saw Blair glance at Barnes's back.

"We're with the Resistance," she said, nodding toward her armband.

"Yeah, we've heard of you," Preston said. "You connected with any particular group?"

"You have a radio?" Barnes asked.

"We have a receiver, yes."

"Then you might have heard our boss," Barnes said. "We're with John Connor."

Hope exhaled in a quiet huff, a shivery thrill running through her. She'd hoped that the visitors would be from the Resistance, but she'd never dared to hope that they'd come from Connor himself.

Her father wasn't nearly so impressed.

"Really," he said, his tone neutral. "Can you prove that?"

"Like how?" Barnes countered. "You want a special tattoo or something?"

"I'm wondering about your convenient timing," Preston said suspiciously. "We get a T-700 knocking on our door, and then suddenly you drop in—"

"There's a *T-700* here?" Barnes cut him off, his eyes darting around. "Where?"

"You claiming you didn't know anything about that?"

"Damn it, Preston, *where*?" Barnes snarled.

"It's by the ford across the Slate River, on the far side of town," Hope told him hastily. That icy look was in his eye again. "But I don't think it's moved since we spotted it."

"Show us," Barnes said grimly, reaching down and picking up the big six-barreled gun and hoisting it up into his arms again.

"Hold it," Preston snapped. "We're not done here yet."

"Yes, we are," Blair said, starting forward again. "Like he said, show us."

Beside Preston, Half-pint Swan raised his gun. Hope saw his finger start to tighten on the trigger—

Without even looking, Hope's father tapped the other's

rifle barrel to the side.

"Easy," he warned. "You too," he added to Barnes. "We've got it under control."

"With *those*?" Barnes snorted, nodding at the hunting rifles pointed at him and Blair. "I don't think so."

Hope caught her breath. In all the excitement she hadn't really focused on which men her father had brought here with him. But now that she did—

"Dad, where's Halverson?" she asked. "Is he still at the river?"

"Yes, along with the rest of the force," Preston said. "I told them not to do anything until I get back."

Hope felt her stomach tighten. If Halverson decided to take on the Terminator without her dad and the others, there could be trouble. Big trouble.

"Dad—"

"That's enough, Hope," Preston said, his voice quiet but firm. "I can't be responsible for everything Halverson does. But I *am* responsible for the town. I can't just let heavily armed strangers walk in without some idea of who and what they are."

"So while you're standing there wondering about us, there's a machine ready to walk in," Barnes growled. "Here's the deal. You got a T-700, you need us. You need *this*." He hefted the big gun.

"And your clock is running," Blair added.

Preston's eyes flicked to Barnes, to Blair, back to Barnes.

"I'll lead," he said, raising the muzzle of his rifle. "You'll follow me, with Hope and my men behind you. You'll keep your guns pointed up unless and until I say otherwise. Any action which might be interpreted as aggressive toward us or anyone in town will be dealt with accordingly. Clear?"

"Clear," Barnes said, heaving his big gun up to rest half over his shoulder and striding toward the others. "How far?"

"To the river?" Preston asked as he waved the rest of the men back and started down the path leading back toward town. "Less than a mile. Let me know if I'm going too fast for you."

"Don't worry," Barnes said. "We'll keep up."

CHAPTER TEN

Jik woke to the sound of gunfire.

For a moment he lay still, his hand groping for the Smith & Wesson lying beside his cot, his eyes and brain fogged by too little sleep. The gunfire was distant, probably a mile or two away. Normally, having some distance between you and gunfire was a good thing, and the more distance the better.

Only in this case, it wasn't. A mile away meant it was coming from the ford over the Slate River.

The Terminators he'd seen heading that direction last night had launched their attack.

And here, a mile away, Jik was completely out of the fight.

He sat up on the cot, wiggling his toes a couple of times inside his boots to get his circulation going, listening closely to the distant cracks. So far all the gunfire seemed to be of the single-shot variety instead of coming in machinegun bursts. That implied that the townspeople were doing most of the shooting, which in turn implied that the machines were low on ammo and had to be careful how they spent it.

It could also mean that the town's opposition was so weak that the Terminators weren't even bothering to shoot back. That they were simply killing the people with their bare hands.

Swearing under his breath, Jik squeezed himself through the door. There was no way he could get to the ford in time to help. But maybe there was something he could do from right here.

The Terminators were trying to find him. It was time they succeeded.

The distant gunfire was still going on as he slipped around the final tree and came into sight of the bridge. He'd wondered if the T-700 he'd seen there earlier might have been called to the ford, but Skynet apparently hadn't seen any need for reinforcements down there. The Terminator was still standing its silent guard, right where Jik had left it.

And then, as Jik hesitated, wondering if this was really the best plan he could come up with, the distant sounds from the ford changed as a new weapon joined in the battle.

Only this one wasn't any single-shot hunting rifle. It was the terrifying, lethal stutter of a T-600 minigun.

And Jik no longer had a choice. If the Terminators were bringing that kind of firepower to bear, the people standing against them had literally only minutes left to live. Their only chance was for Jik to give the machines a better, more important target.

The secret of man's being, the old quote ran through his mind, *is not only to live but to have something to live for.*

Gripping his Smith & Wesson in both hands, he stepped into the T-700's view.

"Hey!" he shouted. "Over here!"

The machine turned its glowing red eyes toward him.

"Yes, here," Jik called. "Here I am. Take a good look."

He raised his gun.

"And get terminated."

Aiming between the machine's eyes, he squeezed the trigger.

***

They had just passed through the town, which as far as Barnes could tell consisted entirely of a bunch of ramshackle houses and a couple of larger buildings, when the sound of gunfire erupted from somewhere dead ahead.

Their leader, Hope's father, was off in an instant, breaking into a sprint with his rifle held high in front of him. Grunting, swearing under his breath, Barnes followed. His legs were already feeling leaden from all the weight he was carrying, and the soft, draggy ground beneath him wasn't making things any easier. But he'd told Preston he could keep up and he was damned if he would fall behind now.

Three minutes later, they burst through one final barrier of low-hanging branches onto the scene of battle.

Barnes had seen Terminators picking their way through city rubble, striding across empty fields, even climbing up the outsides of shattered walls. But up to now he'd never seen one standing shin-deep in the middle of a narrow river, plumes of whitewater churning around its legs, trying to push forward against the current and the relentless impact of heavy rifle rounds.

Heavy, but not heavy enough. The T-700's approach was being slowed by the gunfire, but it wasn't taking much damage. There were some dents in its torso and skull, and its gun arm had been dislocated at the shoulder, but that was about it.

Well, Barnes could do something about that. Braking to a halt, he slid his right foot behind him for stability and dropped the muzzle of his minigun into firing position. Lining up the weapon on the Terminator's torso, he squeezed the trigger.

The gun thundered to life, pouring out its stream of destruction. Barnes leaned into the recoil, fighting to keep the hail of lead centered on its target.

He probably wasn't as accurate with the minigun as an actual T-600 would have been. But at this range he was accurate enough. The T-700 staggered back, its arms and legs snapping free of its torso and flying into the churning water, the torso itself denting and then shredding and finally disintegrating under the assault.

And as the machine collapsed into a heap in the roiling water Barnes let up on the trigger.

"Anyone else?" he challenged.

He hadn't expected a response. He got one anyway. On the far side of the river, thirty meters to the north, a pair of bushes were shoved violently apart to reveal a second T-700. It strode to the riverbank and then turned to its right and started downstream toward the ford.

"Look out—there's another one!" someone shouted.

Barnes glanced down at the minigun's ammo belt. There were only about thirty rounds remaining, about half a second at full auto. Best to save those until the machine was closer. He dropped into a crouch and lowered the big gun to the ground.

And as he did so, a burst of gunfire from his left burned through the air above him.

He twisted his head to look in that direction, swinging his shoulder-slung SIG 542 into firing position. A third T-700 had appeared from the trees, this one fifty meters south, also moving along the riverbank toward the ford.

But unlike the one coming down from the north, this Terminator was ready for battle. Its G11 submachinegun was pointed and ready, its metal skull swinging back and forth as its glowing eyes tracked the human defenders scrambling madly for cover.

Sinking a little deeper into his crouch, Barnes swiveled as far around as he could at hips and waist and fired off a three-round burst from the 542. At this range the shots did little but stagger the Terminator back, but it was enough to give the rest of the men time to get to cover.

"Never mind the one to the north," someone shouted over the renewed gunfire. "The south one. Focus your fire on the south one."

As if to underline the urgency of the order, the southernmost of the two T-700s fired again, this burst digging gouges into the side of a wide tree two of the riflemen were huddled behind. Barnes sent another burst bouncing off the Terminator's torso, then checked the T-700 coming from the north. Its gun hand was still hanging at its side as it strode toward the ford, with no indication that it was preparing to open fire.

That would change soon enough, Barnes knew. But for the moment, whoever had called out that order had the situation properly nailed. The second Terminator was the one doing all the shooting, so that was the one they needed to deal with.

From Barnes's left came a familiar thunderclap as Williams opened fire with her Desert Eagle.

"I need to get closer," she shouted to Barnes as her shot staggered the Terminator back. "Cover me?"

Barnes gave a curt nod.

"Go."

He flicked his rifle's selector to single-shot as Williams ducked around behind Preston and his men and sprinted in a broken-field charge for the river. Deliberately, methodically, he pumped slug after slug into the T-700, spacing his shots so as to conserve ammo while still keeping the Terminator off balance and unable to get a clear shoot at the woman running toward it. A few of the other men, Preston among them, caught onto the plan and added their fire to Barnes's, their shots alternating with his.

Ten seconds later, Williams reached the river, her Desert Eagle now holstered and the Mossberg shotgun unslung and clutched in front of her. She was just closing the weapon's action, which told Barnes that she'd exchanged the shotgun round that had already been in place for one of the solid slugs from her ammo pack. The machine turned its G11 toward her, its burst going over her head as she threw herself into a feet-first baserunner slide that carried her to the very edge of the riverbank. The Terminator fired again, this burst also going wide as Barnes and Preston simultaneously hammered it.

And as the machine once again staggered back, Williams's slug blasted at point-blank range into its gun.

Terminators were made of incredibly strong, incredibly hard alloy. The G11s, on the other hand, were not only not as strong, but also had a couple of critical weak points. The gun's receiver was one such weakness, a spot where a heavy rifle or shotgun slug could jam the action and possibly ignite the chambered round. The magazine with the exposed explosive of its caseless rounds was another.

And if you were really, really lucky, those two weaknesses intersected. Williams's round slammed into the gun—

And suddenly the entire magazine went up in a sputtering, multiple flash as the close-packed ammo blew up, each round triggering the one next to it. The T-700 staggered back as the exploding rounds lit up its torso.

"Look out—here it comes!" someone shouted.

Barnes looked away from the sputtering fireworks display. The northern T-700, the one that the earlier voice had ordered everyone to ignore, had reached the ford and started across the river. Cursing, Barnes swung his rifle around toward it.

"Don't shoot!" the same voice called again. "It's not after us. Don't shoot!"

Barnes frowned. Ridiculous. The thing wading through the whitewater toward them was a Terminator. Terminators were always after humans. That was what they did. That was what they were.

But the machine's gun hand was still at its side, its head and eyes angled to the north instead of toward the small group of humans standing against it. From all appearances, it really *did* look like it was ignoring them.

"Don't shoot!" the voice called again.

Barnes swore again, shifting his grip on his rifle. Appearances or not, he didn't trust the damn machine farther than he could spit at it. He would hold onto his ammo for now, but the instant the T-700 stopped pretending and launched its attack he would make damn sure he was ready to blow its head off.

He was still crouching in the grass and dead leaves, waiting for that moment, when the Terminator finished crossing the river, turned north, and headed off again along the riverbank.

Barnes watched its back as it strode stolidly along, an eerie sense of unreality creeping across his skin, until it disappeared among the trees.

A movement caught the corner of his eye, and he looked across the river to see the other T-700 stride past the ford and continue north on the opposite bank. Its gun, he noted, was lying in a tangle of twisted metal on the ground behind it. Its right hand, which had taken the brunt of the multiple explosions, was in impressively bad shape, too.

The Terminator disappeared into the trees and bushes. Slowly, Barnes got to his feet, his 542 still pointed at the spot where the machine had vanished.

"What the *hell*?" he muttered under his breath.

"Agreed," Preston said as he came up beside Barnes, sounding as disbelieving as Barnes felt. "I thought Terminators killed everyone they met."

"That's because you don't understand Terminators."

Barnes turned around. Shouting and speaking voices were sometimes very different, but he knew instantly that the man emerging cautiously from behind a tree was the one who'd been directing their fire. Or rather, their lack of fire.

"Who are you?" he demanded.

"Remy Lajard," the man replied, eyeing Barnes warily. "The question is, who are *you*?"

"His name's Barnes," Preston said. "The woman over there is Blair. They say they're with the Resistance. What exactly is it I don't understand about Terminators?"

"The fact that most of them are programmed for specific jobs," Lajard said. His face and clothes were as rough and rustic as everyone else's, but something about his tone reminded Barnes of a couple of his more annoying teachers back in pre-Judgment Day school. "It was clear that these two—these three, actually, counting the one Barnes destroyed—have a more important assignment than shooting back at people who are attacking them."

"Maybe it's clear *now*," another man put in. This one seemed even scruffier than the rest of the group, as if looking like a mountain hermit was a badge of pride for him. "It sure as hell wasn't clear when we first started shooting."

"And as I *tried* to tell you at the time, Halverson, it wasn't coming for us," Lajard said. "It was clearly just trying to get across the river."

"Clear to whom?" Williams asked as she came up to the rest of the group.

"Clear to anyone who was paying attention," Lajard

said, starting to sound annoyed. "You saw it yourself in that second T-700. Its gun hand was down, and it was looking at the riverbank, not us, as it crossed. It was obviously evaluating footing and route."

"So what happened with the other one?" Barnes asked, jerking his head toward the spot where Williams had blown away the T-700's gun. "Didn't it get the message? *It* sure as hell was shooting at us."

"*It* was just giving the other one cover fire," Lajard retorted. "After you destroyed the first one, it needed to draw your attention long enough for its companion to get across." He snorted. "You really think it would have missed *everyone* if it had actually been trying to kill us? You may not have seen what a G11's caseless ammo can do—"

"Yeah, we've seen it plenty," Barnes cut him off. "Fine, so it missed everyone. Why?"

"I just told you—"

"I think he means that if it was going to shoot to distract us anyway, why not shoot to kill?" Williams put in.

"And while you're at it, why were you so hot on us not destroying them before they got away?" Barnes added.

Lajard took a deep breath.

"For the first," he ground out, "I already said they're obviously on some important mission, and Skynet is smart enough not to simply waste ammunition. As for the second, see part two of my answer to question one."

"Oh, I see," Williams said, an edge to her voice. "You just didn't want us wasting ammo. Even though they were right there, in the open, where we could get them."

"You shoot every bear you run across, whether it's attacking you or not?" Lajard countered. "You'll probably never even see those particular Terminators again."

"Or we might," Barnes said.

Lajard rolled his eyes. "If that happens, and if they shoot at you, you have my permission to blow them to scrap," he said condescendingly. "Happy now?"

Barnes looked at Williams, caught the sour twist of her lip. Unfortunately, the man had a point. Several points, actually.

"So what kind of special mission could they be on?"

Lajard shook his head. "Haven't a clue," he conceded. "I don't even know what a group of Terminators would want out here in the middle of nowhere."

"Actually, Oxley and I were talking about that last night," Preston said. "We were wondering if they might be after someone."

"You mean someone like *them*?" Lajard asked, pointing at Barnes.

Barnes tightened his grip on his rifle. But Preston shook his head.

"Seems unlikely," he said. "At least one of the T-700s was already in position by the ford last night, long before Barnes and Blair showed up." He frowned suddenly at Barnes. "Unless there's some reason Skynet might have known you were coming?"

"Not really," Barnes said, throwing a quick warning glance at Williams. His original plan, once the Terminators had been dealt with, had been to ask Preston if he knew about any underground cables passing through or near the town.

Now, though, he was starting to think that might not be such a good idea. Hopefully, Williams would take the hint and keep her own mouth shut.

She did. Her forehead wrinkled briefly, but she kept quiet.

"Besides, their positioning clearly shows they were expecting their quarry to come from that side of the river," Preston continued. "No idea who it might be, though."

Halverson grunted. "Maybe they've taken over Buzby Jenkins's old property," he muttered. "Probably just don't want us hunting on that side of the river."

"Then why did they head upriver *away* from the ford just now?" Lajard asked. "Come on, Halverson—if you can't be logical, at least try to be consistent."

Halverson's face darkened. "Look, *professor*—"

"I have a question," Williams spoke up quickly. "Do you get a lot of Terminators out here?"

"I just *said* we didn't," Lajard said testily.

"Then how come you know so much about them?"

Barnes looked back at Lajard. That was a damn good question.

"Well?" he prompted.

Lajard's lip twitched, some of his arrogance melting away.

"I have a certain familiarity with them," he said evasively. "It comes of having—"

"It comes of him having worked for Skynet since Judgment Day," Halverson said. "Just say it, Lajard."

Barnes felt his face go rigid.

"You *what*?"

"It wasn't *all* the time since Judgment Day," Lajard said hastily, flinching back from Barnes's glare. "And it wasn't like I had a choice, either. None of us did."

"*None* of us?" Barnes echoed. "How the hell many of you *were* there?"

Lajard sighed. "About a hundred in all," he said. "If it makes you feel any better, I think the three of us were the only ones who made it out before the attack."

"Out of where?" Barnes persisted. "Where were you? San Francisco?"

Lajard shook his head. "No, we were in the big research center in the desert southeast of here."

Barnes felt his eyes narrow.

"Not a chance," he said flatly. "No one made it out of there alive. Connor said so."

It was Preston's turn for widened eyes.

"That was *Connor's* group that blew up the lab?"

"Connor's group attacked it," Barnes said. "Skynet blew it up." His eyes flicked across the other men and women grouped silently around them. "You said there were three of you. Who are the other two?"

There was a brief pause.

"I'm one of them," a woman's voice came from behind him.

Barnes turned. It was Susan Valentine, the woman who'd been on backstop duty when Preston's kid had tried to get the drop on him and Williams.

"Who else?"

"Nate Oxley's the third," Preston said. "And Lajard's right. The people who were working there didn't have a choice."

"There's always a choice," Barnes growled.

"Right—we could have let the Terminators kill us," Lajard retorted.

Barnes shrugged. "Like I said. There's always a choice."

"*Look*—"

"How about we hear the whole story?" Williams suggested. Her voice was carefully neutral, Barnes noted, but he could see his same suspicions lurking behind her eyes.

Because people under Skynet's control didn't walk away from that. They just didn't.

"Certainly," Preston agreed. "But we'll have to go back to town if you want all three of them—Oxley's helping Doc Meade set up an emergency trauma center." He looked at the pile of broken Terminator pieces still visible above the river water. "In case we needed it."

"Yeah, well, we still might," Halverson growled. "Somebody needs to stay here and guard the ford. And we ought to track those Terminators, too, and figure out where they're going." He looked pointedly at Lajard. "You know. In case they decide to come back."

"I was just going to suggest that," Preston agreed. "Chris, Pepper, you two stay here. Trounce—"

"Trounce, you stay here with Chris and Pepper," Halverson interrupted. "Ned, Singer—you two are on chaser duty. Find the machine that's on this side of the river and keep it in sight."

"But don't get too close," Lajard added. "And *don't* shoot at it."

"Not unless it shoots first," one of the men said grimly. Hefting his rifle, he headed off along the riverbank, another man following close behind.

Barnes looked back at Preston. There was a fresh tightness at the edges of the man's mouth as he watched the two men disappear into the woods. But he merely turned back to Barnes and gestured.

"Shall we?" he invited. Without waiting for a reply, he started back down the trail toward town, his daughter Hope beside him.

Picking up his minigun, Barnes dropped into step behind them. The rest of the crowd shambled their way into the procession behind him.

He'd made it out of sight of the river when Williams wandered casually up alongside him.

"What do you think?" she murmured.

"I don't know," Barnes muttered back. "But I don't like it."

"Me, neither," Williams agreed. "I've never seen a machine deliberately shoot to miss."

"Or just walk off when one of its buddies gets its gun and half its hand blown off."

"Or leave any wreckage behind," Williams added. "Especially with so many of them lying around in pieces in San Francisco." She hissed between her teeth. "What the hell have we gotten ourselves into here?"

"Damn good question," Barnes agreed. "Let's see if Preston can give us a damn good answer to go with it."

CHAPTER ELEVEN

There was a long line of people waiting at the mess tent when Kyle and Star arrived for breakfast a little after dawn. Most of them were members of the Resistance, men and women Kyle had already met or at least recognized.

But a number of them were strangers, more of the seemingly endless supply of tired and hungry civilians who'd been cautiously emerging from the hills and woods around San Francisco ever since Connor and the others had set up their temporary camp here.

They reminded Kyle of the people he'd left behind in Los Angeles. People who'd been there, just like they were here, mainly because there was nowhere else to go.

He could feel their eyes on him as he and Star walked past to the front of the line. He didn't like doing that, but he didn't really have a choice. Vincennes and some of the other men and women were already seated at one of the tables, and they were watching him and Star. Vincennes had made it clear that Resistance people on duty had first claim to whatever food was available.

Fortunately, none of the civilians said anything. Maybe they knew the rule, too.

Still, orders or not, Kyle could see that the mess servers

were doing their best to stretch their supplies as much as possible. The small tin dishes they handed him and Star were less than a third full.

Which was all right with Kyle. He could still feel the civilians' eyes on him, and he was willing to make do with a little less.

By the time they reached Vincennes's table, the other Resistance men had finished their own meager breakfasts and headed out, leaving Vincennes alone.

"Morning, Reese; Star," the older man greeted them.

"Hello," Kyle said for both of them. Star didn't say anything—Star never said anything. But Vincennes knew that. "Are we late?" he added, looking at Vincennes's empty dish.

"No, not at all," Vincennes assured him. "Doesn't matter anyway. You've been pulled off hunting and paired with Callahan for special scavenger duty. You know Rob Callahan, right?"

"Yes, sir," Kyle said, a sudden lump forming in his throat. "We lived together in Los Angeles."

A flicker of something crossed Vincennes's face.

"Oh—right. The Moldavia Building."

"Yes, sir," Kyle said again, looking sideways at Star. She was gazing down at her tray, her eyes staring at and through the food there. Probably thinking, just as he was, about that one, terrible day.

The day when Kate Connor had come calling at their colony of refugees in the former Moldavia Los Angeles building. The day that Rob Callahan, Zac Steiner, and Leon and Carol Iliaki had all answered Kate's call for Resistance recruits. The day that Kyle and Star had also left, sent off by their friend, mentor, and protector Sergeant Justo Orozco.

The day the Terminators had come and killed everyone who was left.

"Sorry," Vincennes said quietly. "Sorry, Star. I didn't mean to bring up memories. It's just—" He nodded toward the line of refugees. "We've gotten so many new people over the past week that I sometimes lose track of where they all came from."

"It's okay," Kyle said. "What are we scavenging?"

"The debris from last night's Terminator attack," Vincennes replied, looking relieved to be back on less painful ground. "We had a team out early this morning making sure they were all dead, and they reported a lot of ammo the machines hadn't had a chance to use. Bill Yarrow and Zac Steiner are going out to collect everything they can find, and I want you and Callahan out there with them."

"Okay," Kyle said, pleased they were trusting him with that kind of job. Ammo was always in short supply, and the Resistance needed every bit of it they could get. "You want us to scavenge the guns, too?"

"No," Vincennes said. "The team said it was all G11s, plus the minigun the T-600 was carrying, and they're all way too heavy for you to lug back on foot. You see something that's still in decent shape, tag it and we'll send a jeep to collect it later. Your job is just to get the ammo."

He gestured toward the armorers' station that was Star's current assignment.

"Pick up some backpacks when you drop off Star. Yarrow, Steiner, and Callahan will be meeting you at the south checkpoint, and you can head out together."

"Should we take any weapons?" Kyle asked.

Vincennes shook his head.

"Grab a shotgun if it makes you feel safer, but you're well within the daytime perimeter, and that area's already been swept. You'll have plenty of weight to carry on your way back as it is."

"Yes, sir," Kyle said.

Vincennes's eyes drifted over Kyle's shoulder to the line of hungry refugees.

"And while you're out there, keep an eye out for anything that might mark a food depot."

Star pressed against Kyle's side, and even through all his layers of clothing he could feel the shiver that ran through her small body. Both of them had vivid memories of being herded together in this place with the rest of Skynet's human captives.

"Skynet wasn't feeding anyone very much," he muttered.

"No, but it was giving them *something*," Vincennes said. "Whatever the machines had stashed away, we want it."

"Understood," Kyle said, pushing back the memories.

Vincennes dug into his pocket and pulled out a folded slip of paper.

"Yarrow has the whistle for your team, but he'll need the code for that part of camp—I forgot to give it to him. It's a little different from the one the hunter teams use, so have him check it before he whistles anything."

Kyle took the paper. He didn't mind the whistle code nearly as much as some of the others. Barnes, for one, made no secret of his disgust with it. But even Kyle was starting to question its efficiency.

"Any idea when the radios will be up and running again?"

"About two minutes after we find out where the damn interference is coming from," Vincennes said sourly. "And don't bother volunteering to blow it up when we find it. I've already got a waiting list."

Star tugged at Kyle's sleeve, and he looked down. *What does the noise machine look like?* she signed.

"It's probably not an actual machine," Vincennes said when Kyle had translated the question. "More likely just a high-voltage short-circuit that's creating big, noisy sparks. Probably some big underground motor that was damaged enough to leak current but still has enough connection to a power supply that it hasn't run dry yet."

Star tugged at Kyle's sleeve again. *Maybe it's not an accident*, she signed. *Maybe the machines are trying to keep John Connor quiet.*

"Could the interference be deliberate?" Kyle asked Vincennes. "Star thinks Skynet may be trying to keep Connor's broadcasts from getting out."

"Oh, Skynet wants to stop his broadcasts, all right," Vincennes agreed. "You can bet a week's meals on that one. But you can't do that by flooding the airwaves with interference at the source. Your jamming needs to be at the receiver's end, not the transmitter's. Or so the tech guys tell me."

He looked out at the devastated landscape around them.

"No," he went on. "As soon as Connor feels well enough to start broadcasting again, he will. Nothing Skynet does has ever stopped him before. It's not going to stop him now."

"I hope you're right," Kyle said, thinking back to that single broadcast that he, Star, and Marcus had heard back in Los Angeles. "The people out there need to hear him."

"They will," Vincennes promised. "Very soon." He gestured at Kyle's half-empty plate. "Eat up, and get to work. Connor's not so weak that he can't still kick your butt halfway to L.A. if he catches you loafing."

The fireball that had consumed Skynet Central had

barely faded away when Connor ordered his Resistance team in for search and clean-up duty. In the middle of all that barely controlled chaos, Star had been scooped up by the mess tent people and assigned to dishwashing duty.

That job had lasted exactly two hours, the length of time it had taken Kyle to find someone to listen as he described Star's skill at disassembling, cleaning, and reassembling firearms. The woman had taken Star to the armorer station for a test, and fifteen minutes later the mess people were back to looking for a new dishwasher.

This morning the armorers were as busy as always, stripping, cleaning, and repairing the group's impressive array of firearms. Kyle got Star settled behind her usual table and helped her get all her cleaning fluids and cloths arrayed in their proper places around her work area. He collected four backpacks and then, just because he didn't feel right without it, also picked up a sawed-off shotgun. Slinging the weapon over his shoulder, he headed for the south checkpoint.

Callahan and Zac were waiting when Kyle arrived, along with a smallish man Kyle didn't recognize.

"You Reese?" the man asked as Kyle came up.

"Yes, sir," Kyle said. "Sorry if I'm late."

The man grunted. "Bill Yarrow. Pass out the bags, and let's get started."

"Yes, sir," Kyle said again, eyeing Zac as he handed each of them a backpack. He hadn't seen the thirteen-year-old since the day Zac and the others had walked out of the Moldavia Building. But the months he'd spent with Connor since then had clearly been good for the kid. Like Callahan, Zac was harder, leaner, and more muscular than he'd been back then. Better fed, too.

"First pass will be to pick up the live ammo," Yarrow

said as he looped his backpack over one shoulder. "If we've still got space, we'll go back and collect as much empty brass as we can carry. Clear?"

There were three murmured assents.

"Good," Yarrow said briskly. "Let's go."

"For me, it happened two years after Judgment Day," Susan said, shifting uncomfortably in one of the plain wooden chairs that Hope had brought in from the kitchen to help accommodate the unexpected crowd currently standing and sitting around their living room. "There were half a dozen of the big walkers, the ones I found out later were T-400s, plus a couple of T-1 tanks that had come along for support. I was living in a sort of group house—it was the only building in our neighborhood that hadn't fallen down or been scavenged for lumber."

Hope threw a surreptitious look across the room. Blair was listening closely to Susan's story, just as she had Oxley's and Lajard's, an intense but otherwise neutral expression on her face. Barnes was listening just as closely, but his expression was one of outright suspicion.

And every so often he turned that suspicious look toward Hope and her father.

"At first I thought they were going to kill us," Susan continued. "I'd heard the rumors that they were doing that in some of the other neighborhoods. But they didn't. They just walked up to the house, and one of them put a radio up against the door so that I could hear there was someone trying to talk to me."

"That someone being me," Lajard put in. "As I said, I'd been with Skynet for a year at that point. We needed a good metallurgist, I'd found Susan in what was left of the university database, and sent a team out to get her." He looked over at Barnes. "And for the record, the term *Terminator* originally meant that their job was to terminate the chaos and crime that had become endemic across the world since the war."

"The war that *Skynet* started," Barnes growled.

Lajard shook his head. "I'm not convinced of that."

"I don't give a damn whether you are or not," Barnes said flatly. "I was one of the people the Terminators were hunting. I saw what they did."

"And *I* say that all of that happened later, after the gangs ramped up and started terrorizing the rest of the populace," Lajard countered, just as firmly. "Maybe Skynet just got tired of trigger-happy vigilantes wrecking its machines. Machines that were only trying to protect people."

"What about the prisoners in Skynet Central?" Barnes countered. "Or the ones in that underground facility, the place you claim you were working in? Connor said they were living in cages while Skynet did experiments on them."

"I never saw anything like that," Lajard insisted. "Maybe Connor misinterpreted what he saw. Maybe they were refugees that Skynet had taken in."

Hope sighed. It was an argument that had been going on ever since the three scientists first arrived in town three months ago. Despite all the stories and rumors that had filtered into Baker's Hollow over the years, Lajard stubbornly refused to believe that Skynet was actively and deliberately slaughtering the scattered remnants of humanity. He insisted that, even now, Terminator killings were either gang-related, self-defense, or rare and atypical accidents. In his view, all the anti-Skynet bias was propaganda driven by lies from dangerous malcontents like John Connor.

Susan and Oxley weren't as dogmatic in their support as Lajard was. Susan, in particular, seemed to straddle the line. On one hand, she agreed that she and the other humans working in Skynet's underground lab had been treated quite well. On the other hand, though, she'd seen the Terminators react instantly and strongly to anything they perceived as a threat. For her, the question seemed to boil down to what exactly Skynet considered a threat these days.

Most of the townspeople, with no direct knowledge either way, generally ignored the question. Whatever was happening in the world beyond Baker's Hollow seemed distant and academic.

Only it wasn't. Not anymore.

Hope's father was clearly thinking along the same lines.

"Whatever Skynet's original plan might once have been is irrelevant," he said. "The question is what it's doing now. More specifically, what it's doing here in Baker's Hollow."

"The Terminators are here to kill," Barnes growled. "Wherever they go, they're *always* there to kill."

"That's paranoid nonsense," Lajard scoffed. "As long as it doesn't perceive us as a threat, we'll be fine."

"What kind of non-threat do you want us to be?" Barnes demanded. "You mean like we just sit back and watch while it tracks down and kills whoever is out there?"

There was an uncomfortable shuffling of feet from the crowd. Hope looked around, studying the various faces, trying to gauge their moods. Those who'd seen the Terminators in action clearly weren't thrilled at the thought of going up against them again. But they weren't any happier with the idea of simply abandoning whoever was out there.

"Who says they're planning to kill him?" Lajard countered. "Maybe it's a search and rescue operation. You don't have any proof they're trying to kill anyone."

Barnes snorted. "They have guns, right?"

"So did the T-700s who were with us before our accident," Lajard said. "So do you. So do half the people in town. In case you hadn't heard, there are big, hungry predators prowling around out here."

"Sure are," Barnes said. "And the worst of them are made of metal—"

"Tell us about the accident," Blair cut in.

"There's really not much to tell," Susan said. "We were working at the lab on something called the Theta Project. We'd developed a new type of hip and lower spine system—new materials as well as new stance-maintenance software—and we needed to field-test it. The biggest question was how it would do on steep terrain, so the three of us and the prototype were loaded aboard a transport and flown up into the mountains about twenty miles northwest of here. We'd landed and gotten out, and the T-700s were starting to unload our equipment, when an avalanche came down and buried everything."

"We escaped most of it," Oxley added. "But we didn't have a radio we could use to call for help. Or any food or shelter, either. We hung around the site for a couple of days, but no one came."

"Eventually, we realized we were going to have to get back on our own," Susan said. "We started hiking back down the mountains, but it was deep forest, and we didn't have any maps. We got lost."

"*Seriously* lost," Oxley agreed. "We were on pretty much our last legs when Susan spotted some smoke rising from a mountainside in the distance. We changed course and headed that direction."

"They nearly didn't make it, either," Preston put in. "One of our hunting parties ran across them thrashing weakly through a row of thorn bushes. All three were suffering from exposure and malnutrition."

"Most of that last part is a blur," Susan admitted, a flicker of memory crossing her face. "At least, for me. I think it was a week before any of us could even get out of bed."

"Bottom line is that we owe these people our lives," Lajard said firmly. "We're not going to repay them by bringing destruction down around their heads." He eyed Barnes warningly. "Or by letting anyone else do it, either."

"Fine," Barnes said calmly. "We got the message. Nice meeting you all." He stood up and headed for the door. "Come on, Williams."

"Wait a minute," Preston said, jumping to his feet. "Where are you going?"

"We're leaving," Barnes said. "You heard Lajard. He says we're putting you at risk."

"Lajard doesn't speak for the town," Halverson spoke up brusquely, throwing a hard look at Lajard as he stepped away from the wall into Barnes's path. "Anyway, we're not sending you on your way until you've had some food and rest. We owe you that much."

"He's right," Preston seconded. "Let me show you to our rooms while Hope and I get something together for you to eat."

"My place is more comfortable," Halverson said. "And Ginny's already got food ready."

"They'll be fine here," Preston said, locking eyes with Halverson. "It won't take long."

"They're coming to my place," Halverson said in the voice he always used when he'd made up his mind about something. He gestured to Barnes. "Come on—it's a few houses down."

"Mayor?" Blair asked.

Hope looked at her father, noting the familiar tension in his jaw. But he merely nodded.

"It's all right," he said. "Go ahead."

"Fine," Barnes said, eyeing Preston closely as he gestured to Blair. "We'll grab our stuff and be right with you."

They headed out, Halverson striding along in the lead. With the meeting clearly over, the rest of the crowd began to file out behind them. A minute later, Hope and her father were alone.

"That might not have been a good idea," Hope said hesitantly.

"You mean letting Halverson push me around in front of everyone?" Preston responded, his voice tight as he crossed to the window and peered out. "That happens all the time."

"I was thinking Barnes and Blair might rather have stayed here with us," Hope said.

"They'll get over it," Preston said, still gazing out the window. "As for Halverson, for once he did exactly what I was hoping he'd do."

Hope frowned. "You *wanted* them to go with him?"

"What I wanted was to be left alone for a couple of hours." Preston left the window and headed to the corner where he'd propped his rifle. "You remember that bridge I told you about a long time ago, the one that one of the summer kids and I built over the river?"

Hope had to search her memory.

"The one you made out of rope and a bunch of boards you swiped from the Pennering building site?"

"That's the one," Preston said, nodding. "I think whoever's out there has crossed that bridge."

"How would he know it was there?"

"Only two ways I can think of," Preston said. "Either

he happened on it by accident, or else he's the one who helped me build it."

"Whoa," Hope said, feeling her eyes widen. "You mean some kid who visited here thirty years ago is *back*? That's really... unlikely."

"Unlikely as in the scratch end of zero," Preston agreed. "I know. And for the record, it was closer to forty years ago. But I can't think of any other reason why those two T-700s would suddenly decide to head up opposite sides of the riverbank. Whoever they're hunting must have gotten across the river, and that's the only other place for miles where that's possible."

"That assumes the bridge is still there, of course," Hope warned. "Rope bridges and mountain winters don't exactly go together."

"Which is why I want to go up there and take a look," Preston said. He checked his rifle's magazine, then headed for the door.

"What if the Terminators are waiting?" Hope asked, scooping up her bow and quiver and hurrying to catch up.

"They won't be," Preston assured her. "The bridge comes off a narrow path at the bottom of a steep defile. Even if the machines know where it is, they're not going to be able to get down there without dumping themselves into the river. Best they can do is look down on it from above, and even that's iffy." He stopped, eyeing her as she came up beside him. "Where exactly do you think *you're* going?"

"With you," she said. "First thing you taught me was that the forest can be dangerous, and that you don't go out there alone."

"I meant that *you* don't go out there alone," he countered.

"We should make up a survival pack before we go," Hope said, ignoring him. "Whoever's out there may need food or medical care." She cocked her head. "And if it turns out he needs carrying, we'll need two of us there anyway."

"No," Preston said firmly. "There are Terminators out there."

"And they can't get down your path, remember?" Hope said. "Besides, if Lajard is right, they're not after us, which means we don't have anything to worry about."

"And if Barnes is right?"

"Then we're all doomed anyway," Hope said calmly, "and it doesn't matter whether I'm out there with you or back here in town."

Her father made a face.

"Did I ever tell you that you inherited your mother's sense of logic?"

"No, but I'll take that as a compliment," Hope said.

"You would." Preston sighed. "Fine. Go pack a food bag. Nothing too heavy—we'll be going up and down some tricky slopes. Let me go double-check that I have all the ammo we've got for this thing."

He nodded toward her quiver.

"And you'd better bring all the rest of your arrows, too. Just in case."

CHAPTER TWELVE

Ginny Halverson was a small, thin woman with a quiet manner that was in stark contrast to the bluster of her loud and borderline-bullying husband. She accepted Halverson's sudden imposition of guests without complaint, showed Blair and Barnes to a bedroom, and assured them that a meal would be ready soon.

"We must really look tired," Blair commented as she looked over the room. Like the couple of rooms she'd seen in Preston's home, this one was only sparsely furnished, with a large bed piled high with bear skins, a dilapidated chest with two of the drawers missing, and a chunk of log serving as a side table with a large partially burned candle stuck to its top. On the walls beside the room's single window were more bear skins, probably there as insulation. Clearly, Halverson liked to hunt.

"What was that?" Barnes asked as he lowered his minigun to the floor with a muffled thud.

"I said we must look tired," Blair repeated. "Everyone here seems to think we need to go rest somewhere."

"Or else they just don't want us going anywhere," Barnes growled as he slid his rifles off his shoulders and propped them against the wall beside the minigun. "Not until they've figured out what to do with us."

Blair felt her stomach tighten. She'd been thinking pretty much the same thing.

"So you think they're up to something, too?"

"*Someone's* sure as hell up to something," Barnes said darkly. "I don't care what that idiot Lajard says. Mission or no mission, if Terminators have ammo to spend, they spend it. On people"

"Mmm," Blair said noncommittally. In general, he was probably right.

On the other hand, she'd seen plenty of H-Ks veer off for strategic or tactical reasons even when they still had something to shoot with. "Maybe Lajard's right about Skynet being concerned about its ammo supply," she suggested. "There can't be a lot of places out here where they can reload."

"Yeah, and that's another thing," Barnes said. He paused by the bed long enough to test its softness with his hands, then continued on to the window. "Where the hell did those machines come from, anyway?"

"Good question," Blair agreed. "You think it's possible they're a search party?"

"Three whole months after they got lost?"

"Point," Blair admitted. "Maybe they're remnants from the lab explosion, then. Some perimeter guards or scouts that survived Connor's attack."

"Then where were they going?" Barnes countered. "You saw them—they weren't just wandering around waiting for instructions. They were heading *somewhere*."

"Which brings us back to some kind of special mission," Blair said. "Maybe they didn't shoot at Preston and the others because there wasn't any point in doing so. It's not like their guns were doing a lot of damage."

"At least, not until we showed up," Barnes said thoughtfully. "And they *did* shoot at us. They shot at me, anyway."

Blair thought back to the brief battle.

"The southern one shot at me, too," she said slowly. "Nothing really came close, but that was mostly because you were keeping it off balance."

"That's the same one that blew off a piece of sky over my head when I was putting down the minigun," Barnes said, peering back and forth out the window.

"Because we were the ones who were a threat."

"*Or* because we were the only strangers in the group," Barnes said.

Blair frowned. That was a possibility that hadn't occurred to her before.

"You think Skynet's leaving the locals alone for some reason?"

"Why not?" Barnes asked. "Lajard made a deal with Skynet. Maybe the whole damn town did, too."

"But why?" Blair persisted. "I can see Skynet wanting human scientists to work for it—there are still things even the smartest computer can't do. But what can these other people possibly have that that Skynet would want or need?"

"Don't know," Barnes said. "But I can tell you right now that Lajard's story doesn't hold water. If they were worth hauling in to work in that lab, they were worth sending out an H-K to look for them."

Blair nodded. "So either the three of them *aren't* worth anything, or else Skynet deliberately left them out here for some other reason. Some experiment out in the woods, maybe?"

"You're the one who found the fancy cable," Barnes reminded her. "What could they be doing that they'd need a data transfer back to the lab?"

"It could be almost anything," Blair admitted. "You ever hear about this Theta Project Lajard mentioned?"

Barnes shook his head. "No. But if Skynet had a hundred scientists on it, it must have been pretty damn serious about it."

"Yeah." Blair chewed at her lip. "I'm starting to think it might be time for a strategic withdrawal. Whatever's going on here, it may be more than we can handle on our own."

"Too late," Barnes said. "Whatever Skynet's got going, it's bound to have a guard on the chopper by now." He gestured out the window. "But we *could* follow Preston and see what he's up to."

"Preston?" Blair echoed, frowning as she circled the end of the bed and joined Barnes at the window.

Sure enough, Preston and his daughter were walking quickly through the middle of town, heading toward the path to the river. Preston had his rifle slung over his shoulder, while Hope had her bow and a very full quiver of arrows at her side.

And both of them were wearing small ragged backpacks.

"Maybe they're just relieving the watch at the river," Blair suggested.

"Or maybe they're not," Barnes said, stepping back from the window and studying its frame. "Let's find out." Turning the lock, he carefully pushed the window open. "Go get the guns."

Blair looked back at the door, wondering what Halverson would say if he caught his guests sneaking out the bedroom window.

"The minigun, too?"

"Yes," Barnes said, heading back toward their stack of weapons. "Never mind—I'll get them. You go on through."

The open part of the window was narrow, and the

glass looked extremely fragile, and Blair had a couple of bad moments as she worked her way through. But she made it without breaking anything. By the time she was on the ground Barnes had returned to the window with everything except the minigun.

"Here," he said, poking the butt of her Mossberg through the opening.

"No minigun?" Blair asked as she took the shotgun.

"Too big to fit through," he grunted, poking the SIG 542 toward her. "But I took the rest of the ammo belt."

Thirty seconds later the weapons, backpacks, and Barnes were all outside with Blair.

"Head around that side of the house," he ordered, pointing, as he pushed the window closed again. "Long as Halverson and his wife stay in the kitchen they won't see us."

They made their way through the town, managing to avoid the handful of people also moving around outside. Preston and Hope were out of sight by the time they reached the edge of the forest, and Blair took special care to keep an eye on the woods around them as they made their way down the path. It was only an assumption, after all, that the Prestons were going all the way to the river.

Five minutes later, they reached the rushing water.

"What now?" Blair asked as she and Barnes peered from behind a screen of branches at the woman and two men standing apprehensive sentry duty at the ford.

"We could ask them where Preston went," Barnes said doubtfully. "But if the whole town's in on it, they'll probably lie."

"Then let's not ask them," Blair said, thinking hard. "In fact, let's just forget about Preston."

Barnes eyed her suspiciously. "If you didn't want to

follow them, this is a hell of a time to bring it up."

"I was thinking we might try a different approach," Blair said. "Whatever's going on in Baker's Hollow, it has to be connected somehow to the cable. We know the cable was running along the far side of the river, or at least the last vector we had on it suggested it was running along that side. If Skynet's playing games, maybe part of that game is to keep us on *this* side of the river."

For a moment Barnes didn't reply. Blair braced herself, waiting for the inevitable scornful blast...

"Let's see if I've got this straight," he said, his eyes narrowed in concentration. "You're saying Skynet heard us talking about the cable through all those pieces of broken machine lying around outside the lab. It wanted to stop us there—*tried* to stop us there—only it couldn't. So it grabbed all the T-700s it had in the area and put them over there. Not to keep someone from getting across from that side, but to keep *us* from going across from here."

"Exactly," Blair said, wondering if he was seriously considering her suggestion or just setting her up for a harder fall.

"What if we'd put down on that side instead of this side?"

"We couldn't," Blair said. "There weren't any clearings big enough to land the Blackhawk, not for miles. Skynet would know that if we wanted to look around over there we'd have to come from here."

"So why pull the machines out, then?" he persisted. "Why send them upriver?"

"I'm not sure," Blair admitted. "Maybe it wanted to get them under cover before we could blast them."

"Or maybe it figured that the town could handle us," Barnes suggested. "Maybe it thought that once they spun us that story about someone on the run we'd be so busy trying to find him that we'd forget about the cable."

"Could be," Blair said cautiously. She was still having trouble buying Barnes's notion that everyone in Baker's Hollow was in on some grand conspiracy. But as one of her old wingmen had often said, just because someone was paranoid didn't necessarily mean he was wrong.

"And by sending one Terminator up each side of the river, it makes us think there's another way across upstream," she added slowly. "Which forces us to search both sides for our refugee."

"Yeah, I guess that makes sense," Barnes concluded. "Worth checking out, anyway. You got a plan?"

Blair braced herself. Was this where he was going to cut her down?

"If Skynet doesn't want us crossing the river," she said, "I say we do precisely that."

Once again, he surprised her.

"Okay," he said. "Go ahead—I'll cover you in case the guards give you any trouble. Once you're across, you can cover me."

"Right," Blair said, eyeing the guards. For their sake, they'd better not give her any trouble. "Keep an eye out for Preston and Hope, too. There's no guarantee they're actually ahead of us."

With the three guards focused on the river, Blair got within five paces before one of them noticed her and snapped a warning that brought the others spinning around, rifles held at the ready.

"It's all right," Blair said hastily. "Blair Williams. I came with Barnes on the helicopter."

"What's happened?" one of the men asked, looking anxiously over her shoulder. "Did that Terminator find the town?"

"No, not as far as I know," Blair assured him. "It occurred to me that no one's tracking the T-700 that's still on the other side of the river. I thought I'd go over and see if I can figure out where it's gone."

"Sounds dangerous," the woman said.

"Also stupid," the first man said brusquely. "We sure as hell don't want you drawing it over to this side."

"I won't," Blair promised, a thought suddenly occurring to her. "I could use a guide, though. One of you want to come along?"

The first man shook his head. "Halverson told us to stay on guard here."

"You always do everything Halverson tells you?"

"Damn right," the first man growled. "You listen to experts, you stay alive longer." He gestured. "And one of the things experts say is not to go into a forest alone."

"Oh, I'm not alone," Blair assured him, glancing back over her shoulder. "I guess he's fallen behind a little." She looked back at the others. "Last chance for one of you to come along and help out."

"Just go," the man growled. "And if you hear a whistle—three shorts, three longs, three shorts—get back here as fast as you can."

"We will," Blair promised, wincing at the thought of a T-700 rampaging through Baker's Hollow. "I'd better go—Barnes can catch up whenever he catches up. By the way, Preston *did* head up the east side of the river, right?"

"Preston?" the first man repeated, frowning.

"He was ahead of us," Blair said. "You didn't see him?"

"Haven't seen anyone since you all headed back to town."

"He might have taken another route," the woman offered. "There are a couple more paths heading upstream off the main one that you can't see from here."

"That's probably where he went," Blair said. "See you later."

Blair had seen the river depth at the ford when the T-700 was crossing, and had already calculated that her boots would be high enough to keep out most of the water. What she *hadn't* anticipated was the sheer raw strength of the river's current. Over the twenty-five-foot trek she had to stop four times to consolidate her balance, and even then nearly had her feet knocked out from under her twice. The water was *cold*, too, and by the time she stumbled up onto the bank her bad leg was throbbing and her feet felt like chunks of ice. She climbed up a short embankment, found a convenient tree where she would be out of sight of the guards, and drew her Desert Eagle.

She'd barely gotten settled when Barnes appeared, striding toward the river as if he owned it. He didn't stop to chat with the guards, but merely exchanged nods with them and headed across.

Headed across quite effortlessly, in fact, to Blair's annoyance. He stopped only once, at one of the spots where Blair had nearly been knocked over, but aside from that simply walked straight through.

Of course, he *was* massive compared to her. An*d* he'd had the chance to watch her cross first and see where all the trouble spots were.

Blair backed up a few steps as he reached the riverbank, waiting until he'd entered the relative safety of the trees before holstering her gun.

"Anything from the guards?" he asked, turning to look behind him.

Blair shook her head. "They weren't even watching you, let alone targeting you. I invited one of them to come along with us, too, just to see how they'd react."

"And?"

"No interest," she said. "If they're worried about us stumbling across something we shouldn't, they're more worried about disobeying orders."

"*Halverson's* orders."

"He *does* seem to be the real power in town," Blair agreed. "Makes you wonder why they even bother with a title like mayor. Or why Preston's the one wearing it."

"Makes *me* wonder why Preston puts up with him," Barnes growled. "Where do you want to start?"

"Let's head up along the river," Blair suggested. "If we keep the water within hearing distance we shouldn't get lost."

"If we head upriver, we might run into that Terminator," Barnes warned.

"If there's something out here Skynet's hiding, we'll probably run into more than just one."

Barnes hefted his assault rifle.

"Bring it on," he invited darkly.

A minute later they were making their way through the trees, the rushing water a constant muffled roar off to their right. As they walked, it occurred to Blair that if Skynet's actual plan was to lure her and Barnes away so that it could hit the town without any serious resistance, they were playing right into its hands.

Still, if Skynet wanted the town destroyed, it could have sent in the T-700s last night. Or this morning, while she and Barnes were walking in from the Blackhawk.

No, there was something going on that she was missing. Some piece to the puzzle she didn't yet have. Maybe they were about to find that piece.

Maybe all they were about to find was more Terminators.

CHAPTER THIRTEEN

From Kyle's vantage point, the Terminators' midnight attack had been short but incredibly noisy, with an awesome display of firepower from both sides.

It was therefore something of a surprise to discover how much ammo the Terminators *hadn't* fired.

Callahan put it into words first.

"Good God, we've hit the jackpot," he breathed as they stood together by the broken machines, gazing at all the extra magazines still strapped to the Terminators' upper arms and thighs.

"That we have," Yarrow agreed. "Callahan, you and Reese take left; Steiner and I will take right. Get the magazines off the T-700s themselves first, then hunt around for anything that might have fallen or been shot off them. Remember that a magazine blown off by a high-speed round can fly and bounce quite a distance."

"Vincennes said to check the guns, too," Kyle said as they fanned out across the thirty or forty meters of last night's field of destruction. "Some of them might be worth tagging for salvage."

"I'm not optimistic," Yarrow said. "T-700s are usually fast enough to wreck their guns before they shut down completely. But sure, go ahead and check—we might get lucky. And don't forget to pull the magazines out of the wrecked guns. If we can't get the weapons, we can at least salvage their ammo."

Yarrow's prediction turned out to be correct. The T-600's minigun was still in decent shape, though two of the six barrels were badly dented. But all of the T-700s' submachineguns either had warped barrels or broken firing mechanisms.

"You suppose that's why they're using this caseless ammo, too?" Kyle called across to Yarrow as he picked up an intact magazine and slipped it into his pack. "Skynet figuring that it can wreck all the guns that can fire the stuff and we won't get any extra brass to reload?"

"Could be," Yarrow called back. "The G11s were still in the prototype stage when Judgment Day happened, so there were damn few guns around that could take their ammo. Skynet must have either severely modified an existing assembly line to build the things, or else created its own from scratch."

"Lucky for us, Chief Armorer Dockery can build anything," Callahan added as he dropped another handful of ammo into his bag.

"You're right there," Yarrow agreed. "I hear he's already got three machine guns up and running that can use this stuff, with six more on the way. Probably why Vincennes wants us to sweep the whole Skynet Central area as fast as we can, so that we can build up a decent stockpile before Skynet catches on to what we're doing and switches weapons and ammo again."

"Ah," Kyle said, a funny feeling in his stomach as he looked down at one of the broken guns. Back when he, Callahan, and Zac had been living at Moldering Lost

Ashes, as they had nicknamed The Moldavia Building in L.A., Kyle had known everything that was going on.

Now, suddenly, he was the new kid in town again. Not the person other people came to with questions, but the person everyone else had to explain things to.

It was embarrassing. More than that, it was dangerous. How could he protect himself when he didn't know how things worked?

How could he protect Star?

"Which could be any time now," Yarrow continued. "Skynet's already fitting the latest H-Ks with those new plasma guns. Dockery says it's only a matter of time before it comes up with a smaller version for the T-700s."

"Or whatever Terminators it's got going by then," Callahan said. "But for now, we can still collect their brass and their caseless rounds and send some fresh lead back at them."

"In the old days we called that recycling," Yarrow said with a touch of humor. "Callahan, you and Reese finished with that side yet?"

"I think so," Callahan said. "Should we start on the brass now?"

"Go ahead," Yarrow said. "Same sweep pattern as you did on the ammo."

The unspent ammunition had been well consolidated, either strapped to the Terminators or else in magazines lying in plain sight. The spent brass, in contrast, was anything but. The casings were all over the place, some of it scattered as far as ten meters away from where the Terminators had fallen, much of it half buried in tangles of wire or under exposed rebar or mixed into the piles of concrete dust that the restless breezes had funneled into nooks and crannies around the exposed concrete blocks.

It was long, boring, backbreaking work. Small wonder, Kyle thought more than once, that the team that had confirmed the Terminator kills had passed off the duty to someone else.

The sun had crossed over into the western sky when Kyle heard a shout over the distant sounds of sporadic gunfire coming from the hunting teams.

"Hey! Everyone!" Zac called. "Come here a minute."

Kyle turned, wiping sweat and dust off his forehead. Zac was crouched beside what was left of the rubber-skinned T-600 that had led the midnight charge. Hefting his half-full backpack onto one shoulder, Kyle slung his shotgun over the other and headed across.

Yarrow was squatting beside Zac when Kyle and Callahan reached them.

"Down here," Zac said, gesturing.

Frowning, Kyle lowered himself down beside the others. As far as he could tell, the shot-up T-600 looked pretty much like any other shot-up T-600.

"What are we looking at?" Yarrow asked.

"Underneath it, all the way down," Zac said, pointing at the spot where the Terminator's back was resting against the cracked masonry. "I was going for a casing that was pressed against its back, and it slipped down here and fell."

Trying not to flinch, Kyle pressed his palm against the T-600's side and pushed back the ragged clothing and rubbery skin as far as he could, about a quarter-inch worth. There was a gap down there, all right.

"Must have hit pretty hard when it fell," he commented.

"There's more," Zac said, and this time Kyle could hear the cautious excitement in the younger teen's voice. "When that casing fell, I'm pretty sure it took almost a second to hit anything."

"Really," Yarrow said thoughtfully as he stood up and walked around to the other side of the Terminator. "That would mean a drop of four or five meters."

"That's what I was thinking," Zac agreed. "It was a little hard to tell with all the shooting going on over there, but I'm sure it was at least half a second."

"Which would mean there's another whole level down there," Yarrow said, crouching down. "Yes, you can see the hole on this side, too. Reese is right—it must have hit really hard to break through that much concrete."

"Has to be more of the complex down there," Callahan said, standing up and getting a grip on one of the Terminator's outstretched arms. "Let's see if we can move it."

Yarrow took the machine's other arm.

"On three."

But T-600s were heavy, and not even the four of them straining together could lift or roll it from its resting place.

"That's not going to work," Yarrow said breathlessly, straightening up. "We'll need to find another way down."

"Wait a second," Kyle said. "You want to go *down* there?"

"Why not?" Yarrow said, looking around. "If there's an actual room down there, there might still be some useful stuff in it."

"Like what?" Callahan asked.

"Guns and ammo, maybe," Yarrow said. "Or food. Wouldn't that get us some smiley points if we brought back a few cartons of food." He pointed at an angled, meter-wide section of broken concrete pipe sticking half a meter out of the ground. "That looks promising. Let's take a look."

The top of the conduit had been crushed inward, possibly from an impact with a piece of girder lying nearby. The broken section was connected to the rest of the cylinder by twisted pieces of the pipe's metal reinforcement mesh, and was hanging in a loose flap that covered most of the opening.

"Might be clear," Yarrow said, shading his eyes as he looked in past the concrete flap. "Can't tell until we get this stuff out of the way. Either of you bring any tools?"

"I've got a knife," Kyle offered.

"Me, too," Callahan added.

"I was hoping for something more along the lines of a pry bar," Yarrow said.

"How about my shotgun?" Kyle suggested.

"Better than nothing," Yarrow said. "Let's have it."

It took a few tries, but he finally found the right combination of positioning and angle to pry the dangling concrete away from the opening.

"Wish we had a light," he muttered as he stuck his head and torso as far into the cylinder as he could. "Looks like it goes all the way down. Bend this flap a little higher, will you, Callahan?"

"What are you going to do?" Kyle asked as Yarrow handed the shotgun back and got a grip on the sides of the conduit.

"I'm going in for a quick look," Yarrow said. "You three wait here." Jumping up, he slid his feet inside the opening.

Kyle looked at Callahan. His expression was troubled, but he didn't look anxious to challenge a superior's decision. Zac, in contrast, merely looked intrigued.

"Shouldn't we check with someone first?" Kyle asked, feeling his heart starting to beat faster. This didn't sound like a smart idea.

"Like who?" Yarrow countered, grunting as he eased his hips into the duct. "You want to go all the way back to camp and find someone to ask if we can do something other than the job we were assigned? One of the things you need to learn, Reese, is that Connor really likes initiative and bold thinking."

Kyle looked around. With the sentry ring spread out beyond the hills of rubble so that they could cover the whole hunt area, there wasn't a single person in sight. Even the edge of the main camp over half a mile away was deserted, with everyone there out of sight somewhere inside the camp.

"You could whistle it in," he suggested.

"You find me a code for this situation, and I'll be happy to use it," Yarrow said. He was all the way inside the conduit now, gripping the edge as he did a controlled slide down the rough concrete.

"What happens if you get hurt?" Kyle persisted.

"Then you'll come down and get me," Yarrow said. "Relax, Reese—I can see the ground from here. Nothing's going to happen." His head disappeared into the darkness, and then his hands. "Okay, I'm touching bottom," he called, his voice echoing oddly. "Let me see if I can see anything—"

And he broke off amid a sudden crunch of breaking concrete.

"Yarrow!" Callahan snapped, pressing his face into the conduit. "Yarrow! Can you hear me?"

There was no answer.

"I'm going in," Callahan said, grabbing the sides of the opening and jumping his feet inside the way Yarrow had. "Reese, whistle a distress signal, will you?"

"I can't—Yarrow has the whistle," Kyle told him, biting back a curse. So much for initiative and bold thinking. "No, wait—"

But he was too late. With a sliding hiss and a second, quieter crunch of breaking concrete Callahan was gone.

"What do we do?" Zac asked anxiously.

Desperately, Kyle looked around again. But there was still no one visible. If both Yarrow and Callahan were injured, or even dead—

"Reese?" Callahan's voice floated up hollowly from the cylinder.

"I'm here," Kyle called back, sticking his face into the opening. It was too dark down there to see anything. "You okay?"

"Yes, but Yarrow isn't," Callahan called grimly. "He must have hit his head on the way down—there's some blood on the side of his face and he's not really conscious. And his leg's jammed."

Kyle clenched his teeth. *Great.*

"How far down are you?"

"Not very," Callahan replied. "It's less than three meters from the floor to the base of the pipe, plus the two meters of the pipe itself. If you and Zac can find a rope or something we can tie up there and then tie under his arms, I think the three of us can get him back up by ourselves."

"Right," Kyle said, looking around again. "Let me think."

"How about the backpacks?" Zac suggested.

"Worth a try," Kyle agreed. "Dump 'em ."

It took half a minute for them to dump all the scavenged ammo and brass out of the four backpacks. Kyle tied their shoulder straps together, then took the sling off his shotgun and added it to the makeshift rope. A quick knotting of the sling to one of the bits of metal mesh protruding from the edge of the conduit, and it was ready.

"Here it comes," he called, and lowered the packs down. "You need any help down there?"

"Yeah, and a lot of it," Callahan called, his voice grim. "I can't get his leg free. It's bleeding, too, pretty bad."

"We've got to get some help," Zac breathed.

Kyle nodded. "Callahan, I'm sending Zac back for the medics," he called into the conduit.

"There's no time," Callahan said. "We have to get him back up before we can treat him, and I'm going to need both of you down here for that. Once he's up and we've got room to start bandaging, *then* Zac can go for help."

Kyle grimaced. But if Yarrow really was bleeding badly, Callahan was probably right. The main part of the camp was a good mile away, which meant at least a fifteen-minute round trip, plus whatever time it took to find a medic.

"Hang on," he said. "We're coming."

"I'll go first," Zac volunteered. Before Kyle could say anything, the younger teen grabbed the edges of the conduit, swung his legs inside, and slid out of sight.

Grimacing again, Kyle rested his shotgun against the side of the conduit and got his legs up inside. Holding on with one hand, he retrieved the weapon and shoved the barrel awkwardly down the waistband of his jeans. He shifted his grip to the sling and slid carefully down the pipe.

There wasn't a lot of light down there, but as Kyle worked his way down the line of backpacks his eyes adjusted enough to see that he was heading into a relatively narrow area lined by more of the tangled debris that littered the surface. Callahan and Zac were crouched beside a hunched-over Yarrow, and Kyle had to splay his feet to either side as he came down to avoid landing on any of them.

"How is he?" he asked as he came to a halt on the uneven ground.

"I think he's starting to come to," Callahan said, his voice grim. "He's moaned a couple of times. Come on, give me a hand with his leg."

Kyle looked down. Yarrow's leg was jammed up to his shin between a couple of blocks of broken concrete. Even in the dim light Kyle could see the man's pant leg was soaked with blood.

"Right," he said, gingerly getting a grip around Yarrow's thigh. "I've got the leg. You two see if you can pry apart the blocks."

"Shee—!" Yarrow hissed suddenly.

Kyle jerked in surprise, but managed to keep his grip on the leg.

"Yarrow?" Callahan asked anxiously. "You all right?"

"It *look* like I'm all right?" Yarrow bit back between clenched teeth. "What the hell are you doing to my leg?"

"Trying to get it free," Kyle said. "Hold on to my shoulder."

"Wait!" Zac said suddenly. "Shh."

They all froze. Kyle kept his grip on Yarrow's leg, trying to take some of the man's weight onto himself. He looked around, wondering what Zac had heard.

And felt his blood run cold. He'd assumed Yarrow had crashed into some sort of chamber, some accidental gap randomly formed by the blast, shockwave, and collapse that had devastated Skynet Central. But this wasn't simply a gap.

It was a tunnel. A twisty, meandering tunnel that wound its way haphazardly between huge slabs of concrete or around twisted tangles of metal or broken machinery. Its floor was littered with debris and pieces of broken concrete. Its roof was even more irregular, and at places there were pieces of girder or twisted nets of rebar that had been pressed into service to hold up sections of the ceiling.

This wasn't something that had happened randomly in the explosion. This had been deliberately, carefully built.

And there was only one possibility as to who the builders were.

"Terminators," Zac breathed. "I can hear their footsteps. They're coming."

"Get out of here," Yarrow murmured. "All of you, get out. Now."

Kyle looked up at the line of backpacks hanging down from the conduit. If the Terminators were close enough for Zac to hear...

Callahan had come to the same conclusion.

"There's no time," he murmured back. "Zac, find us a place to hide. Reese, give me a hand with Yarrow."

"No," Yarrow, said, pushing Kyle away. "No time." He looked around. "There—that gap at the edge of the floor. See it?"

Kyle looked around. The gap was little more than a darker shadow at the side of the tunnel a dozen steps away.

"Yes."

"See if it leads someplace where you can hide," Yarrow ordered. "*Go.*"

Clenching his teeth, Kyle headed toward the shadow, trying not to trip on the uneven ground. He reached the gap and looked down.

They were in luck. The hole opened into a deep drop-off, deep enough that the faint light trickling down from the broken pavement above them showed no sign of a bottom. He couldn't see if there was any place for them to stand, or whether they would have to hold on to concrete or rebar until the Terminators went away. But at least they would be out of sight.

He hurried back to the others.

"It opens into some kind of pit," he reported. "I can't tell how deep."

"You'll have to chance it," Yarrow said firmly, wincing in pain. "All of you—down the rabbit hole. Now."

"Just as soon as we get you out," Callahan insisted.

"It's too late," Yarrow said, his voice suddenly as cold as death. "Besides, they'll see the backpacks. They'll know someone's here."

"I can cut them down," Kyle offered, reaching for his knife.

And froze. Yarrow had drawn a Colt from inside his jacket and was pointing it squarely at Kyle's face.

"I gave you an order, Reese," he said. "It's too late for me. It's not too late for you. Get your butts into hiding."

"But—" Callahan began.

"Because you have to get back alive," Yarrow cut him off. "The machines aren't digging this damn tunnel for the fun of it. It's heading straight for the camp. You're the only ones who can warn Connor."

"We can't just leave you," Callahan said, his voice pleading now.

"You have to," Yarrow said. "Besides, it was my stupid mistake. I'm not going to have you paying for it." He waved the gun. "Now go, before I have to die with your deaths on my conscience."

Callahan's face was screwed up like he was going to cry. But he jerked his head in a nod.

"Go," he told Kyle.

A few seconds later, they were at the gap.

"I'll go first," Callahan said, sitting down on the edge of the hole and sliding his legs through the gap. "See if I can find some footing." Half turning, he dropped down into darkness.

Kyle looked back along the tunnel, at Yarrow leaning against the wall, the Colt in his hand pointed down the tunnel toward the heavy footsteps Kyle could now hear coming toward them.

"There's a ledge," Callahan called softly from the hole.

Kyle tapped Zac on the shoulder.

"Go."

The younger teen dropped and maneuvered himself into the opening. Again Kyle looked over at Yarrow, suddenly aware of the shotgun tucked into his waistband. If he and Yarrow together had enough firepower to disable the machine— "Reese?" Callahan whispered.

"Reese, move it," Zac hissed. "They're almost here."

Kyle caught his breath. *They?*

And then, abruptly, the approaching footsteps seemed to leap into focus. Zac was right—there wasn't just one set there, but several.

Turning back to the gap, he hurriedly slipped his legs into it. One Terminator they might have been able to handle. But not a group. All Kyle could do from Yarrow's side, with or without the shotgun, was put his death on Yarrow's conscience.

His head was still above ground when he caught a distant glimpse of red Terminator eyes around a bend in the tunnel.

Flinching, he ducked down, nearly losing his balance as his feet hit the narrow ledge and almost slid off. For a second he fought for balance before Callahan and Zac grabbed his sleeves and steadied him. The edges of the hole itself were jagged and broken, with twisted pieces of exposed rebar on the underside of the slab. Kyle got a grip on one of them—

Just as the boom of Yarrow's Colt thundered through the tunnel.

He tensed, squeezing the rebar hard. There were two more shots, then three more in rapid succession.

And then, silence.

Kyle looked beside him at Callahan. The other's face was tight, his mouth working wordlessly. Zac, on Callahan's other side, had his face pressed against his upper arm as he held tightly with both hands onto the rebar. The silence stretched like a piece of old cloth...

And then, Kyle heard the footsteps start up again.

He felt his throat tighten. Had the machine he'd glimpsed as he dropped into the hole spotted him, as well? Yarrow should have been blocking most of the Terminator's view, but with Terminators you never knew. The footsteps came closer... closer... reached the hole...

And passed by without breaking stride.

Kyle stole another look at Callahan. He was facing up and over his shoulder, his eyes focused on something back there. Kyle followed his line of sight, and spotted the faint shadows passing across the hole as the Terminators filed by.

There was a long line of them. T-700s, Kyle guessed, from the clink of bare metal on the concrete above them. Several had gone by before it occurred to Kyle that he should probably be counting the shadows. Another eleven of the machines made it past after he started his count.

Finally, the last one passed, and the sound and vibration of their footsteps faded away. "Eighteen," Zac breathed, his voice trembling. "There were *eighteen* of them."

"Where do you think they were going?" Callahan asked.

"You heard Yarrow," Kyle said. "The tunnel's heading into the camp."

Callahan muttered something under his breath.

"Come on," he said, shifting his grip to the edge of the tunnel floor. "Let's get out of here."

"Hold it," Zac said suddenly, grabbing his hand and pulling it back down out of sight. "There's more coming."

Kyle froze, holding his breath as he listened. A few seconds later, he heard the metallic footsteps again headed in their direction. He looked up at the wall, waiting for the shadows to appear.

A minute later they did.

Only this time they were heading the opposite direction.

Kyle peered up at the shadows, a risky plan starting to take shape in the back of his mind. He had no idea what kind of peripheral vision T-700s had, and sneaking a single eye out of cover to see what was going on could conceivably get all three of them killed.

But Zac had counted eighteen Terminators in the last pass. If he was right, and if this was the same group heading back again...

He waited, counting until the eighteenth came by. The footsteps changed tone—it was indeed the last one in line. Shifting his grip on the rebar, Kyle eased his head up for a quick look.

It was a T-700, all right. But instead of the usual submachinegun, it was carrying a huge, jagged chunk of concrete. Kyle threw a quick glance behind it, confirmed there weren't any more machines, and craned his head up a little higher.

He was only able to see the last three Terminators in line. But that was enough. All three of the machines were lugging pieces of broken concrete or twisted metal.

Kyle lowered his head again. Callahan and Zac were looking at him questioningly, but he shook his head, nodding toward the retreating line of Terminators.

Once again, the sound and vibration of their footsteps faded away.

"They're not attacking the base," he murmured to the others. "At least, not yet. They were carrying pieces of debris. *Big* pieces."

"Debris?" Zac asked.

"Debris, as in they're still digging," Callahan said. "That means we've still got time."

"The big question is how far they have gotten," Kyle whispered. "The front of the tunnel can't be too far ahead, not with that quick a turnaround."

"Unless this was a different group," Callahan pointed out. "There could be two shifts running, with some place up there that's wide enough for them to pass each other."

"But this doesn't make any sense," Zac objected. "How can Skynet be running Terminators with all the radio interference blanketing everything out there? Skynet uses shortwave to communicate with the machines, right?"

"I guess that means the interference *isn't* blanketing everything," Kyle replied.

"Or the interference has been carefully designed so as to leave the right frequencies open," Callahan said grimly. "That alone shows this plan's been up and running for a while."

"So what do we do?" Zac asked.

"Like Yarrow said, we get out of here and alert Connor," Callahan told him. "Reese, could you see if the backpacks were still there?"

Kyle shook his head.

"The machines were in the way. I'll try now." Carefully, he again eased his head up through the hole.

Yarrow was lying on the tunnel floor, pressed up against the side wall as if he'd been shoved or kicked there. In the faint light coming through the conduit Kyle could see the bright red blood spreading out over the concrete.

Standing over the body, its metal skin shimmering in

that same diffuse light, was a Terminator.

Instantly, Kyle ducked down again.

"Terminator," he whispered urgently.

All three froze. Kyle strained his ears, trying to hear past the thudding of his heart. If the Terminator had seen him, it certainly wasn't in a hurry to come and investigate.

Which, given that it *was* a Terminator, meant that it *hadn't* seen him.

Callahan and Zac were staring at him, their expressions tense. Motioning them closer, Kyle leaned his lips close to their ears.

"It's standing guard over Yarrow," he whispered. "Right under the conduit."

"But it didn't spot you?" Callahan whispered back.

Kyle shook his head, playing back the memory of that quick glance. Now that he thought about it, he realized he hadn't seen the glow of the machine's eyes.

"It was facing the other direction."

Callahan nodded, his lip twisted.

"Skynet's not sure he was alone. But they don't know who else, or how many, or which way. So it's watching both directions for us to come back."

"What do we do?" Zac asked.

Callahan huffed out a breath.

"If we can't go back, the only other direction is forward," he said.

"You mean go in *further*?"

"Skynet's trying to punch this tunnel into the camp, right?" Callahan said. "Then sooner or later, it has to open up the far end. If we can get up there, maybe we can find a way to crack it open ahead of them and get out."

"We're sure not using the tunnel with that T-700 back there," Kyle warned.

"I know," Callahan said. "That means we'll have to go that way." He pointed downward. "There's empty space down there—you can feel the air flow. Maybe we can travel underneath the tunnel and find a way back up some place where the machine back there can't see us."

"And if we can't?" Zac asked.

"Then we won't be any worse off than we are now," Kyle said. "I'm game."

Zac sighed. "Me too."

"Okay," Callahan said. "Any idea how we get down there without bringing the whole metal nest down on top of us?"

"We could wait until the next group is marching by," Zac suggested. "Their footsteps should cover any noise we make."

Ten minutes later, as the Terminators again went marching back toward the front of the tunnel, the three of them slipped down the angled piles of debris into the darkness. Distantly, Kyle wondered what they would find down there.

Or whether any of Connor's people would ever find them.

CHAPTER FOURTEEN

Barnes and Williams had been trudging through the forest for over an hour, and Barnes was starting to regret he'd ever agreed to go on this little nature hike, when they found the bridge.

"What do you think?" Williams murmured as they crouched in the undergrowth about thirty meters away.

Barnes eyed the structure through the branches, wishing he'd thought to grab a pair of binoculars before leaving San Francisco.

"Looks solid enough," he murmured back. "I suppose someone *could* have crossed on it."

"Mm," Williams said. "Pretty hard to tell how solid a bridge is without trying it."

"Go ahead," Barnes offered. "I'll wait here."

Williams grunted. "Funny. What do you want to do?"

Barnes looked around. Aside from the bridge, there was nothing here but more forest, the same as the stuff they'd already tromped through. No people, no buildings—no Terminators.

"I guess we could look around a little," he said doubtfully. "See if we can find some trace of this visitor Preston's so hot to bring in. Or just call it a bust and go back."

"Can't say I'm overly thrilled by either option," Williams said. "But you're right. You want to flip a coin—?"

"Shh!" Barnes hissed, snapping his head around to the left. Something had rustled over there, loudly enough to be audible over the noise of the river churning through the deep gorge beneath the bridge.

Williams froze, her Mossberg already pointing that direction. Barnes kept his eyes moving, sweeping the area where the sound had come from, while also keeping an eye on their flanks. A nice, loud rustling in the bushes was the oldest trick in the book...

The noise came again. This time Barnes spotted its source: a small rippling in the branches of a thorn bush forty meters away.

"If that's a Terminator, it's awfully small," Williams said softly.

"Aerostats and hydrobots aren't exactly huge," Barnes reminded her. It would be just like Skynet to have seeded the forests with some new kind of ground-hugging nasty that they hadn't run into before. "Stay here—I'll check it out." Watching the rippling bush and the ones right beside it, searching for the glint of metal, he started to rise from his crouch.

"Freeze," a quiet voice ordered from behind him. "Don't turn around."

Barnes hissed a curse. And he'd been *watching* for this trick, too, *damn* it. "Easy, friend," he soothed.

"What makes you think I'm your friend?" the voice countered. "Who are you?"

"Barnes, she's Williams. You from the town back there?"

"What makes you think that?"

"Your friendly approach to strangers," Barnes growled. "They say hello with hunting arrows."

"So you're not from Baker's Hollow, either," the man said. "What are you doing here?"

"We were heading home when we spotted the smoke from the town," Williams said. "You may have heard our helo coming in early this morning. What's your name?"

"Where's home?" the man asked, ignoring the question.

"At the moment, San Francisco," Williams said. She twitched her left arm, jiggling her red armband. "We're with the Resistance."

"Yes, I already saw the armbands," the man said. "If you're Resistance, I assume you listen to John Connor?"

Barnes snorted. "All the time."

"Good," the man said. "What was in his last broadcast?"

Barnes frowned. Connor's last broadcast had been over a week ago, before the attack on Skynet Central. He had no idea what Connor had said in that message, and it was clear from Williams's silence that she didn't either.

"I don't know," he told their captor. "We don't have time to listen to every broadcast. Who does?"

There was a short pause.

"Skynet does, for one," he said. Oddly enough, the tension level in his voice had actually gone down. "That's a point in your favor, actually."

"Wait a minute," Barnes said, frowning. "You think we're *Skynet*? What, we don't look human enough for you?"

"You look very human," the man said grimly. "But that isn't a defining quality anymore." He murmured some sort of curse under his breath. "Unfortunately, aside from cutting you open, I don't know any way to prove you're who you claim."

The skin on the back of Barnes's neck began to tingle.

"Let's not do anything drastic," he said carefully. "There's got to be some way we can prove ourselves."

"While we're thinking, how about telling us your name?" Williams suggested.

There was a short pause.

"Call me Jik," the man said.

"You a pilot?" Williams asked.

"No," Jik said. "Why?"

"*Jik* sounds like a pilot's call sign," Williams said. "Who's your friend out there?"

"My friend?" Jik asked. "Oh. This." The distant bush rustled again. "Some rope tied to a small branch. Simple but effective. If you spotted smoke in Baker's Hollow, what are you doing way out here?"

"Hunting a Terminator," Barnes told him. "It headed up this side of the river, and we wanted to see where it went. Or whether it just gave up and went away."

"Oh, it didn't go away," Jik said sourly. "It's somewhere to the south, I think—I caught a couple of glimpses of it while I was trying to get to the ford."

"So *you're* the one it's hunting?" Williams asked.

"So it would seem," Jik said. "And be advised that there are *two* T-700s on this side of the river, not just one. I shot the other one earlier, during all the gunfire. But I only had one round left, and that wasn't enough to kill it."

Barnes felt a cautious stirring of hope.

"You only had one shot?"

"But I got its weapon away from it before it recovered," Jik said, an edge of warning in his voice. "In case you were thinking I'm bluffing back here."

"No, of course not," Barnes said. "Those G11s are heavy, aren't they?"

"Heavy enough," Jik agreed. "But I'm sure I'd be able to get off a couple of rounds before my biceps gave out."

"What did you mean, looks aren't a defining quality anymore?" Williams asked.

"I mean that Skynet's come up with something new," Jik said grimly. "A human heart and organs wrapped up inside metal."

Williams inhaled sharply. "You mean *Marcus*?"

"Was that its name?"

"*His* name," Williams corrected harshly. "*His* name was Marcus Wright."

"Well, its name isn't Marcus Wright anymore," Jik told her. "I killed it. Or destroyed it, however you want to put—"

"Wait a second," Barnes interrupted. "*You* killed it?"

"I just said that," Jik said.

"Yeah," Barnes muttered.

Only that was impossible. He'd seen Marcus Wright die himself, and it hadn't been at the hands of anyone named Jik.

"When and where'd this happen?"

"Back in the forest, a couple of days ago," Jik told him. "Why? Was it a pet or something?"

Barnes looked at Williams. She was looking back at him, her face gone suddenly pale.

"It wasn't Marcus," she breathed. "My God. There were *two* of them?"

"What do you mean, two of them?" Jik demanded.

"She means the one you killed wasn't the one we called Marcus," Barnes told him. He eased his head to the side, just far enough to see Jik out of the corner of his eye. The man was a little taller and thinner than Barnes, with sunken cheeks, unkempt brown hair, and a scraggly beard.

And he was indeed hefting a Terminator G11.

"Look, can we maybe point the gun somewhere else—?" Barnes began.

And then, right at the edge of Barnes's vision, the dark metal skull and glowing red eyes of a T-700 appeared from behind a tree.

"Behind you!" Barnes snapped, leaping to his feet and spinning his 542 around toward the Terminator. He caught a glimpse of Jik raising his own weapon—

Barnes's rifle was barely halfway to target when a burst of fire from the G11 blasted in his ear. Reflexively, he winced back, his body tensing in anticipation of pain from torn muscle and shattered bone.

But the impact and pain didn't come... and it was only as Barnes took a second look at Jik's face that he realized the man's eyes weren't focused on him and Williams. He was looking at something beyond them, over their shoulders.

Oh, hell.

And then, the barrel of Barnes's assault rifle arrived on target, and there was no more time for thought or worry or wondering how close the Terminator was that was coming up behind him. He squeezed the trigger, firing a round into the T-700's torso that staggered the machine back. A quick flick of his thumb shifted the weapon to three-shot mode, and he fired again. The multiple rounds slammed into the metal chest, this time nearly knocking the T-700 off its feet. Williams was shouting something as Barnes fired another burst, her words lost in the racket of his own fire and the chatter from Jik's weapon. A third burst from the 542 spun the T-700 halfway around, and Barnes finally had enough breathing space to throw a quick look behind him.

The second Terminator hadn't been hiding behind a tree like the one Barnes was shooting at. From its current position at the edge of the gorge, he concluded it had been waiting out of sight below ground level, probably hanging onto the nearly sheer side of the drop-off to the river. It had no doubt climbed up the bank while the three of them were talking, concealing itself in the tall grasses that lined both sides of the gorge.

Only now, the steady hammering from Jik's G11 was threatening to knock it back over the edge and into the rushing water ten meters below.

But only until Jik's gun ran dry. The instant that happened, the machine would get its balance back, and the beleaguered humans would be caught in the middle of a pincer.

Unless Barnes could take out his target first.

He turned back around, to find that Williams had left her position and was heading off in a curved path toward Barnes's target.

Barnes fired again, staggering the Terminator with another three-shot burst. It was essentially the same tactic they'd used back at the ford, with Barnes covering Williams while she got close enough to use her shotgun to its best advantage.

On the plus side, this time the Terminator didn't have a weapon of its own. On the minus side, there wasn't a nice convenient river separating them.

Which meant that if Williams got too close the Terminator could simply reach out and snap her neck.

Barnes flipped his rifle back to single-shot, spacing out his blasts, keeping the machine off-balance while he waited for Williams to get in range.

And then, Jik's chattering gun went silent.

Cursing, Barnes threw another look over his shoulder. With the hail of lead no longer battering it, the other T-700 steadied itself and straightened back to its full height. Its eyes seemed to take them all in...

"Williams!" Barnes snapped.

"I know!" Williams shouted back. There was the boom of a shotgun— "Go—I've got this one."

Barnes spun around, swinging the 542 toward his new target. The T-700 was already on the move, striding through the grass and dead leaves toward them.

And then, as Barnes lined up his sights on the Terminator's torso, the machine gave a sudden jerk, its stride faltering, its body and limbs weaving around as if it was drunk.

And as it turned its head to the side Barnes saw that an arrow had unexpectedly sprouted in the back of the machine's neck.

Dead center in the Terminator's partially exposed motor cortex.

Behind Barnes, Jik's machinegun opened fire again with a new magazine.

"No!" Barnes shouted to him, jabbing a finger back toward Blair's target. "I've got this one."

He glanced back long enough to confirm that Jik had understood. Then, breaking into a full-bore sprint, he charged straight toward the staggering Terminator.

Painfully aware of the terrible risk he was taking.

With that arrow buried in its motor cortex, the T-700's tracking and balance systems were temporarily shot to hell. But the control chip was already rerouting its systems around the damage, and if the machine recovered before Barnes reached it, he would be in the worst and possibly the very last fight of his life.

The T-700 was groping for the arrow now. The skeletal hand found it, snapped off half of the shaft.

And leaping into the air, Barnes rotated his body ninety degrees forward and slammed feet-first into the Terminator's torso.

The machine fell backward, slamming onto its back with enough impact to drive what was left of the arrow even farther into its skull. Barnes jumped back to his feet, lined up his 542 on the metal forehead, and fired.

The Terminator jerked as the bullet slammed into the thick alloy. Barnes fired again and again, each round bending or breaking another section of metal.

On his fourth shot, the glowing eyes finally faded into the darkness of death.

For another couple of seconds Barnes stared down at the dead Terminator, his throbbing ears vaguely aware of the gunfire still going on behind him. He'd already seen Terminators play possum once on this trip, and he had no interest in being suckered a second time.

But the eyes stayed dark. Breathing heavily, he lifted his gaze to the far side of the gorge.

Preston and his daughter were standing there, Preston with his rifle ready, Hope with another arrow in her bowstring. Preston gestured toward the Terminator lying in the grass, and Barnes gave him a thumbs up.

And then, the gunfire behind him stopped.

He turned. Williams and Jik were standing more or less where he'd left them, only with Williams now peering over what seemed to be a ridge or bump in the ground.

"You get it?" he called.

"No," Williams replied. "It fell into the ravine."

Barnes frowned. There was a ravine back there? He hadn't even noticed it through all the trees and brush.

"Can you see it?"

Williams looked back and forth, then shook her head. "No."

"What's the terrain like?"

"Very steep," Jik responded, "with bushes, trees, and

dead logs. We'd need a belaying rope to get down there."

Barnes pursed his lips. In general, it was a bad idea to leave a Terminator alive and loose if there was any chance at all of killing it.

But heading into unfamiliar territory after one while tied to the end of a rope was even more dangerous.

"Skip it," he called. "Time to head back."

He turned to Preston and Hope.

"Thanks for the assist," he shouted over the gorge.

"No problem," Preston called back. "What do you want us to do?"

"Go back to town, I guess." Barnes jerked a thumb over his shoulder toward Jik. "This the guy you were expecting?"

"Not really sure who I was expecting," Preston admitted. "But he'll probably do."

"What about the T-700?" Hope asked, pointing toward the dead Terminator at Barnes's feet.

"I need to make sure it can't be used for spare parts," Barnes told her. "We'll meet you back in town."

Preston nodded. "Watch yourselves." Touching his daughter's arm, he headed away from the gorge along a narrow path. A few seconds later, they were out of sight.

"We're worried about spare parts?" Williams asked, coming up behind him. With the adrenaline rush of the battle over, he noticed, she was limping badly on her injured leg.

"The T-700 you dumped into the ravine was the one whose hand you wrecked when you blew up its gun, right?" Barnes asked.

Williams's lips puckered.

"Right," she said. "Good point."

Barnes grunted and took aim at one of the Terminator's shoulder joints.

"Stand back."

A minute later Barnes had blown all four limbs off the dead Terminator. The right arm required a second try when it fell close enough to the torso after being disconnected that the T-700's automatic electromagnetic recoupling lock was able to draw it back into place. Another shot to the stubborn joint, followed by a quick kick to move the arm out of range, did the trick.

He and Williams were collecting the severed limbs when Jik arrived, coiling a length of fragile-looking rope over his shoulder as he walked.

"Was that Danny Preston?" he asked, peering across the river.

"You know him?" Barnes asked.

"I spent a few summers here with an uncle." Jik nodded toward the bridge. "In fact, Danny and I were the ones who built that thing."

"Really?" Barnes said. "He didn't seem to recognize you."

"I doubt he does," Jik said. "It's been forty years, and they've been kinder to him than they have to me." He nudged the T-700's torso with his toe. "They don't look so tough when you chop off all their limbs, do they? Except those teeth. I always wondered why Skynet bothered putting teeth on its Terminators."

"It's psychology," Williams told him. "It makes their heads look more like human skulls. Awakens those deep, dark fears we all have locked inside us."

"Like Terminators really need more of that than they already have," Barnes said. He lifted one of the severed Terminator arms and wiggled it in front of Jik. "See this? Watch."

He lowered the shoulder part of the limb and touched it to his leg.

"See there?" he asked, pulling the metal limb away and then swinging it past Williams's leg. "See? The electromagnet doesn't stick."

"Were you expecting it to?" Jik asked, frowning.

"*You* were," Barnes countered. "Remember? You were talking about cutting us open to see if we were Terminator hybrids." Turning, he tossed the arm over the edge of the gorge into the river below and reached for the next one. "Just wanted to show you that we aren't."

"Ah," Jik said. "Thank you. Though, I was already pretty well convinced. Someone with a Skynet chip in his head should have been able to quote the last Connor broadcast verbatim." He nodded down at the partially disassembled Terminator. "Besides, you'd hardly have helped me destroy my attackers if you were on their side. A house divided against itself, and all that."

"Yeah." Barnes picked up the final leg and tossed it over the edge. "Let's get out of here." He glanced at Williams.

And paused for a longer look. She was staring down at the limbless Terminator, a sudden tightness to her throat.

"What's the matter?" Barnes asked. "Leg bothering you?"

"Terminator hybrids," she said, her voice as rigid as her throat. "You just called them Terminator hybrids."

"So?" Barnes asked. "That's what they are, aren't they?

"T-600 is short for Terminator six hundred," Williams said, her eyes still on the machine. "T-700 means Terminator seven hundred. Right?"

"Yeah," Barnes said, frowning. Why was she lecturing him on the obvious? "So?"

She looked up at him.

"In that same format, a Terminator hybrid would be *T-Hybrid*, or just *T-H*."

Barnes looked at Jik, who looked as lost as Barnes felt.

"Meaning what?" Barnes asked.

"Meaning that in Greek," Williams said, "T-H is the letter *theta*."

And like a sudden kick in the gut, Barnes got it.

"The Theta Project," he breathed.

"What's a Theta Project?" Jik asked.

"Something a bunch of damn traitors are going to have to do some explaining about," Barnes told him darkly. "Come on. And keep an eye out for that other T-700."

CHAPTER
FIFTEEN

For Kyle, the first hour was the hardest.

It wasn't just the darkness. Darkness was a familiar part of the post-Judgment Day world, and like everyone else he'd learned how to adapt and adjust. Not knowing where they were going, or even if the passageway beneath the Terminators' tunnel would lead anywhere at all, was also not a big deal. Uncertainty was as much a part of life as darkness.

What set Kyle's skin crawling was the periodic rhythmic thumping overhead as the lines of T-700s first marched to the face of the excavation to collect rubble, then headed back again with their fresh burdens to wherever they had found to dump them.

Those were the hard moments. Because those were the moments when a careless move on Kyle's or Callahan's or Zac's part—a slip of a foot, an accidental dislodging of one of the jagged pieces of concrete or metal they were crawling over—would alert the Terminators to the human intruders.

And once the machines knew where they were, they would be dead. All of them.

Just like Yarrow.

Kyle thought a lot about Yarrow as they traveled. He thought some about the man's last big mistake, the mistake that had trapped Kyle and the others down here.

But everyone made mistakes. Mostly, what Kyle thought about was the way Yarrow had done what he could to atone for his error by sending the others to safety.

He also found himself wondering how exactly Yarrow had died.

Kyle hadn't heard any sounds as the T-700s had reached him. Maybe Yarrow hadn't had time, or maybe the rolling echo of his last gunshots had covered up whatever screams or moans of agony he'd made before the end. Kyle hoped it had been quick, that the Terminators had simply broken his neck or hammer-crushed his chest or done something that would let their victim die quickly.

But all he actually knew was that the death had involved blood. A lot of blood.

He also knew that if the Terminators found him, he would probably die in very much the same way.

It wasn't Kyle's own death that worried him. He'd learned long ago not to focus on that, because it did nothing but freeze his will and paralyze any chance of thinking his way out of a bad situation.

But all the mental discipline in the world couldn't stop him from worrying about Star.

What would happen to her if he died down here?

It was a question that had forced itself on him many, many times. At the moment, settled as she was into John Connor's Resistance force, her chances of survival were better than at most of the times in their past together. Certainly better than any place she'd been since they left the Moldering Lost Ashes building.

But things changed. People changed. Connor might be

taking a personal interest in the two of them now, though why he would even care about a couple of inexperienced kids Kyle couldn't guess.

But the Resistance leader had a million other things clamoring for his attention. Sooner or later, he would forget about them.

And even if he didn't, could anyone else ever understand Star, or give her the attention and care she needed? Kyle was the only one who shared their private history. The only one who understood her brand of sign language, appreciated the way she thought and felt, and knew where she hurt.

If he died down here, she would die too. Maybe not tomorrow or the next day, but sooner or later she would give up and die.

But Kyle didn't make that last, fatal mistake as the T-700s passed back and forth overhead. Neither did Callahan or Zac. And as the pathway they were following angled off from directly beneath the Terminators' tunnel the footsteps became more and more distant until they finally faded away completely.

Which didn't mean the going became any easier. Far from it. The explosion that had leveled Skynet Central had sent underground shock waves across the entire San Francisco peninsula. Everything that had been part of that grand complex had been reduced to a tangled mess of shattered concrete and bent or broken support girders. Callahan, who had taken point, was picking his way through the rubble by touch alone, sometimes finding passages barely wide enough to squeeze through, sometimes finding routes that led in the wrong direction. Occasionally he hit a dead end that required them to back up and try again.

Once, they came upon an actual almost untouched room, with slightly buckled walls, a ceiling they could stand upright beneath, and a floor that they could really and truly walk on. It was such a relief to be able to move around like humans instead of moles that they nearly missed the fact that the floor was only half there.

Zac nearly died with that discovery—fortunately Kyle was close enough to grab his arm before he went over the edge. After that, they went back to crawling, no matter how safe the landscape seemed to be.

They'd been going for a couple of hours, and the rumbling in Kyle's empty stomach had become an almost continuous growl, when Callahan called a halt.

"How are you doing?" he murmured as they hunched together in the darkness.

Kyle shivered. How was he doing? He was cold, hungry, thirsty, and scared. His hands were raw and blistered, with a hundred tiny cuts from the rough concrete and shards of metal that lay along their path. His knees were agony, and he could feel the wetness of blood oozing into his pant legs as he crawled along. He had fresh bruises on his elbows and head where he'd missed some protruding obstacle with his groping hands as he crawled. The image of Yarrow's dead body continued to hover in front of his face in the darkness. So did Star's face. How was he doing?

"I'm fine," he said.

"Me, too," Zac seconded.

"Okay." Callahan's groping hand found Kyle's and pressed a small piece of something into it. "I always carry a snack bar with me, just in case something goes wrong. Steiner? Here's yours."

"Thanks," Kyle said, resisting the impulse to wolf down his third of the bar. Better to nibble slowly and make it last as long as possible. "Any idea where we are?"

"Hard to tell," Callahan said. "We took a lot of twists and turns along the way. I'm guessing we've covered around two hundred meters, maybe two-fifty, with the Terminators' tunnel about ten meters to our left. Assuming it went more or less straight, that is."

"Two hundred meters would put us inside the nighttime sentry ring," Zac murmured. "If they're that far in, they could be planning to attack tonight."

"Maybe," Callahan said. "But just getting inside the perimeter isn't going to do much for them. Besides, they're going to way too much trouble for just a raid."

"What trouble?" Zac scoffed. "It's not like they've got anything else to do right now."

"I was thinking about that H-K they threw against the camp last night," Callahan said. "Why bother? Especially since Skynet must have known we had enough firepower to take it down."

"Okay," Zac said. "So why do it?"

"Maybe it was a diversion," Kyle suggested. "No, not a diversion," he corrected himself as the image of those heavily loaded T-700s in the tunnel came back to him. "It was cover. The Terminators needed to do some blasting or heavy work at the tunnel face. Skynet crashed the H-K so we wouldn't hear or feel the other explosion."

"That's my guess, too," Callahan said. "Same idea with the T-600 and the T-700s who came marching into camp. Again, why bother?"

Kyle shook his head. "No idea."

"Think about it," Callahan said. "How did we get down here in the first place?"

"Through the conduit," Zac said, sounding puzzled.

"Except that the only reason we knew the conduit might

lead somewhere was because of the hole under the T-600,"
Kyle said as he suddenly understood. "It didn't make the
hole by falling. It fell so that it could cover the hole."

"You got it," Callahan said. "Remember how its arms
were splayed out to the sides? It fell like that to spread out
its weight so that it wouldn't break all the way through
when it landed."

Kyle nodded, remembering now how the T-600 had
just stood there motionless at the end, defiantly firing and
taking fire until it fell.

"That's also why Skynet sent in a T-600 along with the
T-700s," he said. "T-600s have enough bulk to cover the
hole. T-700s don't."

"Clever, huh?" Callahan said sourly. "And think about
this: if Zac hadn't taken his brass-hunting job so seriously
we might have walked right past it."

"But this is insane," Zac protested. "If Skynet wants to
flatten us, why not just do it? Why bother with a tunnel?
What's it going to do, bring in some really big bomb and
plant it under the HQ tent?"

"I don't know what it's planning," Callahan said. "But
one thing's for sure: whatever the goal is, Skynet must
figure it's worth the effort."

There was a scraping of boots on concrete.

"Come on, let's get moving," Callahan said. "Time to
find a way back to the tunnel and see what Skynet's got
planned for tonight."

The T-700 that had fallen into the ravine hadn't seemed
to Blair to be in particularly bad shape. Given the interest
Skynet had already shown in tracking down the fugitive,
she fully expected the machine to mount another attack
somewhere on their walk back to the ford.

But to her surprise, they arrived without the Terminator making an appearance. Her next guess was that it was lurking somewhere near the ford, waiting until they were slogging through the water before striking, possibly in a pincer maneuver with the T-700 that had gone north earlier along the east bank.

But once again, Skynet passed on the obvious. Preston and Hope were already waiting on the far side of the bank with the three guards as Blair, Barnes, and Jik reached the ford, with no sign of Terminators on either side of the river. Nothing attacked, from either direction, as the three of them headed across.

Only once was there a tense moment, when Jik got his feet tangled with one of the arms from the T-700 that Barnes had shredded earlier with his minigun. Even then, he managed to keep his balance until Barnes reached him and held his arm while he got his feet free. Barnes himself made it across without any trouble at all, and even with her aching leg Blair did the same. It seemed like Skynet had simply given up.

And that worried Blair. A lot. Because Skynet didn't give up, any more than its Terminators did. If it wasn't attacking at this particular moment, it was only because it was playing some other game.

Problem was, Blair had no idea what that game might be.

On the short walk back to town Blair kept an eye on their backtrail, just in case Skynet decided to go with a delayed punch. But again, the Terminators were nowhere to be seen.

They had reached Baker's Hollow when they finally met their first real obstacle.

It was Halverson. And he was furious.

"What the hell's going on?" he snarled as the group

emerged into view along the trail. His eyes flicked across Jik, shifted briefly to Barnes and Blair, then settled on Preston. "We heard gunfire."

"That was us," Preston confirmed. "We were out doing a little hunting." He nodded toward Jik. "We think we've found—"

"What part of them coming to my house didn't you get?" Halverson cut him off.

Blair looked sideways at Preston. His throat was tight, but when he spoke his voice was calm enough.

"They *did* go to your house," he reminded the other. "What happened after that was none of my doing."

"You saying they just sneaked out of my bedroom window on their own?" Halverson demanded. "That you didn't call to them, or invite them, or anything else?"

"I did nothing at all," Preston said. "I didn't even know they'd left your house. If I had, I'd certainly have urged them to return."

"Sure you would." Halverson shifted his glare to Barnes. "My hospitality not good enough for you?"

Unfortunately for him, glares didn't work nearly as well on Barnes as they did on Preston.

"Your hospitality's fine," Barnes told him. "Wish I could say the same about your attitude."

Halverson's face hardened.

"What did you say?"

"I said you're an idiot," Barnes said flatly. "Are you even listening?"

"I'm listening just fine," Halverson shot back. He jabbed a finger at Jik. "If this is the guy the Terminators are after, what the hell are you doing bringing him into town?"

"You really think his presence will affect Skynet's decision about what to do with you?" Preston asked.

"*Not* having him here has worked pretty well so far," Halverson bit back. "So has leaving Skynet alone."

"So that it will leave you alone?" Jik spoke up. "Yes, I've heard that philosophy before. The people who live by it usually don't live very long."

"Maybe you'd like to debate the point with the philosopher himself," Halverson said sarcastically.

Jik smiled faintly. "Indeed I would," he said. "Perhaps you'd like to fetch him for me."

"While you're at it, go get the other two," Barnes added. "Tell them to meet us at Preston's place."

"Forget it," Halverson said. "If we're going to meet anywhere—" He broke off, and Blair saw in his eyes the sudden recognition of what having a prime Skynet target in his home might mean. "Fine," he said. "Preston's house. I'll tell them." With a final glare at Barnes, he turned and strode off.

"My house is this way," Preston said, beckoning to Jik.

"He's right, you know," Jik commented quietly as they set off again. "My presence here *does* put you at additional risk. Whatever happens, I'm afraid your life here will never be the same again."

Preston shrugged, a little too casually.

"That possibility's been hanging over our heads for a long time," he pointed out. "Since Judgment Day, really."

"True," Jik agreed. "The difference is that while I bring danger, I also bring hope."

"What kind of hope?" Blair asked.

"The very best kind," Jik assured her. "Before I go into that, let's hear what these pacifist philosophers have to say."

Blair exchanged looks with Barnes.

"Yes," she murmured. "Let's."

CHAPTER SIXTEEN

For someone who'd seemed as nervous about Terminator attacks as Halverson, Barnes thought more than once, he didn't seem to be in much of a hurry to get Jik out of his town. At their home, Hope had enough time to throw together a quick meal, and they all had enough time to eat it before Halverson finally arrived.

It was just as well they'd opted for Preston's house with its larger living room. Not only had Halverson brought the three scientists, but he'd also grabbed a dozen other men and women. His closest friends and allies, Barnes had no doubt, and all of them armed.

Idiots, Barnes thought darkly as the people settled onto chairs or couches or found sections of wall to lean against. Idiot Halverson for stirring up a turf war; idiot Preston for letting him get away with it. Barnes had seen too much of this sort of political infighting among the group leaders when Connor first moved their team from Los Angeles to General Olsen's Resistance group, and it led to nothing but trouble.

At least the mayor was smart enough to get in the first word.

"Thank you all for coming," he said, nodding to everyone

as if he'd actually invited them all. "I'd like you to welcome our visitor, Jik, who seems to be the man the Terminators have been searching for. We asked you here—"

"They're looking for him," one of Halverson's buddies interrupted, "and you brought him *here*?"

"Don't worry, we've got some time," Jik said calmly. "We know Skynet still has two T-700s in the area. If it was in a hurry to get me, it should have attacked us on our way into town. The fact that it didn't means that it has something else in mind."

"Probably waiting until nightfall," someone else muttered.

"Possibly," Jik agreed. "If they want new instructions or data, that would be the time when Skynet could get it to them."

"Or possibly the whole thing is a misunderstanding," Lajard put in, eyeing Jik curiously. "Who exactly are you, friend?".

"As you say, a friend," Jik said. "Before we go into specifics, I'd like to hear a bit more of *your* story. I'm told you worked for Skynet in that big underground lab to the southeast."

"You make it sound like we had a choice," the woman scientist, Susan Valentine, said quietly. "We were taken from our homes, all of us, and forced to do what Skynet wanted."

"I'm sure Skynet was quite insistent," Jik agreed. "But you *did* have a choice. People always have choices."

Oxley snorted. "You sound like Barnes," he said. "It's all very well to talk about sacrificing your life for a noble cause. It's a lot different to just stand there and get yourself killed."

"I never said all the choices were pleasant," Jik pointed out. "But they're always there."

Oxley snorted. "Right."

"And if more of the people like you had chosen that option," Jik added pointedly, "it might very well be that we'd be facing Terminators that weren't nearly so dangerous."

"That's easy for *you* to say," Oxley growled. "You've got guns—you get to shoot back. We didn't have anything."

"Yeah, we're the lucky ones, all right," Barnes growled. "Tell us about Theta."

The room went suddenly silent. Valentine's face looked all pinched and pained, and Oxley shifted uncomfortably in his seat. Lajard, in contrast, met Barnes's gaze without flinching.

"What do you want to know?" he asked.

"Let's start with the designation," Jik said. "Theta, the Greek TH. Was it a plan for turning human beings into Terminators?"

Halverson's jaw dropped. *"What?"*

"You make it sound sinister," Oxley protested. "It wasn't like that."

"What *was* it like?" Preston asked, his voice as cold as Halverson's.

"Oh, don't be so squeamish," Lajard chided. "It was a solid and practical idea, and it might have gone somewhere useful if people hadn't turned Skynet against them."

"You must be the live-and-let-live one I've heard so much about," Jik said, eyeing Lajard closely.

"What, because I believe humans and Skynet can coexist?" Lajard countered. "Absolutely. And I've yet to be proved wrong."

"We may change your mind," Jik said. "Tell us about Theta."

Lajard shrugged. "Conceptually, it was simple enough. The idea was to enhance basic human abilities to give people a better chance against the harshness of the post-Judgment Day world."

"*Enhancing* them?" Barnes bit out. "You gut a human and stuff him inside a metal body, and you call that *enhancing* him?"

A murmur rippled through the room.

"Absolutely," Lajard said, ignoring the reaction. "A Theta is stronger than a normal human, with more stamina and less need for food and sleep. He's a survivor, in the very best sense of the word."

"And all it costs is his humanity," Preston said.

"*Or* it gives him his humanity back," Lajard countered. "Take our prototype, for example. When Marcus Wright was brought to us, he—"

"So *you're* the ones who turned him into a machine," Williams said.

Barnes looked over at her, a shiver running up his spine. Williams hadn't moved, hadn't even raised her voice... and yet, as he looked into her eyes, he suddenly had the sense that he would rather face down an armed T-700 right now than tangle with her.

Lajard, who didn't know her, missed it completely.

"No, we're the ones who took a dead man and gave him a second chance at life," he said irritably. "We rebuilt his brain, created a technique for stripping donated organs of biochemical identity tags so that they could be put together without running into rejection problems—"

"How did you know Marcus?" Valentine interrupted.

"I met him," Williams said, that same graveyard chill in her voice.

"He paid us a visit," Barnes added, watching the scientists' faces closely.

"That's impossible," Valentine said, frowning. "He was our prototype. He never left the lab."

"Well, he did," Barnes told her. "Maybe the explosion opened up his cage."

"No one was kept in a cage," Lajard insisted.

"The hell they weren't," Barnes said hotly. "And Skynet was doing experiments on them."

"Yes, well, until you can actually prove that, I'm sticking with what I saw," Lajard insisted.

"But Barnes raises a good point," Jik said. "You say this Marcus Wright was your prototype. How many more Thetas did you make?"

"None," Oxley said. "We were still working on Marcus when our transport crashed and we got stuck out here."

"Of course, that was three months ago," Valentine pointed out. "It's possible the others finished Marcus's tests during that time and started work on another one."

"Oh, they built another one, all right," Jik said grimly. "I know because I killed it."

Some of the color drained from Valentine's face.

"You *what*?" she breathed. "Another Theta?" She shot quick, startled looks at Oxley and Lajard, then turned back to Jik. "When was this?"

"And where?" Preston added.

"A couple of days ago, on my way here," Jik said.

"What did it look like?" Lajard asked.

"Like a skin-covered Terminator," Barnes told him. "That's what they all look like. That's the *point*."

"I meant what were its facial characteristics," Lajard said with exaggerated patience. "There were other conversion candidates waiting in storage. If we knew which one you ran into, we might be able to figure out how far along the others got before the lab went up in smoke."

"You couldn't have mistaken this one for anyone else," Jik said. "Or any*thing* else, for that matter. It had a scar on its right cheek, and the whole left side of its face looked like it had been burned by acid."

"I don't remember anything like that in the queue," Lajard said, frowning at the others.

"Maybe there was an accident during the procedure," Oxley suggested. "There was a fair amount of hydrochloric and other acids involved in the tag-stripping process."

"You were the one who handled the bio-medical aspects?" Jik asked.

"One of them, yes," Oxley said. "Susan was with the metallurgical group, while Remy worked on programming."

"What programming?" Preston asked. "You said these hybrids were nothing but enhanced people."

"*You* try hooking up a human brain to a set of metal limbs and internal servos and see what happens," Lajard growled. "You need an interface chip to handle data transfer between neurons and electronics, and that chip has to be programmed for the job."

"With a few other enhancements thrown in," Williams said.

"What enhancements?" Preston asked.

"Location and ID data," Williams said. "Secret mission parameters and profiles. Complete Skynet control."

"Now you're being ridiculous," Lajard insisted. "I *worked* on the damn chip, remember? There was nothing like any of that in the programming."

"Then why did that Theta try to kill me?" Jik asked. "Or are you suggesting it's pure coincidence that the Theta was running the same agenda as the T-700s out there? T-700s that we *know* are under direct Skynet control?"

"I don't know," Lajard said stiffly. "But as long as we're pointing suspicious fingers, I might mention that we've only got your word that there even *was* a hybrid out there, let alone that it attacked you."

"Which brings us back to you," Oxley put in. "We've told you about Theta. Let's hear a little of *your* story."

"Oh, come now," Jik said reprovingly, a slight smile touching the corners of his lips. "I'm not surprised you don't recognize me. But surely you at least recognize my voice."

"Your *voice*?" Preston asked, frowning.

Barnes's throat tightened. Ever since Jik had gotten the drop on them out in the forest he'd had the nagging feeling that he'd heard that voice somewhere before. Now, abruptly, his brain made the connection.

Only—

"Of course," Jik said. "*Jik* is just a nickname from my childhood, a name I use when I'm keeping a low profile. It's a blending of my initials, J.C."

He drew himself up, his eyes sweeping the group of people around him.

"I'm John Connor."

CHAPTER SEVENTEEN

A stunned silence descended on the room. Their expressions, Blair saw as she looked around, ranged from stunned to hopeful to flat-out disbelievingly worshipful.

She looked at Barnes. His eyes were focused like twin Gatling guns on Jik, his lips starting to twist into the kind of snarl that usually preceded one of his borderline-suicidal leaps into danger. His eyes flicked to Blair—

Quickly, urgently, Blair gave her head a tiny shake. *Not now*, she pleaded silently. *Later. Not now. Not here.*

His eyes narrowed in silent, impatient question. Blair flicked her eyes to the ring of armed townspeople surrounding them.

Barnes scowled. But to Blair's relief he gave her a small nod and settled back a little into his seat.

Preston was the first to find his voice.

"Well," he said hesitantly. "I… welcome to Baker's Hollow."

"I think what Mayor Preston is trying to say," Lajard growled, "is what the hell are you doing here?"

Preston turned an outraged look at the scientist.

"Lajard!"

"No, I mean it," Lajard insisted. "You've put the whole

town at risk just by being here. Why?"

"I assume you heard my last broadcast," Jik said, gazing unflinchingly into Lajard's glare. "We lost a lot of people in the San Francisco attack. We need replacements, and we need them now."

He waved a hand around him. "You—the people of Baker's Hollow—have managed to survive out here in the wild. Not just survive, but actually prosper. You're exactly the kind of people we need."

He raised his eyebrows slightly.

"In fact, I'll go farther than that. We need a new base, preferably something in this part of the country. Baker's Hollow and the surrounding area may be just what we're looking for."

"What size base are we talking about?" Halverson asked suspiciously. "We've got all the population right now we can supply."

"Don't worry about that," Jik assured him. "If we come, we'll bring our own food and equipment with us. With extra for anyone who joins us, of course."

"Sounds wonderful," Lajard said with only a hint of sarcasm. "In the meantime, your precious Resistance is a long way away, and we've still got a couple of Terminators beating the bushes for you out there."

"So let's deal with them," Jik said firmly. "What resources do you have aside from the guns and bows I've already seen? Any explosives?"

"No." Preston patted his side pocket. "But we've got a little gasoline for fueling our emergency lighters."

"How much?" Jik asked.

Preston looked at one of the other men.

"Ten gallons?"

"Closer to twelve," the other said.

Jik shook his head. "Not enough. What about chains or study ropes?"

"We've got some chains, but they're not very long," Preston said. "We've got a fair amount of good rope, though."

"Chucker's bear traps have chains on them," Halverson offered, gesturing to one of the men across the room.

"You have bear traps?" Jik asked, his eyes lighting up. "How many?"

"I got two that are in decent shape," Chucker said. "There's another one, too, but it's a little iffy."

"Don't worry, we'll make it work," Jik promised. "Go get them, will you? The rest of you grab any chain or thick rope you've got, plus any tools for fixing Chucker's traps. Whose house is closest to the river?"

"Mine," one of the women spoke up.

"Bring everything there, as quickly as possible," Jik ordered. "Along with everyone who has a large-caliber gun and ammo to load into it." He gestured to Preston. "Mayor?"

"You heard the man," Preston confirmed. "Get to it."

"Before you go, Connor," Blair spoke up as the group made a concerted rush toward the door, "could we have a word with you?"

"Certainly," Jik said, sidestepping a couple of men as they hurried past.

"Back here, please?" Blair said, standing up and gesturing toward the bedrooms.

Jik's eyes narrowed slightly.

"Why can't we talk right here?"

Peripherally, Blair saw that a few of the men, Preston and Halverson among them, had paused to listen.

"This would be better discussed in private," she said as Barnes also stood up.

"We're all allies here, Williams," Jik said. "Whatever you have to say, go ahead and say it."

Blair threw Barnes a questioning look. He gave her a reluctant nod.

"Fine," Blair said, turning back to Jik. "As it happens, Barnes and I work with John Connor. The *real* John Connor. You're not him."

The room went utterly still.

"Excuse me?" Jik said into the brittle silence.

"I said we know the real John Connor," Blair repeated. "We don't know you."

"That's interesting," Jik said evenly. "Because I *am* the real John Connor. And *I* don't know *you*."

"Of course you don't know us," Barnes said. "We just said that."

"So what we have here is your classic standoff," Jik said calmly. "My word against yours." He waved a hand that encompassed the people around them. "Except that these people know my voice. They know nothing about you."

Blair looked around. He was right, she realized. Whatever this scam was he was running, he had Connor's voice down cold. A voice that these people had probably been listening to for months.

And if it came down to believing a pair of strangers who'd dropped out of the sky or the man whose exhortations had kept them hoping and working toward a better day, Blair had no doubt which side they would come down on.

But even if they didn't know the truth, she and Barnes did. The man was a fraud, and she had to try.

"We came in a helicopter," she said, speaking now to Preston and the other townspeople. "If we're not Resistance, where did we get that?"

"Could be any number of places," Jik said. "There are still plenty of gangs out there, some with surprising access to resources. There are also some paramilitary groups in the Rockies that aren't affiliated with the Resistance. You could be from one of them."

"Or they could be from Skynet," Halverson rumbled, his rifle pointed openly now at Barnes.

Blair felt her body tense even more. If Jik wanted to get rid of them, tying them to Skynet would be the simplest and surest way to do it.

But to her surprise, Jik shook his head.

"I don't think so," he said, gazing thoughtfully at her. "It's hard to imagine what Skynet would gain by letting them wreck a couple of its Terminators."

He turned to Preston.

"Still, whoever they are, we can't afford to let them wander around without supervision. Can you assign two or three of your men to watch them while we go deal with those last two T-700s?"

"I can do that," Halverson spoke up. "Chris, Trounce—"

"I'd prefer that Mayor Preston assign the guards," Jik interrupted. "No offense, but I'd feel better if this was official."

Halverson grimaced, but nodded.

"Sure. Whatever you want."

Preston gestured to a couple of the men near the door.

"Trounce, you and Smith," he said. "Simple guard duty. You don't need to tie them up—just keep them in the house. Barnes, Williams, over on the couch, please. Unfasten your gun belts first, if you would."

Blair looked around the room. If she and Barnes were fast enough…

But it was already too late. Three others besides Halverson had their guns up and aimed now. She unfastened her gunbelt and lowered it and her beloved Desert Eagle to the floor.

"What if they make trouble?" one of the guards asked as Barnes reluctantly set down his own weapons.

Preston looked at Barnes.

"You're not going to make trouble, are you?"

"Not yet," Barnes said, his voice dark as he eyed Halverson. "Maybe later."

"Just take it easy," Preston advised. "Don't worry, we'll get this all sorted out later."

"If there *is* a later," Blair warned.

"Is that a threat?" Halverson demanded.

"There are two T-700s out there," Blair reminded him coldly. "You don't need any threats from me."

She crossed to the couch and sat down at one end. Barnes took the cue and moved to the couch's other end. Preston and Halverson gathered up their guns and packs while the two guards pulled chairs over to the big window and sat down, their rifles cradled in their arms.

"We'll be back soon," Jik promised as Preston and the remaining townspeople filed out the door. "I suggest you take the opportunity to get some rest."

He paused in the doorway.

"And if you think you can come up with a better story," he added, "you might want to do that, too."

A moment later he was gone.

"What now?" Blair asked quietly.

Barnes gave a long, measuring look at the two guards.

"We wait," he told her. "For now."

CHAPTER EIGHTEEN

Kyle had taken over point from Callahan, and had led them slogging through the underground ruins for another hour, when he rounded a particularly large slab of concrete and saw a light in the distance.

It wasn't much of a light, no more than a sliver of hazy yellowish glow, more oozing than actually shining, coming from the ceiling fifty meters ahead.

But in that first minute Kyle didn't care what kind of light it was. It was *light*, and after hours of straining his eyes in utter blackness it was like a breath of clean air or a long swallow of cold water.

They'd found the Terminators' tunnel again.

Which meant that they'd found the Terminators.

There was a rattle of gravel as Callahan and Zac came up alongside him.

"That the tunnel?" Zac whispered.

"Probably," Callahan said. "Okay. Extra quiet from here on."

Keeping extra quiet turned out to be easier than Kyle had expected. The light, dim though it was, gave enough illumination to show them a little of the uneven ground they were crawling across. They covered the fifty meters more quickly, and more quietly, than most of the previous several hours' worth of travel.

From the positioning of the light when Kyle first spotted it, he had guessed the opening was only a meter or two above the level of their floor. What he hadn't known was that the passageway made a sharp dip halfway along their path before leveling off at a new, lower level. When they reached the light, it turned out to be over three meters above the floor, nearly a meter out of reach.

The good news was that the opening was similar to the one they'd used to escape the tunnel all those hours ago: a gap between the tunnel floor and the wall of debris beside it. Like the other opening, this one also had an angled field of broken masonry below it, tricky but not impossible to climb.

The bad news was that the opening was far too narrow for even Zac to get through.

For a minute they stood together looking up at it, listening to the rhythmic footsteps as the Terminators continued their endless march back and forth to the tunnel face. The marching seemed to go on for longer than it had before, and Kyle wondered uneasily if Skynet had thrown more T-700s into the project. Implying that the breakout was indeed imminent.

Finally, the muffled thudding faded away. Callahan waited another few seconds, then drew the other two in for a close-huddle conference.

"Thoughts?"

"I think we're near the front of the tunnel," Zac whispered.

"How do you know?" Kyle asked.

"Because those Terminators were going both directions," Zac said. "One group coming up empty-handed, the other passing them with their loads."

"Ah." Kyle hadn't detected the difference in direction himself. But Zac had shown several times already that he had the best hearing of the group.

"Sounds like they're gone," Zac went on. "Let me climb up and see if I can see anything."

He started to step away. Callahan, still holding onto his sleeve, pulled him back.

"I'll go," he said firmly. "I'm a better climber, and that slope looks tricky."

The slope was every bit as difficult as Callahan had anticipated, and even with Kyle and Zac standing on either side to brace his arms and legs there were times where he nearly slid back. But finally he was there. Carefully taking hold of the edge of the tunnel floor, he pulled himself up and peered through the opening.

He held the pose for about half a minute. Then, easing himself back onto the debris, he climbed back down.

"We're at the front, all right," he told them when they were huddled together again. "There's a stack of eight bags along the wall that look like satchel charges."

"They're not right at the tunnel face?" Kyle asked.

"No, about three meters back," Callahan said. "There's still a bunch of debris right at the face, so I'm guessing they'll still be lugging and hand digging for a while longer."

"Where's the light coming from?" Zac asked.

"There are a bunch of small holes in the ceiling," Callahan said "The light's pretty diffuse, so I'm guessing it's sifting in through another layer of broken concrete."

Kyle grimaced. He'd been hoping the light meant another big crack in the tunnel ceiling. They might have used an opening like that to get out, or at least to signal the rest of the Resistance people up there.

"So that's a dead end," he said.

"Don't worry, we'll figure out something," Callahan said. "At least we'll have some light if we can get up there."

"How are we going to do that?" Zac asked.

"Not sure," Callahan conceded. "The wall beside the gap is a single slab of reinforced concrete—you can see the rebar sticking out. There's no way we're going to move it."

"What about the tunnel floor?" Kyle asked.

"Well, it's not too thick, and I didn't see any rebar," Callahan said. "Probably used to be a roof or a wall that didn't need to hold up a lot of weight."

"A non-load-bearing wall," Kyle supplied, remembering Orozco talking about things like that while they poked around some of the ruined buildings back in Los Angeles.

"Right," Callahan said. "On the other hand, it's getting stomped on by T-700s all day, so it can't be *that* flimsy. It's also a little crumbly at the edge, so we might be able to make the hole bigger."

"Sounds good," Zac said. "I'll take first shift."

"That's okay," Callahan said, digging into his pocket. "We can start with my knife. When we wear it down we'll shift to Reese's, then we'll just have to use whatever else we can find."

"Wait a second," Kyle said suddenly. "This won't work."

"Sure it will," Callahan assured him. "It'll take awhile, but—"

"No, I mean we can't do it," Kyle said. "The Terminators will see the hole get bigger each time they go by."

There was a brief silence.

"You're right," Callahan muttered. "Damn."

"So what do we do?" Zac asked anxiously. "It'll take forever to go back to the other hole."

"No point in doing that anyway," Callahan said heavily. "The Terminators are bound to still be watching the conduit. I suppose we could try backtracking and see if there's an opening we missed."

"There wasn't anything," Kyle asked, peering up. The underside of the tunnel floor was hard to see in the reflected light coming from the opening. But even so—

"Probably not," Callahan agreed heavily. "But it's all we've got."

"Maybe not," Kyle said, pointing at the ceiling. "Is that a crack up there?"

The others looked up.

"You mean that line angling across there?" Zac asked, his pointing finger tracing out the path.

"Looks like a crack to me," Callahan agreed. "But if you think the Terminators will notice the gap getting bigger, they'll *really* notice if a quarter of the path they're walking on disappears."

"Right, but only if we're the ones who bring it down," Kyle said. "What if we just deepen the crack enough so that the next batch of T-700s breaks through? Maybe Skynet will assume it had too much stress and gave way by itself."

"Of course, if it *doesn't* assume that, we'll have a whole mess of Terminators down here hunting us," Callahan pointed out. "But it's worth a try."

He looked upward again.

"You're not going to be able to reach the crack from the slope. I guess that means you'll be standing on our shoulders."

"Hang on a second," Kyle said, looking behind them. "I think I saw a door frame back there."

"Yeah," Zac said. "It was... there it is, over there."

The frame was partially buried in concrete chips, but it took only a little effort for the three of them to dig it out. A minute after that, they had it in place beneath the ceiling crack, lying on its long side.

"Perfect," Callahan said, testing its balance. "Wide enough to stand on, and all you two have to do is brace it to keep it from falling over. Okay, hold it steady."

"Shouldn't we wait until the Terminators have made their next round?" Zac suggested. "We don't want you making scraping noises while they're on their way in."

"Right," Callahan said reluctantly, sitting down beside the frame. "I just hope we can get this done before they blast through into the camp."

"We will," Kyle said firmly. "We have to."

It took an hour for the people of Baker's Hollow to gather the equipment Jik had asked for, and to then make the necessary modifications for what he had in mind. During that time Halverson's runners brought in three reports from the men tailing the T-700 on the east bank of the river, which seemed to be tracing out a sentry line half a mile north of town that ran from the river to a couple of miles east.

The obvious inference was that the Terminator was guarding something. But neither Preston nor Halverson could think of anything up there that Skynet might be hiding, unless it thought Jik was still out there and was searching for him.

Finally, with the equipment prepped and their ambush positions chosen, they were ready.

Jik had already decided to lean the main, riskier attack. With Halverson and several of the others, he headed north to intercept the Terminator on their side of the river. Preston and the rest went to reinforce the guard at the ford, and to prepare for the moment when the other T-700 returned and tried to cross the river.

And as Jik and Halverson headed toward the spot they had chosen for their ambush, Jik found himself thinking about Barnes and Williams. Thinking, and wondering.

Mercenaries or paramilitary gang members he could understand. They might have spotted Baker's Hollow and come in to scope out its resources for theft or barter. Con artists he could similarly understand, though how a pair of scammers could have gotten hold of a working helicopter he couldn't guess. Still, in either scenario it would make sense for them to come in masquerading as Resistance fighters.

But in neither scenario was there any reason why they would be so stupid as to claim Jik was a fraud.

It made no sense. Even if Jik *had* been a fraud, why would they open themselves up to suspicion and the risk of serious consequences, consequences that had now in fact rained down on them? Why not keep quiet, pretend to be from a distant Resistance unit which had never had any direct contact with Jik, and try to get through the rest of their agenda before anyone figured out who they really were?

There was more depth to this thing than Jik had yet been able to sort out. But he *would* sort it out.

In the meantime, there were Terminators to be dealt with.

They reached the ambush point to find a man and woman waiting for them, the woman crouched beside a tree, the man pacing nervously back and forth.

"About time," the latter said as Jik and the others came up. "This is the path Singer says it's been walking." He gestured, indicating a roughly east-west direction.

"But it doesn't trace out exactly the same path each

time," Jik said, eyeing the tall grass that covered most of the ground area between the trees. "Otherwise it would have worn a more well-defined furrow."

"That's right," the woman confirmed. "Will that be a problem?"

"No, I don't think so," Jik said. "How soon before it comes back this way?"

"Probably ten minutes," the man said. "At least ten. Maybe fifteen."

"Ten should be plenty," Jik said, gesturing to the men lugging the equipment. "Let's get to work."

Eight minutes later, they were ready. Three minutes after that, Jik felt the first subtle vibrations through the ground as the T-700 approached.

"Get ready," he murmured to the others.

And then, there it was, pushing aside low-hanging branches and wading through knee-high grass as it walked its solitary sentry path. Its G11 submachinegun was held ready, its metallic skull and glowing eyes swept methodically back and forth.

Jik crouched a little lower behind his tree, one hand gripping each of the two long ropes he and the others had strung around two other trees, watching the Terminator closely as he tried to track its precise path.

"Needs to go a little north," Halverson murmured from beside him.

Jik nodded and pulled gently but firmly on the rope in his left hand. Twenty meters in front of the approaching Terminator the grasses shifted slightly, the subtle movement camouflaged by their general wind-induced sway. Jik eyed the T-700's path and gave the rope another few centimeters' worth of last-minute tweaking. The machine continued forward...

With a startlingly loud *crack*, the Terminator's right foot hit and triggered the bear trap Jik had maneuvered into its path. The machine came to a sudden, awkward halt, its momentum forcing it to take one final step forward with its left leg. There was a second crack as the second bear trap snapped shut around its other leg—

"Now!" Jik shouted. Letting go of the rope in his left hand, he shifted both hands to the one in his right and pulled. All around him, the other men and women leaped into position from the bushes, grass and trees, some hauling on Jik's rope, others joining with Halverson in pulling on the other one.

Terminators were incredibly strong machines. But their servomotor musculature hadn't been designed with this sort of movement in mind. The T-700's legs were yanked apart, pulled in opposite directions into a gymnast's splits by the two bear traps now clinging to its lower legs.

And with its balance base suddenly gone, it toppled forward to land on its gun and its outstretched arms.

"Belay!" Jik shouted. Not waiting for the others to secure the thick ropes, he snatched up his borrowed G11 and braced the barrel against the side of the tree. He would have just one shot at this.

The Terminator shifted position, leaving its left hand on the ground and bringing up the G11 in its right. It aimed the weapon down and to its right, targeting the bear trap and attached rope.

And with his own gun on full automatic, Jik fired everything he had into the magazine on the Terminator's weapon.

Sometimes, he knew, a sustained blast into that much caseless ammunition would cause a spontaneous cascading that would cook off the close-packed rounds.

That would create a multiple explosion that would wreck the weapon and usually the hand or entire arm of the Terminator holding it.

In this case, Jik wasn't that lucky. But he was lucky enough. The G11 broke apart in the T-700's hand, its firing mechanism shattered and useless.

And with its gun gone and its legs still being held, the machine was helpless.

Halverson was already on his way, running across the grass with Barnes's SIG 542 gripped in his hands. Dropping the empty G11, Jik grabbed the Mossberg shotgun they'd also taken from the visitors and sprinted after him.

He caught up with Halverson twenty meters from the Terminator, which was now trying unsuccessfully to reach the traps pinning its legs.

"Arms first?" Halverson called.

"Arms first," Jik confirmed. "And then we'll see."

"See what?"

Jik grimaced. What he knew, and the townspeople didn't, was that this was the moment of truth. If their ensnared T-700 and the one he, Barnes, and Williams had tangled with across the river were the only two machines Skynet had out here, that second Terminator should even now be charging to the rescue, trying to get here before Jik and Halverson reduced its compatriot to rubble. Two Terminators working together were always more effective than one alone, even if one or both of them were damaged.

But if Skynet still had other resources available or close at hand, it would be foolish to waste the other T-700 in an attempt to save this one. In that case, the other Terminator would remain hidden and out of range as it waited for the reinforcements.

And Terminator reinforcements would be bad. Very bad.

"See what?" Halverson repeated.

"Then we'll see," Jik said, "which part of it we want to destroy next."

Connor had warned Preston that the last remaining Terminator would probably show up before there were any warning sounds of gunfire from Connor's own position north of town. Sure enough, Preston's team had barely gotten themselves prepared when the bushes across the river parted and the dark figure of a T-700 strode into view and headed for the ford.

It was not, Preston noted, nearly as fearsome a sight as he remembered it from earlier that day. The fingers of its right hand were bent and twisted where Williams's shotgun slug and the Terminator's own exploding gun had damaged it. Its left shoulder also looked a little odd, and Preston wondered if it had been damaged by the fall into the ravine during the later fight with Connor and Williams. The limb might even have broken off and had to be magnetically reattached. There were some serious dents on its torso, as well, where Williams's shotgun blasts had nailed it at close range.

But the Terminator's legs, at least, were working just fine. The machine reached the edge of the swirling water and strode in, leaning against the current to keep from being knocked over.

Preston shot a quick look to his left. Three meters away, Hope was standing straight and ready beside her own covering tree, her arrow nocked, a look of nervousness tinged with determination on her face. To Preston's right, Half-pint Swan also stood ready.

Preston turned back to the river, gripping the heavy rope noose in his hands, making sure the rest of the rope trailing from it was free of any entanglements in the undergrowth around him. The Terminator was nearly to the trap now…

It reached the position, then continued past it. Preston hissed viciously between his teeth, wondering what they were going to do now.

And then, the Terminator jerked to a halt, nearly pitching forward onto its face. Apparently, Preston had been slightly off in his estimation of where the bear trap was actually positioned.

But Connor and Halverson were using bear traps against their Terminator, too. With the two T-700s linked via short-range radio telemetry, that meant this one already knew how to deal with bear traps. It didn't waste any time trying to pull out the chain, but simply leaned over at the waist and reached its metal arms into the whitewater to get a grip on the trap's jaws and pry them apart.

And as its eyes shifted downward, Preston leaped out of cover and raced toward it, holding the noose straight out in front of him.

Even with its eyes turned away and the roar of the water in its auditory sensors the Terminator must have sensed Preston's approach. It looked up as he neared the river, its glowing red eyes staring, its useless teeth clenched, its skeletal face an image out of human nightmares.

But there was no turning back now. With the Terminator's leg trapped, its body hunched over as its fingers tried to pry the bear trap open, and its head turned upward, the machine was at this moment the most unmoving it was ever likely to be. Baring his own teeth in defiance, Preston picked up his pace.

The Terminator was still glaring cold death at him when Preston heard a sharp double twang from behind and to either side of him.

And the twin red glows of death abruptly vanished as a pair of arrows jammed themselves into the machine's eyes.

Terminators didn't scream, in pain or rage or anything else. Nor did they get angry. The machine merely jerked back with the double impact, then straightened up, abandoning the task of freeing its leg, and grabbed at the aluminum shafts sticking out of its skull.

It had succeeded in pulling out one of the arrows and snapping off the other when Preston reached it. Jumping into the frigid water, he threw the noose over the machine's head, gave a quick tug on the rope to tighten the loop around its neck, then leaped backward again out of the Terminator's reach.

"Go!" he shouted.

For a single, awful second nothing happened. The Terminator's hands reached toward the noose, fumbling for a grip—

And then the trailing rope snapped upward toward the sturdy branch it was looped over as the men behind Preston hauled on the loose end. The noose twitched out of the Terminator's groping fingers and closed solidly around its neck.

Preston looked behind him as the two big men hidden in the tree leaned backward, one of them above the other, and fell toward the ground.

And as they did so, the rope wrapped around their waists snapped taut, their combined weight pulling upward on the Terminator's neck, stretching the deadly machine between the bear trap around its leg and the noose around its neck.

Instantly, the machine abandoned the noose now snugged too tightly around its neck to be gripped and shifted its attention to the rope itself. But its damaged right hand was unable to get enough grip for it to simply tear the rope apart.

It was still trying when Chris, Dowder, and Pappas came running up and opened fire with their shotguns and Barnes's long sniper rifle. Twenty seconds later, its arms severed from its shoulders, the Terminator was helpless.

Five minutes after that, it was dead.

CHAPTER NINETEEN

"Not too close together," Preston warned as Half-pint started to set one of the Terminator's legs down beside the other. "Magnetic reattachment, remember?"

"Oh. Right." Half-pint took a couple of long steps farther to the side and set down the leg.

Preston looked over the scattering of Terminator pieces spread out on the riverbank. It was an impressive array, all right. Rather like a live-action version of the exploded-machine diagrams from his auto mechanic days.

"So what do we do with all of it?" Half-pint asked.

A movement caught Preston's eye, and he looked over to see Connor and Halverson coming through the trees, their team lugging pieces of their own wrecked Terminator.

"I think we're about to find out," he said.

"Excellent job, Mayor," Connor said as he and the others arrived at the riverside and dumped their fragments of Terminator onto the grass. "Clean sweep. And the fact that Skynet sent in yours to try to rescue ours means it hasn't got any other resources in the area. Good news all around."

"Doesn't mean it won't put together another group and send them in," Halverson warned.

"Life is uncertain," Connor conceded. "But at the very least we've bought ourselves some time. And it's still possible that Skynet will decide you're not worth the effort of rooting out. That certainly seems to have been its assessment up until now."

"Except that things have changed," Halverson pointed out. "For one thing, we've just wrecked four of its Terminators. For another, *you're* here."

"Nothing we can do about the first," Connor said. "As to the second, I won't be here for long."

"What about the base you said you wanted to set up?" Preston asked.

"That's something I still want to explore," Connor told him. "But later. When I return, it'll be with a full Resistance force."

"Why not just stay here and send for them?" Preston persisted. "Skynet's probably expecting you to move on. In that case, staying here might be safer"

"We know you've got a radio you can call them with," Hope added, coming up beside Preston. "You've been making broadcasts."

"A small one, yes," Connor said thoughtfully. "An interesting suggestion, and one I'll have to think about." He looked down at the scattered Terminator pieces. "But first we have a lot of junk we need to dispose of. I don't suppose you have any thermite back in town?"

"We have a pretty decent forge," Halverson offered.

Connor shook his head.

"I doubt it'll melt T-700 alloy. Our best bet is probably to dump the pieces into that ravine west of the river."

"You and Williams already did that," Preston reminded him. "The machine got out just fine."

"Only because it was more or less intact," Connor said.

"As long as we make sure to scatter the pieces far enough apart, we shouldn't have a problem."

"Well, whatever we're going to do, let's do it," Halverson rumbled, looking up at the sky. "I want to be back in town before it gets dark."

"Good point." Connor raised his eyebrows. "Mayor?"

"I guess the ravine's as good a spot as any," Preston agreed reluctantly. "Fine. Everyone? We're heading across the river. Grab something, and let's go."

"We don't need everybody," Halverson said as the men and women began picking up the dented and scarred pieces of metal. "Connor and I can handle this. You can take whoever we don't need and head back."

Preston was used to Halverson throwing his weight around, and he'd more or less become accustomed to it. But doing it in front of John Connor himself was proving far more embarrassing than it usually was.

But until and unless Connor actually brought in his Resistance group—his group, and the food supplies he'd mentioned—Halverson would continue to have all the weight that his expert hunter status gave him.

And in this case he also happened to be right. There was no point in everyone tromping off into the woods if they weren't needed. There was plenty of other work to be done in town.

"All right," he said. "But take a few guards along, too. In case you run into something you can't handle with your arms full."

"Fine," Halverson said. He walked away, tagging a few of the armed men and women who weren't currently hefting a piece of broken Terminator.

"Speaking of which, Mayor," Connor said, "I wonder if I might borrow that sidearm of yours. The .45 you loaned me is empty."

Preston looked down at his waist, where Williams's Desert Eagle was riding snugly in its holster.

"I don't see why not—"

"We should keep that one with us," Hope interrupted suddenly. "You've still got their shotgun, right. Won't that do?"

"Hope—" Preston began warningly.

"That's all right," Connor soothed. "Actually, she's right—we have more than enough firepower already." He smiled at Preston. "We'll see you back in town. And once again, Mayor, you and the others did a superb job today. You should be very proud."

"We are," Preston said, his annoyance at Halverson fading. Whatever points Halverson thought he was scoring with Connor by ordering Preston around, it was clear that Connor was seeing right through it. "Watch yourselves out there."

"We will," Connor assured him.

Walking past the line of waiting townspeople, Connor waded into the rushing water.

"Any particular reason you didn't want me to give him Blair's gun?" Preston muttered to his daughter.

For a moment she was silent. Preston watched as Connor made it across, followed by Halverson and Half-pint.

"I don't trust him," Hope said at last. "Something about him doesn't seem right."

Preston looked sideways at her, his reflexive objection dying in his throat. The only person in town, he reminded himself, whose opinion he genuinely trusted.

"In what way?" he asked instead.

"John Connor's supposed to be some kind of legend, right?" Hope said. "What in the world would someone like that be doing way out here? Especially alone and on foot?"

Preston pursed his lips as an unsettling thought suddenly occurred to him.

"Unless this is all there actually is to the man."

Hope frowned. "You mean like maybe the Resistance doesn't exist?"

"No, I'm pretty sure the Resistance exists," Preston said. "But maybe Connor himself is nothing but smoke and mirrors. Just some high-sounding broadcasts and a bizarre itinerant preacher game."

The team's rear guard was crossing the river, and the people who'd been left behind were heading down the trail toward town before Hope spoke again.

"In that case, why would Barnes and Blair say they work with Connor?" she asked. "Unless they're lying. There has to be a real John Connor out there, a John Connor who really is the big Resistance leader he claims to be."

"So *someone's* lying," Preston concluded. "Of course, we knew *that* two hours ago. The question is who?"

"I think it's Jik," Hope said firmly. "I don't think he's John Connor at all."

Across the river, the last of the townspeople disappeared into the woods.

"Could be," Preston said. "Fortunately, thanks to Halverson, you and I now have a bit of time to explore that very theory."

He picked up the backpack they'd taken from Barnes and slung one of its straps onto his shoulder. With most of its ammo magazines now with Jik and Halverson, it was considerably lighter than it had been.

"Let's head home. I feel like a long, serious conversation."

* * *

"Well?" Barnes asked from his end of the couch.

Blair consulted her watch. Since the last sounds of distant gunfire had died away... "About half an hour," she told him.

Barnes grunted. "Means they got 'em."

"What do you mean?" Smith asked anxiously from his guard post by the window. "Who got who?"

"I mean they nailed the machines," Barnes told him. "If they hadn't, you'd still hear shots every once in awhile from survivors trying to get away."

Smith exhaled heavily. "Thank God," he muttered.

Blair looked sideways at the two men, both of them visibly relaxing with Barnes's news. The other possibility, unfortunately, was that there was no survivors' gunfire because there were no survivors.

But there was no point in bringing that up. If it was bad news, they'd find out soon enough.

"So who do *you* think he is?" Barnes asked.

Blair made a face. She'd been poking at the whole Jik question ever since Preston had stuck them in here, under armed guard.

"My guess is he's a con man," she said.

"Looking for what?"

"Here and now?" Blair shrugged. "Food and shelter would be a decent enough reward for any scammer these days."

"Mm," Barnes said.

Blair eyed him. "You're not convinced."

"You might be right," he said. "Probably are. You like their story about Marcus?"

Blair felt her throat constrict. Was Barnes going to throw that name in her face for the rest of her life?

"I don't see—"

"Because I don't," he cut her off gruffly. "There's

something about it that doesn't add up."

She frowned at him, her reflexive reaction fading away as she belatedly noticed the concentration on his face. For once, he wasn't simply trying to goad her.

And he was right, she realized. There'd been something about the scientists' description of the Theta Project that seemed a little off.

"I agree," she said. "Any idea what it is?"

"For one thing, they were pretty damn casual about the whole thing," he said. "You saw them."

"They wouldn't be the first people to lose their consciences."

"Yeah, but—" Barnes shook his head. "I don't know. Forget it."

And then, abruptly, Blair had it.

"No, *don't* forget it," she said, her breath tight in her throat. "You're right. *Damn* it."

"What?" Barnes demanded.

"They said Marcus was a prototype," Blair said, her mind racing as she tried to make something coherent out of the sudden updraft of thoughts and suspicions swirling through her head. "Remember?"

"Yeah," Barnes said, watching her closely. "So?"

"So Marcus had a mission," Blair said. "He was trying to lure Connor into Skynet Central where the machines could kill him."

Barnes grunted. "Did a damn good job of it, too."

"Which is exactly my point," Blair said. "Prototypes don't get sent on missions. Prototypes don't get used for anything. They're built purely to test out the systems, or to experiment on in the lab, or even just see how the specs look in solid form."

"Unless he was all Skynet had left after it blew up the lab," Barnes suggested.

"And it managed to program the mission into his chip and get him in position to survive the explosion, all on the fly?" Blair countered. "Because the way Connor described it, the start-to-finish window on that mission was pretty damn short."

"So if Marcus wasn't the prototype, what would the prototype have looked like?"

Blair shook her head. "Like I said, its only purpose would have been for study. To show how the interfaces worked, how the living organs handled their job—that sort of thing."

"So if it had a wrecked face, no one would care."

Blair looked sharply at him.

"The Theta that attacked Jik," she said. "Are you saying *that* was the real prototype?"

"Or maybe a couple of steps down the line," Barnes said. "So once you got all the insides working, what would be next?"

Blair studied his face. His tone and expression said he was going somewhere with this. But where?

"You tell me."

Barnes shot a glance at Smith and Trounce, who were leaning forward as they listened intently to the conversation.

"These Thetas are Skynet's new infiltration units, right?" Barnes said. "I mean, why else bother?"

"They're definitely a step up from T-600s and rubber skin," Blair agreed. "A little on the risky side, though. You saw how Marcus was able to break Skynet's programming."

"Yeah, maybe," Barnes said with a grunt. "What I was thinking was that once Skynet got their bodies looking right, it would have to bring their brains in line, too. That means..." He stopped, eyeing her expectantly.

And then, suddenly, she understood. "False memories,"

she bit out. "*That's* what Jik is. He's a *Theta*." She glared at Barnes. "You figured that out, and you didn't *say* something?"

"Hey, I didn't get it until you were in the middle of your big prototype speech," Barnes protested. "And we *both* should have gotten it a lot sooner anyway. Remember when we crossed the river and he got tangled up in that loose T-700 arm?"

Blair felt a shiver run through her as she recalled, "He didn't just get tangled. The arm's reconnection magnet grabbed him, just like that mine at the base got Marcus."

"That's what I'm thinking," Barnes said. "Don't know why he didn't just kill us once we saw that. Probably figured we were too stupid to notice."

"Or he genuinely doesn't know what he is," Blair pointed out. "Marcus didn't." She looked over at Smith and Trounce. "That also explains a few other things."

"Like?" Barnes asked.

"For starters, why Baker's Hollow is still here," she said. "This town—these people—are Jik's test run. His own—" She smiled faintly at Barnes as a piece of last night's conversation flickered up from her memory. "Skynet's own trial by fire."

"What are you talking about?" Smith asked.

"Don't listen to them," Trounce growled. "We're still here because we're smart and tough. A hell of a lot smarter and tougher than the city pansies they're used to."

"Are you?" Blair countered. "Three scientists working for Skynet drop in out of the blue and just happen to stumble onto your town. They say they've been working for Skynet, yet Skynet never comes looking for them. They settle down, get to know the people, let the people get to know them... and then, a couple of months later, this stranger Jik comes wandering into town."

"And they sit back and take notes and see how all the rest of you react to him," Barnes said. "See if you can spot a Theta when it's staring right back into your face."

"That's crazy," Trounce insisted. "Connor said one of those hybrid things attacked him. Why would it do that if they were both on the same team?"

"Because it's no use seeing if people can pick a Theta out of a crowd if they don't know Thetas even exist," Blair said.

"Right," Barnes agreed. "They're infiltration units. They have to be able to pass for human in front of people who know they're out there."

Blair shivered, her mind flashing back over the long, dark years. Skynet hadn't started its war that way. For a long time it had relied on massive, brute-force firepower to take out the survivors of the Judgment Day nukes. But as the Resistance had gotten organized and hardened, it had gradually shifted its focus from T-1 tanks and H-Ks to the subtler but ultimately more effective tactic of infiltration.

The T-600s had been the first, and they'd been bad enough. It was unnerving to see a stranger coming toward you down a dark street, knowing you wouldn't be able to tell whether it was human or machine until it was well within killing distance.

But a Terminator who could walk right up to you without betraying its identity was far worse. If Skynet ever got Thetas into full production it might well be the beginning of the end for the Resistance.

And the end of the Resistance would be the end of humanity.

"Let me get this straight," Smith said. "So Connor shoots up—"

"He's not Connor," Barnes cut him off.

"Whoever," Smith said impatiently. "So him shooting up a Theta is proof he's one of them. But you two shooting up a couple of T-700s is proof you're not?"

"You want proof?" Barnes asked. "No problem. You got any magnets in town?"

Smith and Trounce exchanged looks.

"Maybe," Smith said cautiously. "Why?"

"You heard what we said about Jik getting tangled up at the ford," Barnes said. "There's some magnetic metal in Terminator endoskeletons. All you need to do is get a magnet and run it over him."

"Just make sure you have your guns ready," Blair warned. "And don't let Lajard and the others get away, either."

Smith shook his head. "You two are certifiable," he said sadly.

"Forget it," Barnes growled. "Maybe Preston will listen to reason."

Smith angled his head backwards, peering out the side of the window.

"We'll find out soon enough," he said. "Here he comes now."

Hope hadn't seen Susan and the other two scientists since her father and Jik had rushed everyone over to Annabel's house and started collecting and preparing the equipment for their attack on the T-700s. Knowing Susan, Hope expected her to be waiting when she and her father arrived back in town.

Sure enough, there she was, standing by one of the trees and picking restlessly at its bark.

What Hope hadn't expected was that Lajard and Oxley would be with her.

"So it's done?" Lajard demanded as the two Prestons

came into sight. "You've destroyed them?"

"That's right, we did," Preston said. "Which you could have found out from any of the others who just came through here."

"Yes, well, none of the others seem all that excited about talking to us right now," Oxley growled. "Like this was *our* fault."

Hope looked sideways at her father, wondering if he would point out that it *was* at least partly their fault. Willingly or not, the three of them *had* worked for Skynet.

But as usual, her father was diplomatic.

"That'll pass," he said instead. "We got both Terminators, and no one got hurt. It's over."

Lajard hissed. "Right. No one got hurt except a couple of valuable machines that weren't bothering anyone."

"Give it a rest, Remy," Oxley said sourly. "And it's *not* exactly over yet. We still have to decide what to do with Barnes and Williams."

"We're going to let them go, aren't we?" Hope asked.

"That's up to Connor," Oxley told her. "He's the one they seem out to get." He looked at Lajard. "And since Connor's the one who came up with the plan to take down the T-700s, I'd say he's proved his credentials."

Again, Hope looked at her father. Again, he passed up the obvious comment.

"We can discuss it when he gets back," he said. "In the meantime, Hope and I need to go home and clean up."

"Actually," Susan spoke up hesitantly, "I was wondering if I could borrow Hope for a while."

"What for?" Preston asked, frowning.

"What else?" Susan bent over and lifted her bow and a quiver of arrows. "Someone needs to keep the food coming. With everyone else busy with the Terminators, I thought she and I could see if we could find some game."

"That's very generous of you," Preston said. "But we should have enough food in town to handle a night or two."

"I'm not so sure," Oxley warned. "I was talking to Vic earlier, and he said the cupboard's looking pretty bare."

"If I can't have Hope, can I go out alone?" Susan persisted. "I'd like to do *something* today to earn my keep."

Preston looked at Hope. "What do you think?"

Hope hesitated. The Terminator battle had left her pretty worn out, emotionally as well as physically. On top of that, she really wanted to be there when her father talked with Blair and Barnes.

But the forlorn, desperately eager look on Susan's face was impossible to ignore.

"It's okay," she said, suppressing a sigh. "I'll go with her."

Her father looked at Susan, then reluctantly nodded.

"All right," he said. "But I don't want you going any farther than Crescent Rock. Clear?"

"Clear," she confirmed.

"Get going, then," he said. "And be careful."

"Don't worry, she'll be fine," Susan promised. She gave Hope a tentative smile. "We'll both be just fine."

CHAPTER TWENTY

The concrete turned out to be tougher than Kyle had expected when he'd suggested the plan. Callahan did his first shift, digging away with his knife until his arms were too weary to lift anymore. Kyle had taken over from him, then Zac. After that it was back to Callahan and once again to Kyle.

Along the way they ruined both Callahan's and Kyle's knives, first dulling the edges and then grinding down or breaking the blades themselves.

It was on Kyle's turn, as he was dragging a piece of bent metal through the enlarged groove, when it finally happened. The section of slab abruptly shifted, the end swinging down half an inch as if on hinges, closing the groove and trapping the end of their cutter.

"Got it," he whispered down to the others, trying to blow out the concrete dust that had settled into his lungs without the noise of a cough.

"Okay, get down," Callahan whispered back. "Hurry—they'll be back any minute now."

Carefully, Kyle climbed down from his perch on the door frame, wincing at the fresh cuts and scrapes on his hands as he steadied himself on Callahan's and Zac's shoulders.

"Wait—you left the cutter up there," Zac said, pointing urgently.

"I couldn't get it out," Kyle told him. "It's wedged in too tight."

"But—"

"It's okay," Callahan said. "It shouldn't fall until the slab breaks. Once it's mixed in with the rest of the rubble, there'll be no way for Skynet to make a connection."

"Assuming we're not in the open at the time," Kyle said. "Where are we going?"

"Over here," Callahan said, picking his way quickly across the debris. "Watch your step."

Callahan's hiding place turned out to be all the way across the chamber, behind a heavy and nearly intact slab of concrete that was leaning up against another equally impressive piece. The angle between them wasn't very big, but there was enough room for the three humans to squeeze in between them.

Kyle shivered as he wedged himself into place just inside the open end, sitting with his knees pressed up against his chest and Zac pressed against his side.

"It's like cold storage in here," he muttered.

"Cold is good," Callahan murmured back from over on Zac's other side. "Helps mask infrared signatures."

"Shh!" Zac hissed. "Here they come."

For a few seconds there was silence. Then, once again, Kyle heard the familiar rumble of metal feet overhead. He listened closely, wondering just how fragile the slab was. Wondering whether this line of T-700s would do the trick or whether they would have to wait here pressed against cold concrete until the next cycle before the floor gave way.

And then, abruptly, with a thunderous crash, it did.

A crash that was followed by utter silence.

Kyle froze, staring out at the underground chamber, wanting desperately to lean an eye far enough out of their shelter out to see what was going on.

He fought back the temptation. If any of the Terminators happened to be looking in his direction at the time, that would be the last mistake Kyle would ever make.

So he sat there quietly, listening to his thudding heart and waiting for something to happen. The silence stretched out...

And as Kyle strained his eyes, he spotted a small, subtle red glow out in the chamber. Not a stationary glow, but one that slowly swept across the walls and rubble.

The glow from a Terminator's eyes as it carefully and systematically scanned the chamber.

Kyle's reflexive impulse was to press closer to Zac and get as far away from the opening beside him as he could. Once again, he resisted the urge. The Terminator out there might pick up his heat if he stayed where he was, but it would certainly pick up any noise he made while trying to change position. The glow brightened as the Terminator's sweep reached the slab in front of them, then disappeared as it passed by. Kyle held his breath...

And then, from the direction of the collapsed tunnel floor came the soft scrabbling of metal on concrete.

Kyle hesitated. But this time, risky or not, he had to look. If the Terminator had spotted them, and the scrabbling sound was more of the machines coming down from above, he and the others would need the next few crucial seconds to get clear of their hiding place and try to make it to an exit that was too small for the Terminators to chase them through.

Keeping his movements slow, he leaned his head out of cover.

His first, horrifying thought was that his fears had been right, that it was all over and he and the others were dead. A T-700 was dangling down through the hole in the tunnel floor, its arms held by two more of the machines standing on opposite sides of the gap. A fourth Terminator, obviously the one that had fallen through, was balancing on the remains of the broken slab, its back turned toward Kyle.

And then, to Kyle's relief, the Terminator took hold of the hanging T-700's ankles and climbed smoothly up its legs and torso to the hole in the ceiling. Shifting its grip to the edge, it pulled itself the rest of the way up and out. The two Terminators on top pulled up the one still dangling, and all four machines moved away out of Kyle's view.

A few seconds later, what looked like a metal door was lowered across the opening, blocking off most of the dim light.

Most, but not all. As Kyle's eyes once again adjusted to the relative darkness, he saw that there was still a gap between the ceiling and the wall. It was narrow, but it might be big enough to squeeze through.

The soft thud of footsteps resumed their familiar cadence as the Terminators headed back down the tunnel with their latest loads of debris.

"Reese?" Zac whispered anxiously.

"It's okay," Kyle whispered. "Quiet, now."

The march seemed to take longer this time. Possibly the Terminators were avoiding walking on that section of presumably weakened concrete, which would affect the flow and efficiency of their passage. Possibly it was just Kyle's imagination, driven by his impatience to get over there and see whether or not their gamble had paid off.

Finally, the vibrations faded away, and the Terminators were once again gone.

Kyle frowned, a shiver running up his back.

Or were they?

He held his breath, listening hard. He didn't have Star's hyper-sensitivity to Terminators' presence, but years of dodging the machines had amplified and trained the small bit of that sensitivity that he did posses.

And right now, that sixth sense was screaming a silent warning.

On Zac's other side, Callahan started to stir.

"Shh," Kyle breathed, quickly reaching past Zac to touch Callahan warningly on the arm. The other froze in place, tapping Kyle's hand twice in acknowledgment.

Kyle held still, counting off the seconds. Two minutes passed, then three, then four, then five.

And as his count reached its sixth minute, a sound finally drifted into the silence wrapped around them. The sound of Terminator footsteps.

Only they weren't coming from somewhere in the distance, marking the return of the digging crew. These footsteps were coming from somewhere near the hole. As Kyle listened, he heard the Terminator head back down the tunnel in the direction the others had gone.

He looked across at Zac and Callahan, their faces just barely visible in the faint reflected light. Both expressions were tense, but Callahan's lips were also twisted in a wry smirk. *Cute*, he mouthed silently.

Kyle nodded. *We sit tight?* he mouthed back.

We sit tight, Callahan confirmed. *Let's see if Skynet was smart enough to leave two of them.*

Kyle nodded, resting his forearms on his knees and turning back to gaze out at the rubble of the chamber.

And trying to ignore the cuts and bruises and hunger and weariness.

The already long afternoon was getting even longer...

From the kitchen came the sound of an opening door.

"Trounce?" Preston's voice came.

"In here," Trounce called back.

Barnes looked at Williams. She returned the look, a grim downward turn to her mouth. This was their last chance, and she knew it as well as he did. If they couldn't convince Preston there was a Theta lurking under his nose, they were probably dead.

And not just him and Williams. Probably the whole town.

Preston walked into the room, his expression that mixture of satisfaction and weariness that Barnes had seen on dozens of Resistance fighters over the years.

"You get them?" he asked the mayor.

Preston nodded, glancing at Smith and Trounce as he dropped into the big overstuffed chair directly across from Barnes and Williams. He winced a little as the holstered Desert Eagle dug into his side, and reached down to adjust it.

"Two T-700s, freshly converted into pieces of junk, which Halverson and the others will soon be dumping into the ravine on the far side of the river," he said. "The whole thing wasn't nearly as bad as I was expecting, actually. I hope you managed to get some rest."

"Kind of hard to rest when there are Terminators nearby," Barnes told him.

"I suppose," Preston conceded.

"No resting, but they've been doing a lot of talking," Trounce reported. "So Connor came through, huh?"

"He did indeed," Preston said, his eyes on Barnes. "Two Terminators down, and we didn't lose anyone."

"Good," Trounce said. "'Cause these two have come up with the world's craziest idea." From the direction of the kitchen came the sound of a knock on the door. "They think—"

"Hold that thought," Preston interrupted, frowning in the direction of the door. "Who is it?" he called.

"Oxley and Lajard," a faint voice came back. "We need to talk."

"Mayor, we need to talk, too," Williams spoke up quickly. "In private."

"Oh, no, you gotta let them in," Trounce said before Preston could reply. "You gotta see their faces when Barnes drops his theory on them."

"Mayor?" Williams repeated, her voice urgent. "Please."

"Hello?" Lajard called again from outside. "Can we come in?"

Preston gazed hard at Williams.

"Make it quick," he said.

And then, suddenly, it was too late. Across the room came the sound of an opening door, and Oxley and Lajard walked through the kitchen into the living room.

"I didn't say you could come in," Preston growled.

"Didn't you?" Oxley asked innocently. "We thought we heard you."

Preston's lips compressed briefly. "What do you want?"

Oxley gestured toward Barnes and Williams.

"Now that Connor has proved himself, it occurred to us that our other guests might want to make some revisions in their story."

"When exactly did this grand proof happen?" Williams asked.

Oxley snorted as he crossed to the window behind Trounce and Smith and took a quick look outside in both directions.

"Wrecking a pair of T-700s without losing anyone is all the proof *I* need," he said.

"You're remarkably easy to please," Williams told him.

"You got any other theories, we'd love to hear them," Lajard invited, walking over to Preston and coming to a halt behind the mayor's chair. "But do try to keep them simple. We'll have to explain it to Susan later, and twisted conspiracy theories always confuse me."

"She'd have been here with us, but she went out hunting," Oxley put in, a subtle edge to his voice as he turned back around to face the room. "She's with Preston's daughter Hope."

"Though personally I don't really care who you are," Lajard added with a nonchalant shrug. "You're trouble, and I'd be just as happy to see you get on that helicopter of yours and go away."

An icy sensation settled onto Barnes's back. So he and Williams had been right. This whole thing—this whole damn town—was nothing but a big Skynet test lab. Now that Jik was firmly established in his John Connor role, the scientists in charge of the lab rats were hoping to kick the two visiting troublemakers out of town so that they could get their little experiment back on track.

And just in case the troublemakers were tempted not to cooperate, Lajard had layered a bit of extra extortion to their demand: Hope, somewhere out in the woods, with an armed woman who Hope thought was her friend.

He looked at Williams. She'd gotten the message too, both parts of it, and Barnes could see the fire simmering behind her eyes.

But if Williams could occasionally get overemotional, she also wasn't stupid. A quick flight back to San Francisco, a quick report to Connor, and they could be back here by dawn tomorrow with a full Resistance strike team. Whatever experiments Lajard and the others were planning, surely they wouldn't be ready to close up shop before then. The best thing Barnes and Williams could do right now would be to confess that they were con artists, or mercenaries, or whatever it took to satisfy Preston, and get the hell out of here.

And then, before he or Williams could speak, the decision was snatched away from them.

"This'll kill you," Smith spoke up sardonically from the window. "They think Connor is one of these Theta Terminator things, and that all you have to do to prove it is wave a magnet at him. And they say that you—" he shot a glance over his shoulder at Oxley "—and *you*, and Valentine are running the show for Skynet."

Lajard shook his head. "*Now* it's gotten ridiculous," he said.

"Probably," Preston agreed. But his voice was thoughtful, and his eyes were steady on Barnes. "Easy enough for Connor to clear away any doubt, though. Maybe when he and the others get back we'll go see if Chucker has a magnet stashed away in one of his junk drawers."

"Well, if you want to play games with these lunatics, that's up to you," Lajard said. "*Fortuna favet fortibus*, as they say. Personally, I have better things to do." Patting the top of Preston's chair once, he headed toward the kitchen.

"Just a minute," Preston said, standing up and turning to face Lajard, his hand dropping to the grip of his holstered gun. "What's your hurry?"

And abruptly, Lajard's measured pace became a flat-out run as he sprinted toward the kitchen and the door beyond.

"Kill them!" he shouted over his shoulder.

"Watch it!" Barnes snapped, leaping off the couch and grabbing the arms of the chair Preston had just vacated.

"Smith, Trounce—behind you!"

He was too late. Standing behind the two thoroughly bewildered guards, Oxley reached up and caught each of the men just above their shirt collars.

And as Barnes heaved Preston's chair off the floor, Oxley gave a quick double twist of his wrists and snapped both men's necks.

Barnes swore viciously as he charged toward Oxley, his legs shoving hard against the floor, putting every bit of speed and power into his attack that he had. Out of the corner of his eye he saw a flurry of motion as Williams grabbed one of the wooden chairs near her, ran to the kitchen door, and hurled it at Lajard's retreating back. There was a crash and a muffled curse, and Lajard was gone. In front of Barnes, Oxley let the two dead guards drop to the floor and reached for the rifle Trounce had dropped.

With the chair pressed to his chest like a combination shield and battering ram, Barnes slammed straight into him.

The impact threw Oxley backward, and for a stretched-out second the two men and the chair moved together toward the window, Oxley's feet scraping across the floorboards, his arms trapped between the chair's legs. He managed to get one hand free and reached around the side, trying to get to Barnes's arm.

He was still trying when he and the chair went hurling backwards through the window.

Barnes nearly went through with them. He was scrabbling for balance when a hand grabbed his arm and yanked him back.

"Come on!" Preston snarled. Letting go of Barnes's arm, he snatched up the two rifles from the floor, shoved one of them at Barnes, and sprinted across the room toward the kitchen.

Williams was already in there, looking cautiously out the open door.

"Clear," she announced as Preston reached her. "What's the plan?"

"Go to ground while we figure out what the hell is going on." Preston handed his rifle to her. "Here."

Williams shook her head.

"Keep it," she said as she reached over and plucked her Desert Eagle from the holster around Preston's waist. "I'll take this."

"Right," Preston said, peering past her out the door. "Let's go."

"Wait a second," Barnes said as he caught sight of his backpack lying on the floor beside the kitchen table. Grabbing the straps, he slung it over his shoulder and followed Williams and Preston outside into the late afternoon sunlight.

"This way," Preston said, making a sharp left-hand turn toward the back of the house. They ran between two dilapidated houses, rounded a third, and finally came to a thick, chest-high hedge at the western border of a small garden. Preston ran them around to the other side and motioned for them to drop down behind it.

"Okay," he panted. "We should have a minute. What the hell is going—?"

"No, we don't have a minute," Williams cut him off, throwing a quick look around her end of the hedge. "We missed a step, Barnes."

"What step?" Barnes asked. "What did we miss?"

"In the Theta program," she said. "You wouldn't start by installing a complete, floor-to-ceiling false memory like Skynet did with Jik. You'd start by giving one of them a few little pieces of false memory. Patches that cover over any parts of genuine memory you don't want him remembering."

And then, Barnes got it.

"Like the memory of getting hauled out of your nice little Skynet lab and turned into a Terminator," he snarled. "You're right. *Damn* it."

"What are you talking about?" Preston demanded.

"Oxley is like Jik—he's a Theta," Barnes told him. "He's been in Baker's Hollow as Skynet's grand experiment to see if Thetas could mingle with normal people without being spotted."

"It's been ramping up this whole time," Williams added. "First you see if people can tell there's something wrong with your Theta, even if they can't guess what that is. That was Oxley's role. *Then* you tell them what Thetas are, and see if they can spot one. That's what Jik's doing."

"Only now that we've crashed it, the party's over," Barnes said. "I'm guessing their next job will be to clean out the lab."

"Wait a minute," Preston said. "You said Oxley was a Theta. What about Lajard and Valentine?"

"Not Lajard," Williams said. "He was genuinely hurt when I nailed him with that chair."

"Valentine?"

Barnes saw Williams wince. "Probably."

"Damn," Preston breathed. "We've got to get to her—"

"Mayor?" Oxley's distant voice came. "Mayor Preston? Come now, you're being foolish. You can't fight us, and there really isn't anywhere to run. Come on out and take it like a man. I promise I'll make it painless."

"Don't answer," Williams whispered urgently.

Preston shot a look at her, his jaw muscles tight. But he kept silent.

"If you'd rather do it the hard way, that's okay with me," Oxley's voice came again, possibly a bit closer this time. "We'll just kill however we have to, painful or otherwise. Here's an idea—we'll start with your daughter."

Watching his face Barnes saw the disbelief and horror were starting to fade away, and Preston was starting to think again.

"If you want to blame someone, blame your friends there," Oxley continued. The voice was definitely closer now. "They're the ones who forced our hand. We'd have been perfectly happy to keep things going the way they were."

"He's lying," Williams muttered. "None of them had the slightest idea of what Skynet had turned them into."

"Why the hell is he talking so much?" Preston muttered.

"He's buying time," Williams said. "You saw how Lajard took off back there. If he's the one real human among them, he's probably the only one who *did* know what they were."

"He was the experiment's observer?"

"And its controller," Williams said. "That Latin he spouted just before Oxley's attack was probably the code to activate them."

"And to put them under his and Skynet's control," Barnes added.

"Right," Williams said. "I think Oxley's stalling to give Lajard time to get to cover."

"Wait a second," Preston said, frowning. "If the Latin was code, then Oxley should be the only one who got activated."

Williams shook her head. "Sorry. They're all linked via short-range radio through the control chips in the backs of their heads. When he activated Oxley, he activated Valentine and Jik, too."

Preston hissed a sigh. "And Valentine's got Hope."

"Yes," Williams said grimly.

"Mayor?" Oxley called.

"You know how to kill these things?" Preston asked.

"We know how to make them hurt," Barnes said, thinking back to his target practice with the chained-up Marcus. "They've got human skin, and all the nerve endings that go with it."

"It's a start." Preston took a deep breath. "Okay. We don't have a whistle signal for a situation like this, so the quickest way to warn everyone in town will be to fire off a few shots. We might was well put those shots to some use. Get ready."

He stood upright and looked over the hedge.

"Oxley?" he called. "You want me? Come and get me."

Barnes felt his lips pull back in a tight grin. He'd seen first-hand how tough Thetas were, as tough as any other Terminator model Skynet had come up with. With these wholly inadequate weapons, and with a lot of the town's best hunters out of reach across the river, he and Williams were going to have a serious fight on their hands.

But at least they finally knew who their enemies were. That was worth something.

He hefted the rifle, throwing a quick glance behind them and then settling down with his eyes and weapon toward the town.

Bring it on, he thought silently toward Skynet. *Bring it on.*

CHAPTER TWENTY-ONE

"They hate me, don't they?" Susan asked quietly as Hope led the way along the path toward Crescent Rock.

"What?" Hope asked, most of her mind on the forest around her. They hadn't hunted this area for a while, which meant there was a chance that some of the bigger game might have returned.

"The people in town," Susan said. "I saw the way they looked at me when they came back from the battle with those T-700s."

"I think everyone's mostly just tired," Hope assured her. "They'll get over it."

"I'm not so sure," Susan said. "You heard what Connor said earlier, back at your house. If Nathan, Remy, and I had died instead of letting Skynet pick our brains, maybe there wouldn't even *be* T-700s for them to have to deal with."

"I didn't think you ever worked on the T-700s."

"You know what I mean." Behind her, Hope heard Susan sigh. "I wish to God I was you, Hope," she said. "With my whole life still ahead of me. Instead of—" She broke off. "I'm sorry, Hope. I'm so very sorry."

"It's okay," Hope said. She looked back over her shoulder. And froze. Susan was staring straight ahead, her face suddenly cold and rigid and agonized. Hope threw a quick look in the direction the older woman was staring, wondering if she'd spotted a bear or another Terminator. But there was nothing there.

"Susan?" Hope asked carefully, looking back at her.

Slowly, the cold eyes turned to focus on Hope.

"I'm sorry, Hope," Susan said again as she started forward. "I have to kill you now."

For a moment Hope just stared at her, the words buzzing around her ears like angry hornets.

"What are you talking about?" she asked as she started to back away.

But it was too late. Susan didn't seem to be hurrying, but her stride was longer than Hope's, she was walking forward instead of backward, and she was rapidly closing the distance between them.

"Susan, please," Hope said, trying desperately to think. "What are you doing?"

"Don't you understand?" Susan asked, a quiet horror filling her voice. "I'm one of them. God help me. I'm one of them."

"One of what?" Hope asked, trying to keep her talking. To her left, her hand brushed against the branches and leaves of a sapling. "I don't understand," she continued, pressing her palm against the slender trunk and bending the young tree over as she continued backing up.

"I'm a Theta," Susan said, her voice shaking now. "I didn't know. God, I had no idea. But I am. I'm a Terminator. I'm a *Terminator*."

"You don't have to be," Hope told her, slowing her backward pace as she felt her hand nearing the top of the sapling, holding it down with every bit of her strength and weight. "You can fight it. You don't have to do what Skynet tells you."

"But I do," Susan said sadly. "You don't understand. I'm so very sorry." She reached out a hand toward Hope's throat.

And jerked backward as Hope released her hold on the bent tree, sending it snapping up to slap against Susan's chest and face.

An instant later, Hope was dashing through the trees, running as fast as she could. The horror of Susan's revelation hovered at the edges of her mind, but she pressed it back into the shadows. There was no time to think about that now. No time to think about anything except survival.

There was a crash behind her, and she spared a quick look over her shoulder. Susan was coming after her, her expression ice cold, her face crisscrossed with small red lines where the sapling's branches had cut into her skin.

Human skin. Not metal. *Human* skin.

It was a small chance, Hope knew. But at the moment she didn't have anything better.

Watching her footing with one eye, looking for the right spot with the other, she drew an arrow and nocked it to her bowstring. This was going to take careful timing.

Ahead and to the right she spotted a large, thick-boled oak. Shifting direction, she headed toward it.

Susan was maybe ten paces behind her when Hope reached the oak. She ducked around it, ran another five paces, then jerked to a halt. Spinning around, she raised the bow and pulled the arrow back to her cheek.

And as Susan came around the tree she sent the arrow whistling into the woman's right arm. The arrowhead punched through the leather of Susan's jacket and the human flesh beneath it, skittered its way around the unyielding metal beneath the skin, and reemerged through flesh and leather to bury itself solidly in the oak.

Susan gasped, a sharp, eerily inhuman sound as the arrow pinning her to the tree brought her to a sudden halt. She tried to tug her arm free, her face contorting with pain and anger as the movement dragged more of the arrow through her skin. Half turning, she got a grip on the arrow shaft with her left hand.

And gasped again as Hope's second arrow flashed through her left thigh and pinned her leg to the tree.

A second later Hope was again sprinting through the trees, heading back toward town as fast as she could. The arrows wouldn't hold Susan for long, and she'd heard enough stories about Terminators—many of them from Susan herself—to know she wasn't going to take one down with nothing but a quiver of arrows.

But her father was in town, and Barnes, and Blair. They would know what to do. *Please, God*, she thought desperately. *Let them know what to do.*

She was nearly to the edge of town when she heard the first sounds of gunfire.

In a single flick of his eyelids, Jik abruptly saw the awful truth.

The men and women trudging through the forest around him weren't his friends or his allies. They were his enemies. People who had sworn to destroy him and the Resistance.

People who had lured him out here into the wilderness to kill him.

But that wasn't going to happen. Not if John Connor had anything to say about it.

Halverson was the closest, striding along beside Jik a few feet away. Casually, Jik angled his own stride in that direction, watching the other out of the corner of his eye.

He was within reach when the big man finally seemed to notice Jik's presence.

"Trouble?" Halverson asked quietly.

Reaching over, Jik wrenched Halverson's rifle from his hands and slammed the weapon's shoulder stock into the other's rib cage.

With a choked gasp, the man folded around himself and collapsed to the ground. Rotating the rifle into firing position at his hip, Jik spun around to face the rest of the traitors marching along behind him and opened fire.

The first four went down without so much as a yelp. Jik was taking down the fifth when the rest finally burst into action, dropping the pieces of broken Terminator they were carrying and either returning fire or scattering madly for cover like ants from a poked anthill.

Jik strode back through the cowering ranks, coolly squeezing off shot after shot until Halverson's rifle was empty. Dropping it, he picked up two more weapons from men who no longer needed them and kept going. When those were empty, he dropped them and found two more.

The bullets were beginning to fly now as the would-be assassins finally got their own weapons up and set their murderous plan into action. Most of the shots buzzed harmless past Jik's head and body before one actually found its target, slamming into his chest and sending a jolt of agony through him.

A blow like that would have killed a lesser man. But John Connor was made of stronger stuff. Regaining his balance, he put a round into the offending shooter and continued on his way.

Those who remained had now gone to ground behind trees, rocks, and bushes. Steadily, methodically, he went to each hiding place in turn.

The traitor called Pepper pleaded with him, calling his name over and over as if it was a magic spell that would drain him of his will and purpose. The one called Singer died with a curse on his lips, uselessly calling down the wrath of God. The one called Half-pint simply stared silently at Jik with fear and agony in his eyes.

But Jik knew better than to listen to any of it. He was John Connor, and these were his enemies and the enemies of humanity. They deserved to die.

So he killed them.

By the time he lowered his last rifle a total of seven rounds had found him, each slug adding a new splash of throbbing pain. But none of the blows was powerful enough or accurate enough to kill him.

Dropping his last empty weapon, ignoring the agony burning through his body, he did a quick but careful survey of the bodies scattered across the blood-stained greenery around him. It had been close, but once again he'd managed to cheat death. Skynet's agents, all of them, were dead.

All except one. He'd only disabled Halverson at the beginning of his preemptive counterattack, knowing that the wounded man could wait until Jik had finished dealing with the others. Time now for that final loose end to be tied off.

He'd paid close attention to the firefight, and had already concluded that all the rifles and pistols scattered across the ground around him were empty. But he still had Williams's Mossberg M500 slung over his shoulder, and the shotgun had one round left. Giving the dead assassins one final look, he turned and headed back to the front of the line.

To find that Halverson was gone.

So were the bow and quiver that one of the dead men nearby had been carrying.

Jik gave a contemptuous snort as he looked around. Did Halverson seriously think he could take down John Connor with nothing but a bow and a few arrows?

Apparently not. There was no sign anywhere of the injured hunter. Instead of staying to fight, he'd taken advantage of Jik's preoccupation with the others to run like a rabbit.

Jik snorted again. Let him run, because there really wasn't anywhere for him to run to. Now that Jik had finished his own defense, he could hear the sounds of fresh gunfire coming from the town itself.

That would be Oxley, also refusing to simply roll over before the Resistance-hating assassins. Jik had no doubt that he would carry the day there, just as Jik had done here in the forest.

In the meantime, some of the townspeople had probably escaped into the trees. They would have to be tracked down and eliminated.

He shook his head. It would be a long and wearisome task, but it had to be done. All of Baker's Hollow had heard the false accusations Barnes and Williams had brought against him, and those treasonous thoughts could not be permitted to survive. The reputation of John Connor had to stay clear and clean if he was to lead the people of the Resistance to victory over Skynet.

And toward that end Jik would need to leave soon. The Eugene group had been one of those who had defied Command's order to activate their transmitters during the climax of Skynet's grand scheme to destroy its enemies. As a result, they'd been one of the few Resistance groups to have survived. They deserved recognition for that.

They deserved a visit from John Connor himself.

Unfortunately, that meant Jik couldn't be here to help Oxley and Valentine with their task of cleansing the area around Baker's Hollow.

But as he'd reminded his colleagues so many times, there were always options. If Jik couldn't help personally with the hunt, he could at least arrange for a substitute.

The wreckage from the T-700s was scattered around the forest where the traitors had dropped or thrown them. Slinging the shotgun over his shoulder again, Jik began gathering those pieces back together.

"Come on, Oxley," Preston shouted, slapping the barrel of his rifle against the top of the hedge for emphasis. "Oxley?"

Blair peeked out around her end of the hedge, gripping her Desert Eagle tightly. Oxley had to know that Preston's invitation was a trap. The question was, would he—or rather, the massive Skynet computer that had programmed him—be arrogant enough to take them up on it?

And then, from somewhere in the near distance came the muffled sound of a woman's scream.

"*Damn,*" Preston snarled. Jumping to his feet, he dodged around Blair and took off toward the gap between the buildings that they'd come through less than three minutes ago.

"Wait!" Blair snapped. She'd seen Marcus Wright in action, and running around randomly out there was an invitation to get killed. "Preston!"

"I have to warn them," Preston called back over his shoulder. "They don't even know what they're facing."

"He'll kill you!" Blair bit out.

"Then you kill him back." Preston ducked between the buildings and disappeared.

Straightening out of her crouch, Blair headed after him.

She made it around the hedge and about four steps toward the gap Preston had used when Barnes caught up with her.

"No—there," he grunted, pointing instead toward a different opening off to the left. Without waiting for a reply, he angled away, heading for a space to their right.

Blair swore under her breath. But he was right. She veered to her left. That scream might have been Oxley's idea of bait, a way of drawing them back into town. If the Theta was waiting for them to return along that same route, Preston was about to die.

But it could also be that Oxley had simply decided to get on with the task of slaughtering Baker's Hollow's civilians, figuring that he could deal with Preston whenever and wherever he chose to surface. In that case, Barnes's plan for the three of them to hit the town from different directions was the right move. If one of them could spot Oxley and open fire, the others would know where he was.

Blair felt her throat tighten. No, not *him*. *It*. Oxley wasn't Marcus Wright, who'd protected Blair and gone on to sacrifice himself for Connor. Oxley had given up what was left of his humanity when he murdered Trounce and Smith.

He—*it*—was a Terminator.

There were two more screams before Blair finished weaving her way through the outlying houses to the main part of town. A dozen people had spilled out of the buildings, a couple of them with guns, a few with bows, most neither. All of them were looking around nervously.

"Go!" Blair snapped at them. "Oxley's a Theta—a Terminator that looks human. He's already killed at least two people. If you don't have a gun, get out of town right now and find a place to hide."

"Look out!" someone shouted, jabbing a finger past Blair's shoulder.

Blair spun around. Oxley had slipped out of the house directly behind her and was headed in her direction, his arms pumping as he ran, his hands flinging off droplets of bright red blood. His eyes were shining with maniacal energy, his lips curled back in a death's-head smile in anticipation of his next kill.

Desperately, Blair tried to bring her Desert Eagle up and around. But Oxley was too close, and the heavy gun had too much inertia, and she knew she would never get it lined up in time.

She tried to get out of his way, to dodge clear of those bloodied hands. But she'd been caught flatfooted, and there was no time for that, either. She threw herself sideways toward the ground, still trying to get her gun lined up.

He was nearly on her when a stutter of rifle shots rang out, blowing off bits of cloth and skin from Oxley's chest and face and bringing him to a sudden and surprised-looking halt.

And as a second volley staggered him a step backward, Blair finally got her Desert Eagle in line and fired point-blank up under his chin.

The force of the blow snapped Oxley's head back and sent him tumbling onto his back. He hit the ground hard, throwing a spray of red mist from the gaping wound. The shot had disintegrated a fist-sized patch of skin, some of it coming off the chin, the rest coming off the throat, revealing the blood-dulled metal beneath it.

But it took more than that to stop a Theta. Oxley had barely slammed to the ground when he was starting to sit up again. His maniacal smile was gone now, replaced by an expression of cold fury.

But getting to his feet was suddenly proving difficult. The air filled with the sound of gunfire as more and more of the townspeople joined the battle. The rounds hammered relentlessly into Oxley's body, the heavier slugs knocking him over, the lighter ones digging fresh wounds into his skin.

Blair pressed herself closer to the ground, not daring to try to get up through the fury of the attack. She squeezed off round after round, mostly targeting Oxley's face, wondering distantly whether she would have time to get clear when all the guns thundering away out there ran dry.

It wasn't an idle concern. What was left of Oxley's skin was bleeding profusely, the multiple trickles soaking his clothing and the grass and leaves around him. But he had a Terminator's single-minded doggedness, and even as the trappings of humanity were stripped away he was still struggling to get up and continue his mission. The volley slowed for a moment, and he managed to lurch to his knees. Behind the last scraps of forehead skin his glowing red eyes locked on to Blair.

Then, to her surprise, he fell onto his side and lay still.

And as the gunfire resumed its hammering at the bloodied metal body, she finally understood.

Lajard had told them that Theta organs were specially bioengineered to avoid rejection problems. She also knew from Kate Connor's work on Marcus that Theta skin regenerated quickly. The Skynet scientists had undoubtedly also fiddled with the hybrids' blood chemistry, giving it extra oxygen-carrying capacity and super-quick coagulation.

But there were limits to how fast even bioengineered blood could clot. No matter how fast Oxley's broken veins and capillaries sealed themselves off, the sheer number of bleeders had finally taken their toll.

Skynet's T-600s were slow and obvious, but they had to be physically destroyed before they could be stopped.

Skynet's Thetas, the ultimate infiltration units, could simply bleed to death.

The barrage faltered, and as the noise faded away Blair could hear someone shouting for the remaining shooters to cease fire.

Eventually, they did.

"Williams?" Barnes called.

Blair looked back to see him and Preston hurrying toward her. Beside Preston, to Blair's surprise and relief, was Preston's daughter.

"I'm all right," Blair called back as she got to her feet and went over to what was left of Oxley.

No movement of limbs or head. Blood still trickling from the wounds. No pulsing or even quivering from the carotid artery, partially visible behind the metal mesh shielding around the Theta's neck.

"Well?" Barnes asked as the others came up beside her.

"It's dead," Blair confirmed, looking at Hope. "Are you all right?"

"I'm fine," the girl said, her voice shaking a little.

"Not from lack of trying on Valentine's part," Preston growled, looking apprehensively behind them. "Hope was able to get the drop on her and pin her to a tree with a couple of arrows."

"Nice," Barnes commented. "Not going to hold her long, though. You need to get these people out of here before she makes it back."

"No argument there." Preston beckoned to one of the women nearby. "Jessie, get everyone out of town, right now."

"Where do we go?" Jessie asked.

"Head for the old Glaumann cabin," Preston told her.

"It's as good a meeting place as any, and I don't think Lajard or Valentine has ever been there."

Jessie nodded. "What about you?"

Preston looked in the direction of the river. "Someone needs to go see what happened to the people who were with Jik," he said. "That should probably be me."

"I'll go with you," Barnes said. "Let me stop by Halverson's first and get the minigun."

"You still have ammo for it?" Preston asked.

Barnes nodded, patting the strap of his backpack.

"About thirty rounds. Should be enough to take down a Theta."

Blair grimaced. That was true enough.

Unfortunately, there wasn't just one Theta on the loose out there. There were two of them.

"You'll need more than that," she said. "I'll get the Blackhawk. Where should I meet you?"

"How about the ford?" Preston suggested. "Jik has to come that way if he's going to link up with Valentine."

"Sounds good," Barnes confirmed. "There should be room enough on the riverbank for you to put down to let me aboard." He raised his eyebrows. "Unless you want me to go back to the chopper with you."

Blair focused on Preston's expression. He knew what he was going to find out there, all right. Not just a killer Terminator, but the bodies of his friends and neighbors.

"I'll be fine," she said.

"What about Susan?" Hope asked. "You'll need a route to your helicopter that she doesn't know about."

"No," Preston said flatly. "You're going with Jessie and the others."

"She'll never find the snaky on her own," Hope said, just as bluntly.

"What's the snaky?" Blair asked.

"It's a route through some of the thickest undergrowth in the area," Hope told her. "We sometimes go there to hunt rabbits and quail. Susan and Lajard don't know about it, and they probably couldn't get through it even if they did."

"We don't *know* that they don't know about it," Preston warned darkly. "And there's nowhere for you to go once you're inside. If they catch you in the middle, you'll be sitting ducks."

"If we don't destroy them, we're all dead anyway," Hope said, fear and anger and determination swirling together in her voice and face. "We need Blair and her helicopter, and she needs me to get to it."

Preston muttered something. "Williams?"

"She's right," Blair said. "For whatever it's worth, she'll be as safe with me as she'd be with Jessie. Or with you."

"And we don't have time to argue about it," Barnes put in, digging around in his backpack.

Preston sighed, then nodded. "Be careful," he said, giving his daughter a quick hug. "Both of you," he added, looking at Blair.

"We will," Blair promised.

"Here," Barnes said, holding out his hand.

Blair blinked in surprise. Clutched in the man's hand were two spare magazines for her Desert Eagle.

"Where's you get those?" she asked.

"I always bring extra ammo for all the guns on a mission," he said, an almost embarrassed gruffness in his voice.

"Good idea." Taking the magazines, Blair slipped them into her pockets. "Thanks."

"Watch yourselves, and good luck," Preston said. "Come on, Barnes. Let's go get your minigun."

CHAPTER
TWENTY-TWO

The T-700 convoys had made four more round trips to the tunnel face before Callahan finally decided it was safe enough to risk a quick recon.

As usual with tasks that included climbing, this one fell to Callahan. Much of the debris slope he'd used earlier had been collapsed and scattered by the falling concrete slab, but together the three of them were able to build it up enough for him to clamber up to the opening.

The hole itself was smaller than Kyle had estimated earlier, too small for any of them to squeeze through. But Callahan managed to get his head through. Gripping an exposed piece of rebar with one hand and the metal door with the other, he eased up for a look.

He stayed there for a good ten seconds, and in the light seeping down from above Kyle could see his neck moving as he turned his head back and forth. Finally, he pulled his head back through the opening and made the precarious climb back down.

"No watchdog," he whispered as they all huddled again. "But it looks like they're almost ready to go with the next blast. They've got two of the satchel charges at the base of the tunnel face, and they've moved the others way back down the tunnel."

"Like they're going to do a second blast further back, too?" Zac asked, frowning.

"No, like they don't want a second blast at all," Kyle told him. "Sympathetic detonation—Orozco told me about that once. If you put a bunch of explosives—"

"If you put explosives within four or five feet of each other, triggering one of them triggers the rest along with it," Callahan finished for him.

"So if everything's ready, what's Skynet waiting for?" Zac asked.

"Nightfall, probably," Callahan said. "The light coming through the roof is pretty weak, so it's probably getting close to sundown. Maybe Skynet's planning another attack like last night to cover the noise."

"Leaving more debris for the Terminators to haul away tomorrow," Kyle said. "So if we don't want to spend tonight and most of tomorrow down here, we need to make our move now."

"The problem is that there aren't any openings up there, at least none I could see," Callahan said. "If we want a hole, we'll have to make our own."

"You mean with the explosives?" Zac asked.

"Exactly," Callahan said. "We'll take the charges, plant them down the tunnel a ways, and blow all of them at once."

"Wait a minute," Kyle cautioned. "You know anything about how to place charges for that sort of thing?"

"Zac and I have both had training," Callahan told him. "And you worked pretty closely with Orozco on some of his demolition stuff. Between us, we should be able to bring down the roof to give us a way out. With a little luck, we might also knock down enough of the roof to seal the Terminators in the other part of the tunnel."

Kyle winced. And if they had no luck at all, the blast might collapse their end of the tunnel and kill all three of them.

But Callahan was right. Skynet knew someone was down here, and they couldn't stay hidden from the Terminators forever.

"Okay, but maybe we should wait a little longer," he said. "If it's still light outside, most of the fighters and all of the big guns will still be working out by the daytime perimeter. If the blast lets any of the T-700s get out, they could kill a lot of people."

"It's a risk, I know," Callahan said heavily. "But if we push things too far, we may be trapped down here by Terminators making last-minute checks and adjustments."

"And if we let Skynet blow the tunnel on its schedule, we *know* a lot of people will die," Zac added.

"He's right," Callahan said. "This is the best window we're going to get. I think we need to go for it."

There was a moment of silence.

"I'm in," Zac said.

Kyle took a deep breath. "Me too."

Callahan nodded. "Let's do it."

The first job, getting up into the tunnel, was easier said than done. The metal door the Terminators had laid over the broken concrete was too heavy for Callahan to push it clear by himself.

In retrospect, Kyle realized as he and Zac made the precarious climb up the debris alongside their companion, that shouldn't have been a surprise. Not only did the door have to handle the weight of T-700s walking over it, but also the extra burden of whatever chunks of metal or concrete those T-700s were carrying.

Fortunately, with all three of them pushing, the door finally moved, and without any of the teeth-jarring screeching that metal on concrete often made.

A minute later, for the first time in hours, they were back in the tunnel.

"We'll start with those," Callahan whispered, pointing to the two charges sitting against the tunnel face. "You two get them—I'll head down the tunnel and look for a place to set them up."

"You want this?" Kyle asked, pulling his shotgun from his belt and offering it to Callahan.

The other shook his head. "Maybe later." Checking his footing, he headed down the tunnel.

Kyle turned back to the explosives, a hard lump forming in his throat. He'd dealt with the stuff several times back when the three of them were living in Los Angeles. But those had all been pipe bombs or something similar, with flammable fuses. Canvas-wrapped packages with a fist-sized box wired into both bombs were way outside his area of experience.

"You know anything about these things?" he asked Zac as the two of them crouched down beside them.

"A little," Zac said, gingerly picking up the small box and turning it over in his hand. "This is the detonator. Not sure what type—I'll have to pull off some of this outer wrapping to see what's inside."

"Is that safe?" Kyle asked, forcing himself not to edge away as Zac started carefully peeling away the plastic.

"Should be," Zac said. "Let's see what we've got."

He angled the partially open package toward the light coming in through the ceiling.

"Looks like a solenoid plunger system," he said. "We use this type, too. It's pretty simple…"

He trailed off.

"What?" Kyle asked.

Zac visibly braced himself.

"It's a plunger," he said. "That means it has to get physically pushed in to trigger the bomb. The solenoid coil around it is just there to do the pushing. Radio controlled, probably—this thing here looks like a receiver."

"You mean Skynet could set it off right now?" Kyle asked, his skin crawling a little.

"You're missing the point," Zac said, his voice suddenly gone brittle. "It's a plunger, and we don't have a radio to set it off. That means one of us will have to stay behind and push it."

Kyle looked down at the short wires running from the detonator to the charges.

"Could we make the wires longer?" he asked.

"If we had more wire, sure," Zac said, looking around. "But I don't see any." He stood up, holding the detonator gingerly in one hand as he picked up one of the wrapped explosives with the other. "Let's get these back to Callahan. Maybe he'll have an idea."

"Okay," Callahan said after Zac had explained the situation. "Let's focus on getting these things placed. Then we'll figure out where to go from there."

"Meaning what?" Kyle asked suspiciously.

"That we'll figure out where to go from there," Callahan repeated, an edge to his voice. The same edge, Kyle noted, that Yarrow had had when he'd pulled his gun and ordered the three of them to cover. "There are six more charges, right?"

"Meaning you'll stay behind and trigger the detonator?" Kyle asked.

Callahan looked him straight in the eye.

"When Yarrow died, I became senior man here," he said flatly. "If it comes to that... yes."

Zac stirred. "We should probably draw straws or something," he suggested hesitantly.

"Or maybe we should pretend we're Resistance soldiers who follow military procedure and chain of command." Callahan held up a hand as Kyle started to speak. "And if we stand around arguing until the Terminators get back, we lose by default. Now go get the rest of the charges like I told you while I get these positioned."

Clenching his teeth, Kyle turned and headed back down the tunnel. Zac lingered another moment, then followed.

"What are we going to do?" the younger teen muttered as he caught up to Kyle.

"You heard him," Kyle said grimly. "If it comes to that, he's going to take the job."

They got another three paces before Zac spoke again.

"So we just have to make sure it doesn't come to that."

"You got it," Kyle said. "So get busy and think. Think hard."

He glanced over his shoulder at Callahan's shadowy figure as he knelt down by the explosives. "And think fast."

There was no way to know how far the disposal group had gotten before Lajard's activation code had turned Jik from a John Connor pretender into a killer Terminator. There was also no way to know how long it had taken the Theta to finish its bloody task. Probably, knowing Terminators, not very long.

Which meant Barnes and Preston should have run into the machine again somewhere between Baker's Hollow and the river.

Only they hadn't.

"What now?" Preston asked over the roar of the water as he and Barnes stood in the partial shelter of the trees near the river. "Go on, or go back?"

"You're the expert," Barnes said, frowning as he eyed the far bank. Was something moving behind the foliage over there? "Are there any paths he could have used to get past us?"

"Not unless he headed up to the bridge and crossed that way."

"Yeah," Barnes said, consciously letting his eyes move away from the area where he'd seen movement. Jik had already caught him and Williams that way once. "What's with that bridge, anyway? He told us he helped you build it."

"*Someone* helped me build it," Preston said. "But that was forty years ago, and I don't remember the kid's face well enough to know whether that was Jik or not." He grimaced. "But even if Jik isn't him, Skynet must have had access to the real guy somewhere along the line. Otherwise how could Jik have known about the bridge?"

"All of his Connor memories were false," Barnes pointed out. "Maybe the childhood ones are, too."

Preston hissed between his teeth.

"More likely they found him somewhere, dredged out his memories, and then killed him. They might even have deliberately searched him out because he'd been in Baker's Hollow and they were using us as their damned—"

"Hold it," Barnes cut him off, dropping the minigun's muzzle from chest-rest into firing position. There was definitely movement over there, too much for Jik's rope-and-stick gimmick. "Jik?" he shouted. "Hey, you! Terminator!"

For a moment, nothing happened. Then, a pair of bushes parted—

And Halverson stepped into view.

But it wasn't the swaggering, arrogant, overconfident Halverson who'd left Barnes and Williams prisoners in Preston's living room while he went off hunting T-700s. He was limping as he made for the river, his face contorted with pain. Instead of a rifle, a bow and quiver dangled loosely from his right hand. His left hand was pressed against his right side.

He was barely in sight when Preston broke from cover and sprinted to the river, slinging his rifle over his shoulder as he ran. He splashed through the rushing water to Halverson, taking the man's left arm and laying it over his own shoulder. He wrapped his other arm carefully around Halverson's back and side, then half led, half carried the injured man across the river and back to the trees where Barnes was waiting.

"Give me a hand," he grunted as he put Halverson's back to one of the thicker trees and started to ease him to the ground.

"No—don't," Barnes said, catching hold of Halverson's arm and pulling him upright again. "If you sit him down, you'll just have to stand him up again in a minute."

"He needs to rest," Preston insisted.

"Not here he doesn't," Barnes countered.

"But—"

"No, he's right," Halverson said, shrugging off Preston's hand. "Besides, I think a couple of my ribs are cracked," he added, making a face as he again pressed his left hand to his side. "I sit down now, I probably end up with a punctured lung."

"Fine," Preston gritted out. "What happened back there? No—dumb question. I mean—"

"You mean did anyone else make it out alive," Halverson said bitterly. "The answer is no. He killed them. All of them."

"How'd he miss you?" Barnes asked.

"Does it *look* like he missed me?" Halverson retorted. "He took my gun, clubbed me with it, then started shooting everyone else."

"Probably planned to come back to you later."

"You think?" Halverson said acidly. "Only I saw how it was going. I saw there was nothing I could do. Badger was already down, so I grabbed his bow, just to have *something* if he came after me. Then I took off to try to warn the rest of you."

Barnes grunted. "Nice thought. A little late, though."

"What are you talking about?" Halverson asked, frowning. "He couldn't have gotten past me."

"He didn't have to," Preston told him. "Oxley was already there."

"Oxley?"

"And Valentine," Preston said. "Remember those Terminator hybrids we were talking about earlier?"

Halverson's face went rigid.

"Oh, God. Did he—is Ginny—?"

"Ginny's okay," Preston hastened to assure him. "It looks like he only got a couple of people before we were able to take him down." His throat tightened. "The full count will have to wait until later."

"Where is she?" Halverson asked. "Ginny. Is she still in town?"

"No, they're all heading to the Glaumann place," Preston said. "You think you can make it that far?"

"I can make it," Halverson said. He looked at Barnes. "What about your partner? Is she okay?"

"She's fine," Barnes said, a small part of his mind wondering how he felt about Williams being called his partner. "She's headed back to the chopper to get us some extra firepower."

"Hope's taking her via the snaky," Preston added. "With luck that'll get them past Lajard and Valentine."

"Yeah, what's with Lajard?" Halverson asked. "You didn't mention him before."

"We think he's pure human," Preston said. "Possibly the Thetas' controller and observer. But that still leaves Valentine on the loose."

"And Jik," Barnes said, frowning at the river. "Where the hell is he, anyway?"

Halverson shook his head. "Last I saw, he was collecting all the T-700 pieces we were supposed to dump in the ravine."

"Collecting the *pieces*?" Preston asked, frowning. "What for?"

"How the hell should I know?" Halverson snarled. "All I know is that he was picking them up and laying them out like a jigsaw puzzle. I only got the one glimpse."

"Maybe he's trying to scavenge enough parts to put together a working machine," Barnes said. "How badly damaged were they?"

"They looked pretty bad," Preston said. "But now that we know it was all for show, maybe they weren't as bad off as we thought."

"What do you mean, it was all for show?" Halverson asked. "We nailed those damn machines."

"Are you blind, or just stupid?" Preston said sourly. "The only reason Skynet let us take them down was to prove Jik's credentials as the great John Connor. How better to do that than let him help the brave little locals wreck a couple of fearsome Terminators?"

"That doesn't make any sense," Halverson protested. "Why even bother if the damn Thetas were just going to shoot up the town anyway?"

An unpleasant sensation ran up Barnes's back.

Suddenly, the pieces were starting to fall into place.

"Because that *wasn't* the plan," he said. "What did Oxley say back there, Preston? That they would have been perfectly happy to keep things going the way they were?"

"Something like that," Preston said, frowning at him. "You saying the plan was for them to stay in Baker's Hollow?"

"I think so," Barnes said, his mind racing furiously. "Only they'd be here with Jik joining them as John Connor. Did he ever say whether he had a radio or not? Or access to one?"

"He said that he had a small one," Preston said. "I never saw it, but from the size of his backpack it couldn't have been very big."

"Perhaps he left a bigger one out in the woods," Halverson suggested.

"Or maybe it's both," Barnes said. "He's got a small transmitter with him, but it's only sending as far as a bigger version out there in some hidden Skynet base."

"Somewhere out in the mountains?" Preston asked, frowning.

"Somewhere right here in this area," Barnes growled. "Probably where Jik came from, in fact, Jik and those four T-700s. Maybe even the H-K that attacked us outside the wrecked Skynet base last night."

"We heard an H-K last night, too," Preston said. "It could have been the same one."

"Where did it come from?" Barnes asked.

Preston pointed across the river.

"Somewhere to the west of here, heading southeast."

"If this base had an H-K, it would have to be in a clearing," Halverson offered. "You can't land those things just anywhere."

Barnes fingered the minigun thoughtfully. Only

Williams had said there weren't any clearings near town on that side of the river. Which meant—

"It's been camouflaged," he told the others. "Probably with camo netting strung between treetops. You two know the area. Where could it be?"

Preston and Halverson eyed each other.

"Has to be somewhere with mostly flat ground," Preston said. "That leaves out the two on Beelee Ridge."

"Also has to be some place where we haven't been hunting lately," Halverson added.

"Maybe someplace you have a good reason to avoid?" Barnes suggested.

Halverson cursed viciously.

"Klein."

"Damn it," Preston said, just as viciously. "Bear Commons."

"Bear Commons?" Barnes asked.

"A big clearing where one of our hunters, Billy Klein, got mauled to death by a bear about six months ago," Preston told him. "Or rather, mauled to death by something we *assumed* was a bear."

"We haven't let any hunting parties go near that area since," Halverson added.

Barnes nodded. Six months ago would put it three months before Lajard and the others arrived in Baker's Hollow. Plenty of time for Skynet to throw something small together out here and run a data cable to it.

"Sounds like the place," he said. "How do I get there?"

"By following me," Preston said. "You'll never find it on your own." He peered back toward town. "Do we go now or wait for Williams to get here with the chopper?"

"We go now," Barnes said. "A Terminator support base is usually stocked with extra guns and ammo. We need to get there before Jik finishes putting that T-700 back together and heads back to rearm."

"You'll never get past him," Halverson warned. "There's not enough room between the river and the ravine for you to sneak by without him hearing you. You'll have to go around the southern end of the ravine."

"Or we go up the east side of the river and take the rope bridge," Preston said.

"The forty-year-old bridge?" Barnes said, doubtfully. "The one put together by a couple of kids?"

"That's it," Preston said. "Unless you'd rather go toe-to-toe with another Theta."

For a moment, Barnes was tempted. Thirty minigun rounds ought to be enough to make quick work of the damn Theta.

But only if he got a clear, clean shot. Given the mass of tangled undergrowth he'd already seen clogging that side of the river, it was a dangerously big *if*.

"No, we'll try the bridge." He turned to Halverson. "You wait here. When Williams gets here with the chopper, tell her where we've gone."

"Like hell I'm staying here," Halverson growled. "With Terminators on the loose and my wife out there with a bunch of useless shirt-makers? Forget it. She needs me."

"She needs our Blackhawk and its M240 machineguns a hell of a lot more," Barnes retorted. "And she needs them in the air, not sitting here with Williams wondering where the hell we went."

"Can't you call and tell her?" Halverson asked. "Even Jik's got a radio. Don't you?"

"Usually, yes," Barnes said. "But in the last week—" He broke off. *"Hell."*

"What?" Preston asked sharply.

"Nothing," Barnes said, cursing his thick-headedness. So *that* was why Skynet had been jamming all the radios in San Francisco. "No, we don't have radios. That means you're staying here. Even if I have to nail you to a tree."

Halverson's face darkened.

"Look—"

"What if we told her we aren't here anymore?" Preston cut in. "Would she be smart enough to come find us?"

Barnes hesitated. Williams was smart, all right. And she knew the cable ran up that side of the river.

"How do we do that?"

"With this," Preston said, reaching into his shirt and pulling out a whistle. "You might want to cover your ears—it's pretty piercing."

It was piercing, all right. But with the proliferation of whistles in the San Francisco camp these days, it was hardly something Barnes hadn't heard before. Preston blew a quick succession of short and long bursts, paused, repeated the sequence, then slipped the whistle back into his shirt.

"That's the best I can do. Ready?"

Barnes resettled the minigun on his arm.

"Ready."

"Good luck," Halverson said.

"You too," Preston said. He hesitated, then reached down and took Halverson's bow and quiver. "Here," he said, pressing his rifle into the other's hand. "You can't use a bow, not with broken ribs. You might be able to use a rifle, though."

"Thanks," Halverson said softly. "I see Lajard or Valentine, you're damn right I'll be able to use it."

A minute later, with the roar of the river on their left, Preston and Barnes left the open area at the ford and once again plunged into deep undergrowth.

"What was that about the radios?" Preston asked over his

shoulder. "Something you didn't want Halverson to hear?"

"No, just something that wasn't worth wasting time talking about," Barnes told him. "I just figured out why Skynet's been jamming our radios in San Francisco. It wasn't just to annoy us, but to keep us from hearing the fake John Connor broadcasts Jik's been making."

"Because if you heard them, you'd send someone to investigate," Preston said, nodding. "Lucky for us— well, lucky in the long run—you came anyway."

Barnes winced. Except that they wouldn't have if Williams hadn't gotten her back up on tracking that cable.

"Yeah," he said. "Why do you put up with him?"

"Who?"

"Halverson," Barnes said. "You're supposed to be in charge. Why do you let him tell your people what to do?"

Preston's shoulders hunched in a shrug.

"That's just Halverson," he said. "He was a master hunter out here long before Judgment Day, and he likes to think he knows how to do everything better than any of the rest of us."

"And you just stand there and let him think that? Why?"

"Because he *is* a master hunter, and we need him," Preston said. "More than that, we need the rest of the expert hunters who look up to him."

"So you just let him walk all over you," Barnes bit out. "You let him make you look like a fool."

"I suppose you could say that," Preston said calmly. "But letting him play his games is what keeps this town functioning and its citizens alive. I think that's worth a little wounded pride, don't you?"

He gestured. "We'd better be quiet from here on. We don't want to reach the bridge to find Jik waiting at the other end."

CHAPTER TWENTY-THREE

The distant whistle call was faint, just barely on the edge of hearing. But the dots and dashes were distinct.

From the puzzled look on Hope's face, though, the message itself wasn't nearly so clear.

"Well?" Blair asked quietly.

"I don't know," Hope murmured back. "That was one of our hunting codes. It means an assigned area has come up dry, and that the hunt team is moving on to the next one. But why would anybody be out hunting *now*?"

Blair looked around through the fading light at the densely packed tress and bushes hemming them in from all sides. The snaky, Hope had called this route. Blair would probably have named it 'the claustrophobic.'

"You said *the* hunt team. But you'd normally have more than one out at a time, right?"

"Right," Hope said. "Yes, I see—the team leader's code should have been attached. But there wasn't one."

"So it probably wasn't talking about a normal hunt team," Blair said.

Hope pondered that a moment.

"You think they're telling us to give up?"

"More likely that Barnes and your father are leaving

the river ford," Blair said.

"To go where?"

"I don't know," Blair said. "Maybe once we're in the air we'll be able to figure that out. How much farther?"

Hope looked around them.

"Ten minutes," she said. "Fifteen if we want to be extra quiet."

"Let's make it fifteen."

Blair's best-case scenario was that Lajard wouldn't have been able to locate the Blackhawk at all. Her next-best hope was that he would locate it, but decide to set up an ambush along the trail from town that Hope's route through the snaky would circumvent.

No such luck, on either count. They arrived at the edge of the clearing to find Valentine already in the Blackhawk, sitting straight and tall and motionless in the pilot's seat.

The way a Terminator would sit.

"We're too late," Hope whispered, her whole body slumping.

"Easy," Blair soothed, frowning. They'd come out on the helo's portside bow, and between the portside door and the broken windshield she could see into most of the cockpit. Valentine was there, but where was Lajard?

And then, she heard a soft, metallic click.

"Try it now," Lajard's voice came faintly.

Valentine stirred, hands moving across the controls.

"Nothing."

There was a muffled curse from the cockpit, and Blair smiled tightly. Lajard wasn't off somewhere on some dangerous errand. Instead, he was lying on his back under the control panel.

Trying to figure out how Barnes's kill switch worked.

Blair looked up at the sky, her smile fading.

Unfortunately, the stalemate wasn't going to last much longer. The minute the sun was fully down and long-range transmitters began to function, Skynet would probably download every scrap of data it had on Blackhawk piloting and tech into Valentine. At that point, it would be simple for the Theta to sort through Wince's jury-rigs and patches and figure out where Barnes had diverted the starter circuit.

And when that happened, the game would be over. Lajard and Valentine would fly out of here, rendezvous with Jik somewhere, and they'd all be off to play the John Connor charade in front of some other trusting and doomed Resistance group.

There was only one way Blair could think of to stop them. One nasty, bloody way.

"We can't let them leave here, Hope," she murmured. "We have to take them out. Both of them. Do you understand?"

For a long moment the girl was silent.

"Yes," she said at last. Even in a whisper her pain and grief were clearly audible. "What do you want me to do?"

"I need you to stay right here while I work my way around the tail to the other side," Blair told her. "Once I'm there, I'll find a way to get Susan to turn in my direction. Remember that shot you made across the river this afternoon, where you hit the T-700's motor cortex?"

Hope's breath came out in a strangled huff.

"Oh, no," she breathed. "Please. I can't do that."

"I know it'll be hard," Blair said gently. "But we have no choice. You saw what Oxley did to those people in town. If Susan and Lajard get away, they'll do the same to other people somewhere else. Maybe hundreds of other people. It has to stop here."

Hope didn't answer. Her face was lowered toward the ground, her eyes squeezed shut.

"That isn't Susan Valentine," Blair said. "Not anymore. It's a Terminator. But if you can nail its control chip, about an inch above the spot where you shot the T-700, there's a chance that Susan may be able to come back out."

"And then die?"

Blair sighed. Unfortunately, she was probably right. Shooting the T-700 had disabled the cortex but done little additional damage to the metal skull and processor banks behind it. In Valentine, though, the space inside the metal skull was occupied by a human brain.

Marcus had managed to disable his chip without doing any further damage. But Hope's arrow probably wouldn't be that selective. If it hit a seam in the armor and slipped through, Valentine would almost certainly die.

But it had to be done.

Hope knew it, too. The girl took a deep breath and raised her head again.

"All right," she said, opening her eyes. "But you should stay here. I'll go around to the other side."

"It'll be dangerous to move around this close to the helo," Blair warned.

"I know this forest," Hope reminded her. "You don't. I'll go."

Blair hesitated, then nodded.

"Okay," she said. "But once you're there, stay under cover until I get their attention to me. How long will it take you?"

"Fifteen minutes," Hope said. "Maybe twenty. I'll have to go straight out into the forest, out of sight, then do a big circle around the clearing."

Blair looked up at the sky. Twenty minutes, with sundown less than an hour away. It was going to be tight.

"Take whatever time you need to keep from being seen," she said. "And be careful."

Hope nodded. Holding her bow vertically in front of her where it wouldn't snag on anything, she slipped silently away into the forest.

The minutes ticked slowly by. Gazing at the helo, listening to Lajard's cursing, Blair found herself staring at the motionless Valentine.

Wondering what was going on behind the Theta's stolid expression.

Marcus hadn't known he was a Theta until the magnetic mine at the Resistance base had blown his body open. Even then, he hadn't realized he was operating under a secret directive until he reached Skynet Central and Skynet itself revealed the truth to him.

Did Valentine understand what had happened to her? Had the memory of her transformation been erased from her mind, the way Jik's entire false John Connor memory had been put into him? Or had she always known who and what she was?

Marcus had hated the thought of what he'd become. Oxley, in contrast, had seemed to revel in his new power, strength, and supposed invulnerability.

What was Valentine thinking? The last five minutes, Blair knew, would be the most dangerous, as Hope made her approach back toward the Blackhawk's starboard side. Blair gave the girl ten minutes, then lifted her Desert Eagle with both hands to point at the cockpit and took a deep breath.

"Lajard?" she called.

There was a moment of silence. Then, beside Valentine, Lajard cautiously raised his head above the control panel, just far enough to see through the broken windshield.

"Williams?" he called back.

"Having trouble starting my helo?"

"Just amusing myself while we wait for sundown,"

Lajard said. "I prefer flying at night. You know, it's really too bad Smith had to open his big fat mouth. It would have been so much better for you and Barnes to leave peacefully. That way, Susan could have intercepted you along the way and killed you more quietly. Or better, I suppose, after you'd gotten the helicopter started."

"Well, she and I are both here now," Blair pointed out. "You want to see how we do one-on-one, go ahead and send her out."

Lajard chuckled. "What, so that Barnes or whoever's lurking in the bushes can shoot me? Thanks, but I think I'll keep her right here where she is. Speaking of killing, Susan tells me you killed Nathan."

"Baker's Hollow killed Nathan," Blair corrected. "It takes a village, and all that."

"That's cute," Lajard said with a snort. "You think that one up all by yourself?"

"We all have our moments," Blair responded, searching the woods on the other side of the helo for signs of movement. So far, nothing.

"You know, your Thetas aren't nearly as tough as you think. A T-600 or T-700 can take a lot more damage."

"But Thetas are far better at infiltration," Lajard pointed out. "I don't think you've grasped the full implications of our time here in the backwater. My Thetas lived among these people for three months—*three months*—without anyone even suspecting they were anything other than what they seemed."

"Sounds impressive, all right," Blair agreed. "Until you realize that once they knew what to look for they picked them out in two hours."

"Don't flatter them," Lajard said scornfully. "*You* picked them out in two hours. You and Barnes. On their own, Baker's Hollow would have gone another three months without getting a clue."

"While Jik played Connor for everyone within reach of his voice?" Blair suggested.

Lajard snorted. "You really don't understand, do you?" he said contemptuously. "Jik was a late model, a full test of the false-memory system, but programming him to be Connor was pure improvisation."

"And pretty much useless," Blair said, putting some contempt in her own voice. Lajard might be stuck here until sundown, but he really didn't need to be telling her all this. Obviously, the man liked to brag and gloat, and the more detail Blair could goad out of him, the better. "He doesn't look a thing like the real Connor."

"So what?" Lajard countered. "I mean, really, how many people have ever seen the real Connor? All we need is the voice, and you have to admit we got that one down cold."

"Maybe," Blair said. "It's still a pretty weak plan."

"You still don't get it," Lajard insisted. "I already said Jik was a last-minute throw-together. The plan—the *real* plan—was to get hold of Connor himself for that job. The *real* John Connor."

"What are you talking about?" Blair asked.

"Oh, come now," Lajard said his voice loaded with scorn. "Did you really think Skynet had Marcus Wright lure him to Skynet Central just to *kill* him?"

Blair felt her breath catch in her throat. That part of the operation had been bothering her for a week now, ever since Barnes and Marcus came charging out to her helo with a bloodied and battered John Connor stumbling along between them. There had been hundreds of Terminators in that facility, T-1s, T-600s, and T-700s. And yet Skynet had held them all back while it sent a single Terminator against Connor?

Now, suddenly, horribly, it all made sense.

"Skynet was going to turn him into a Theta," she breathed.

"Bingo," Lajard said sarcastically. "That wasn't so hard, now, was it?"

Blair shook her head. "That's insane."

"On the contrary, it's brilliant," Lajard said. "Think about it. You take Connor alive—maybe just barely, but alive—and remake him in Skynet's image. Then we delete all memories of what happened to him, from the moment he walked into Central until the moment he walked out."

"And you send him back to the Resistance."

"Exactly," Lajard said. "With probably a few little enhancements to take with him. Enhancements like wonderful oratory skills, limited tactical abilities, and jealousy of subordinates."

"Especially the more competent subordinates," Blair murmured.

"Of course," Lajard said. "After all, they're the ones we'd want him to destroy. All we do then is let him regain his title as savior of humanity, and watch as he builds, nurtures, and destroys the Resistance."

An eerie feeling spread over Blair's skin. It could have worked, too. Connor had been inside Skynet Central at the exact time that Skynet's little kill-code deception was supposed to annihilate most of the Resistance cells around the world, including Connor's own group. Those few who survived would have more important things on their minds than to wonder where Connor had been during the weeks or months of his Theta transformation.

Lajard was right—it had been a brilliant plan. And it had failed only because Marcus wasn't as firmly under Skynet's control as Skynet had thought, and Connor's distrust of

Skynet's kill-code gambit had left his team in position to swoop in and finish the rescue that Marcus had started.

"I'm sure Skynet would have been very pleased," Blair said. "Not so sure you'd have had such a happy ending. You really think Skynet would have left you and the others alive once the rest of humanity was gone?"

"The others, as in Susan and Nathan?" Lajard asked. "No, I imagine they would have eventually been dumped along with everyone else. Not much call for molecular biology and metallurgy once the Thetas and Terminators have served their purpose. But Skynet's a computer, and I'm a computer programmer. There'll always be a place in this new world for people like me."

"*That's* your shining hope?" Blair scoffed. "To live out your life as Skynet's pet?"

"It's not exactly the way I envisioned my future when I was a kid," Lajard conceded. "But it beats the hell out of being a corpse."

"You may still end up that way," Blair said. "Because Skynet *didn't* get to Connor. And you can forget your improvised substitute, because we *are* going to find and destroy Jik."

"Don't be so sure," Lajard warned. "Nathan was never programmed with tactical skills, but Jik's going to be a much harder nut to crack. And now that we have this nice Resistance helicopter to fly around in, he'll do a terrific job of being John Connor."

"Except that *we* know the truth," Blair pointed out.

"Well, of course we'll have to kill you and everyone else in Baker's Hollow first," Lajard said casually. "I assumed that went without saying."

"Go ahead and try," Blair said, fighting back a sudden shiver. "Even if you succeed, sooner or later the real Connor will figure out what's going on and track you down."

"Maybe," Lajard said, his voice suddenly all sly and amused. "You assume he won't already be on our side by then."

"What's *that* supposed to mean?" she demanded.

"Oh, nothing," Lajard said. "It's just that when you said Skynet didn't get to Connor... well, never assume, Williams. That's all. Never, ever assume."

"How many more are there?" Callahan asked as Kyle and Zac set down their latest satchel charges.

"Just the two," Kyle said, eyeing the four bags Callahan had already placed against the tunnel walls and the two he and Zac had just delivered. "These ought to be enough, don't you think?"

"Better safe than sorry," Callahan said, grunting as he picked up one of the charges. "Go get them."

Kyle frowned. There'd been something in Callahan's voice just then.

"Go ahead, Zac," he said. "I'll stay here and give him a hand."

"Both of you go," Callahan ordered darkly. "I don't want Zac having to lug two charges at the same time."

"Go on, Zac," Kyle repeated.

Zac didn't move.

"What's going on?" he asked suspiciously. "Callahan— oh. No, you *can't.*"

"Then how?" Callahan snapped. "You saw the plunger. One of us *has* to stay here and trigger it. So quit arguing, and you and Reese get your butts back to the front of the tunnel."

"We draw straws," Zac insisted.

"We obey orders," Callahan shot back.

"Wait a second," Kyle said, staring down at the plunger. "It just has to be pushed in, right?"

"Right," Callahan said, frowning. "Why?"

"I need a slab," he said looking quickly around. "Concrete or metal, not too big."

Out of the corner of his eye, he saw Zac stiffen.

"They're coming," he murmured.

Kyle looked down the tunnel. In the distance, he could see the faint glow of red Terminator eyes.

The T-700s were on the move... and if they hadn't spotted the intruders yet, that discovery was only seconds away.

"I need a slab," he repeated, giving the area a second quick sweep. But there was nothing around them of the right size.

"Wait a minute," Callahan said. He took the detonator and turned it over to point at the ceiling, then picked up one of the charges. "Grab that other one," he told Kyle, setting his charge on the ground beside the detonator and angling it to the side so that releasing it would send it falling onto the plunger. "Brace its end against this one."

Kyle obeyed, leaving the two satchels balanced against each other with the plunger beneath them.

"That should do," Callahan said, glancing back at the Terminators as he got back to his feet. "Back to the tunnel face. Reese, you want me to do it?"

"No, I've got it," Kyle said as the three of them sprinted down the uneven ground.

Seconds later, they were at the tunnel face.

"On the floor," Callahan ordered Zac, dropping onto his face between the younger teen and the approaching Terminators. "Reese: *go.*"

Kyle dropped into a crouch, pressing the shotgun's stock to his shoulder. The T-700s were coming up fast, their eyes bright enough to paint the tunnel walls and ceiling in a red glow. Lining up his sights on the satchel he'd braced against Callahan's, Kyle fired.

The blast slammed into the charge, knocking it backward out of alignment and sending the other one dropping toward the plunger. Kyle squeezed his eyes shut—

With an ear-hammering explosion, the whole cluster blew up.

The blast of sound and superheated air slammed into Kyle's face and chest, knocking him backward onto the tunnel floor. For an instant his mind flicked back to the massive gasoline explosion and fire back near the Moldering Lost Ashes building, the one where he'd thought he was dying—

And then someone had his arm and was hauling him back to his feet.

"Look!" Callahan shouted, his voice barely audible through the ringing in Kyle's ears. "It worked!"

Wincing at the grit still swirling past his face, Kyle opened his eyes. Through the floating dust he could see an angled pile of debris where that part of the tunnel had been ten seconds ago.

And at the very top of the pile was a jagged hole and the beautiful light of a late-afternoon overcast sky.

"Come on," Callahan called, urging Kyle forward. Zac was already halfway up the rubble, his feet kicking up dust and little pebble avalanches as he climbed. Blinking a few more times, Kyle followed, with Callahan still gripping his arm beside him.

Hours of toiling their way through twisted passageways and switchbacks had completely ruined Kyle's usual sense of direction. But his assumption as they traveled had always been that the tunnel itself was running more or less straight from where they'd entered it, except for the small curves and jogs that had been forced on the diggers. That direction, combined with the distance they had traveled, should by his estimate have put them inside the nighttime perimeter somewhere near the mess tent.

But, as he clawed his way out into the open air, he found he'd been only half right. They were indeed inside the inner perimeter, but somewhere along the way the tunnel had taken more of a turn than he'd realized. Instead of being by the mess tent, the tunnel had taken them to within fifty meters of the medical recovery tent.

The tent where John Connor was currently lying weak and nearly helpless in a hospital bed.

"It's all right!" Callahan shouted, waving his hands toward the guards by the tent.

But the guards weren't listening. To Kyle's surprise and dismay, they were hastily unslinging their rifles and bringing them to bear.

"It's all right!" Callahan shouted again. "We're your people."

And then, abruptly, Kyle realized the guards weren't aiming their weapons toward him and Callahan. Spinning around, he looked back toward the hole they'd blasted.

Their exit wasn't the only hole anymore. Fifty meters further back along the tunnel, the force of explosion had collapsed another section of the roof.

And clawing its way up to the surface was a T-700.

Kyle looked frantically around them. But the search and clean-up teams were still out working the smoking wasteland, and the perimeter guards hadn't yet pulled back from the outer daytime ring to their nighttime stations. Just as he'd predicted earlier, all the fighters and heavy weapons were miles away.

Against all odds, Kyle and the others had made it out of the tunnel alive.

Just in time to watch the Terminators kill John Connor.

CHAPTER
TWENTY-FOUR

Sweating, Barnes followed Preston across the old rope bridge, trying to ignore the churning water beneath him. Several of the boards were cracked or rotted, and the only safe places to step were the points where they were fastened to the supporting ropes.

But the ropes themselves were sturdy enough, and the young Preston and his visiting friend had done a good job of anchoring the bridge to the banks. Despite Barnes's misgivings, both men made it across.

Equally surprising was the fact there was nothing waiting on the other side. Either Skynet had mistakenly written off the bridge as impossible to cross, or else its resources were indeed down to Lajard, Valentine, Jik, and whatever Jik was in the process of salvaging from the two broken T-700s.

The sun had passed behind the mountains, and the sky was rapidly headed toward dusk, when Barnes and Preston reached Bear Commons.

"Hell," Preston murmured as they crouched behind a thick fallen tree trunk at the edge of the clearing. "I *thought* this was going a little too easy."

Barnes nodded silently. In the middle of the clearing—the exact geometrical center, if he knew Skynet—was a small cabin, similar to some of the houses he'd seen in Baker's Hollow, except that this one was constructed of slabs of metal instead of wood or brick. Above the clearing, strung across the empty space, was a thick camo netting that, as near as Barnes could tell, was a perfect match for the contours and coloration of the ring of fifty-meter-tall trees supporting it.

And squatting silently on the ground at the far side of the clearing, like a dragon guarding its hoard, was the dark metal bulk of an H-K.

"What now?" Preston asked.

"Give me a second," Barnes growled, eyeing the H-K. He'd been hoping that Skynet's bungled attempt to get hold of their Blackhawk the previous night had left it without any more aircraft in the area. He should have known it would be careful enough to keep at least one heavy fighting machine in reserve.

And that lack of foresight was going to cost him and Williams.

Especially Williams.

Preston was obviously thinking the same thing.

"How fast can Skynet get that H-K into the air?" he asked.

"Fast enough." More than fast enough, actually. Even from a cold start, if Skynet kicked in the H-K's ignition ramp-up as soon as it picked up the noise of the Blackhawk's engines, it could probably be in the air well before Williams arrived.

Unless he and Preston could keep it from leaving the clearing in the first place.

Barnes frowned up at the camo netting. The mesh was laid out across a loose crosshatch of cables that looked capable of being pulled out and back along two thicker cables running along the north and south ends of the clearing. Another pair of cables, thinner than the support lines, snaked down one of the trees on either end and ran along the ground to the cabin in the center.

Which implied that either the control or the power for retracting the netting was inside the cabin. And from the sheer size of the netting and its support cables, not to mention the way it was bending in the treetops it was connected to, the covering had to be both strong and heavy.

Strong enough and heavy enough to trap the H-K inside the clearing? Maybe. Especially since the things weren't designed to fire upward.

It was worth a try.

"We're going to make for the cabin," he told Preston. "There should be extra guns and ammo there, plus the controls to the netting." He looked sideways at Preston, the face of Preston's daughter suddenly flashing to mind. "On second thoughts, maybe you'd better stay here," he amended. "I can do this myself."

"We do it together," Preston said firmly. Maybe he was thinking of his daughter, too. "Though we might want to angle a little to the right so the cabin will be between us and the H-K."

"Way ahead of you," Barnes assured him. "Follow me. Quietly."

Keeping an eye on the H-K, Barnes circled around the end of the log and headed toward a gap between trees that should bring them into the clearing at the right spot. He stepped over a mass of brittle-looking dead branches, passed one final clump of bushes—

The swiveling of the H-K's main guns was his only warning.

"Down!" he snapped, throwing himself forward onto the ground.

Just as the thunder of the H-K's Gatling guns shattered the evening calm, stitching a line of death above his head.

Barnes was on his feet again even before the burst ended, hunched over and clutching his minigun to his stomach as he made a desperate sprint for the cabin's gunfire shadow. A second burst hammered through the air at him, and he winced as a sudden slash of pain ripped across his left shoulder. Once again he threw himself forward.

And as he hit the ground he saw that he'd made it. The H-K's Gatlings were now out of view behind the near corner of the cabin.

Or at least they would be until Skynet revved up the engines and got the damn thing into the air. Even with the canopy closed, there was more than enough room in here for the aircraft to hunt down a couple of human targets.

There was a flicker of movement at the corner of his eye, and Barnes looked over to see Preston heading for the cabin. Heaving himself to his feet, Barnes followed.

They were nearly there, and Barnes was looking for where to aim his thirty rounds in order to blast open the wall, when there was another thunder of Gatling gun fire.

And without warning, the wall they were heading for exploded violently outward.

Barnes found himself once again on the ground, this time without any conscious memory of how he'd gotten there. Preston was beside him, his face turned upward, his eyes closed, the right side of his head wet with blood.

"Preston!" Barnes shouted over the roar of the H-K's guns as they continued to rip into the cabin.

There was no answer. Crawling on elbows and knees, Barnes worked his way to the other's side.

"Preston?"

For a moment there was nothing. Then, the man's eyes fluttered open, narrowing again as the pain from his head wound came jarring back.

"What happened?"

"Skynet's decided it really, really wants us," Barnes ground out, throwing a look at the cabin.

Or rather, what was left of the cabin. The entire top half had been shattered, its metal walls turned into shards and splinters by the gunfire still raking systematically across it. Only the lower meter or so of the four walls were still intact.

Cautiously, Barnes eased up enough to sneak a look into the shell that had once been a structure. Sitting on the floor just below the demolished section of the far wall were a pair of generators.

He craned his neck to look skyward. High above the clearing, the canopy was starting to retract.

Snarling under his breath, Barnes rolled up onto his knees and brought the minigun up into firing position. He had maybe five seconds to put the generators out of commission before the canopy opened far enough to let the H-K escape into the darkening sky. He pointed the minigun into the demolished cabin—

"No!" Preston said, grabbing at his arm and pointing toward the edge of the clearing near the H-K. "There. Shoot over there."

Barnes frowned as he searched that section of forest with his eyes. Had Jik arrived? But he couldn't see anything.

"That one—right there," Preston persisted.

Barnes frowned harder. There was nothing there except—

Swinging the minigun around, aiming carefully, he squeezed off his last thirty rounds in a half-second of blistering fire.

And with a crackling groan, the tree whose lower trunk the hail of lead had disintegrated toppled ponderously over and landed with a deafening crash.

Squarely across the top of the H-K.

The echoes faded away, and a new silence filled the clearing. Cautiously, Barnes lifted his head.

The tree's impact had crushed the entire top of the H-K, burying the machine's nose in the ground and jamming the muzzles of its Gatling guns deep into the dirt.

"Nice call," he said, turning back to Preston. "How's the head?"

"I'm okay," Preston said, looking a little shaky as he got to his feet. "What now?"

"We get some fresh firepower," Barnes said, sniffing the air as he dropped the empty minigun on the ground. Now that the stink of the Gatling rounds' propellant was dissipating he could smell the equally pungent aroma of aviation fuel. The falling tree must have ruptured the H-K's fuel tank. Glancing around the clearing, he got up and went over to the wreckage of the cabin.

The equipment inside had indeed included a set of the T-700s' preferred G11 submachineguns. Unfortunately, the weapons had been racked or wall-mounted in the upper part of the cabin—which had just been obliterated by the H-K's firestorm. Barnes could see several of the weapons lying amid the debris, all of them badly damaged. He climbed up onto the broken wall and dropped over to the other side.

And jerked in surprise as his feet landed with an audible splash.

"What was that?" Preston asked, coming up and peering over the wall.

"Aviation fuel," Barnes said, wrinkling his nose. So it wasn't the H-K that was leaking, but the reserve tank he could now see peeking out from beneath a broken slab of metal along one of the other walls. "Stay there—if I find something in decent shape I'll pass it to you."

But, to his frustration, nearly every gun he spotted had been damaged beyond safe use. Midway through the search he found a single functional weapon, but everything else was useless.

He'd seen plenty of Terminators wreck their own G11s rather than let them fall into Resistance hands. Clearly, H-Ks were even better at it than T-700s were.

"Come on, come on," Preston urged, his voice low and strained. "Jik could be here any time now."

"I'm hurrying, I'm hurrying," Barnes responded. Across the cabin, beneath a section of broken ceiling, was what looked like an operating table with a collection of surgical gear scattered around it. Sloshing through the pool of aviation fuel, he crossed over to it and crouched down to look beneath the broken ceiling.

And felt his whole body go rigid. It was an operating table, all right. And lying half buried beneath it...

"Anything?" Preston asked.

"No," Barnes said quickly. Too quickly, but Preston didn't know him well enough to catch it. Straightening up, he headed back to where the older man was waiting. "Here," he said, handing Preston the G11. "I'll see if I can find some more ammo—"

"Barnes?" a voice called from across the clearing.

Barnes spun around, snatching back the G11 and turning it in the direction of the voice.

"Jik?"

"The name's Connor," Jik said sternly.

"Whatever," Barnes said, eyes straining to pierce the gloom. "Welcome home. You like what we've done with the place?"

"I have no idea what you're talking about," Jik said. "I've never been here before in my life."

"You've just forgotten," Barnes said. "Come have a look. Maybe it'll come back to you."

"What are you doing?" Preston asked quietly. "Shouldn't we find some cover?"

"Don't worry, he's not armed," Barnes murmured back. "If he had a gun he'd be shooting, not talking."

"So why are *we* talking?"

"Because I can't shoot what I can't see," Barnes growled. "And because there's a chance we can break Skynet's programming."

"Don't give me that," Jik admonished him. "It's a trick. I told you I've never been here."

"Sure you have," Barnes said. He took a couple of steps farther into the cabin and pointed to the operating table. "Here—right here—is where you were created."

"You're insane," Jik bit out. "My name is John Connor. I was born in—"

"You're a Terminator hybrid that's been code-named Jik," Barnes interrupted him. "Right here is where your memories were loaded into your brain chip and your voice was changed to match Connor's."

There was a pause.

"My voice was changed?" Jik asked, his tone suddenly odd.

"Of course," Barnes said. "Everyone on the continent with a radio knows what Connor sounds like. Skynet had to do some work before it could send you out to play."

"You're talking about throat surgery," Jik said tightly. "And a pain in... I thought a tree branch had hit my throat. I *remember* a tree branch hitting it."

"Another false memory," Barnes told him, feeling a stirring of hope. *It was working. It was actually working.* "I can see what's left of a big transmitter in here, too.

This is where your little radio was sending to. Probably where all your future messages were going to go out of, as well. Come take a look—"

"Behind you!" Preston snapped.

With a curse, Barnes spun around. The oldest trick in the book, and he'd been so focused on breaking Jik's programming that he'd nearly fallen for it.

Not that the T-700 crossing the clearing toward them was breaking any speed records. It was limping badly, its left leg dragging through the leaves and undergrowth. The rest of its body wasn't in much better shape, with large dents at its shoulders and hips, and one arm twisted visibly off.

Still, it *was* a Terminator, and it *was* targeting them, and it needed to be dealt with. Lowering the muzzle of his G11, Barnes fired a short burst into the machine's left knee.

With a screech of shattered metal, the knee disintegrated, sending the T-700 tumbling to the ground.

"Barnes—" Preston snapped.

"I know," Barnes said, turning around again. Across the clearing, Jik had broken concealment and was sprinting toward them, Williams's Mossberg gripped in its hands, its face and body torn and bloodied.

Barnes grinned humorlessly. So Jik *did* have a weapon. Unfortunately for him, it was a big clearing, and shotguns didn't have nearly the range of rifles or even handguns. Hence the T-700's distraction, and Jik's own suicidal dash across open ground to try to get into range.

And it had nearly worked. Another ten paces, and the shotgun might do some actual damage.

Barnes let him get three of those paces, then put a three-round burst squarely into his torso.

The Theta staggered back with the impact, the rounds

ripping clothing and flesh and ricocheting off the metal torso beneath. Before Barnes could line up for another burst, Jik reversed direction, turning and sprinting across the edge of the clearing and disappearing again into the darkening woods.

"Watch it—the other one's still coming," Preston warned.

Barnes looked back at the T-700. With half of its left leg gone, the machine had been reduced to crawling, its skeletal hands gripping the grass as it pulled itself toward them.

"What do we do?" Preston asked.

Barnes looked back to where Jik had again gone to ground. The forest, especially at night, was no place to play hide-and-seek with a Terminator. Even one armed only with a relatively short-range shotgun.

But hanging around a wide-open area with a semi-functional T-700 crawling around wasn't any better.

"We find ourselves some cover," he replied, climbing back over the wall out of the cabin. "You know of any defensible places nearby?"

"I don't know," Preston said. "That's not something we usually think about."

"Then it's time you started," Barnes said grimly. "Let's go take a look."

The conversation between the helicopter and the woods went back and forth, back and forth. Blair continued to probe for information from behind a tree across the clearing, while Lajard crouched out of sight beneath the control board and bragged about how clever he and Skynet had been.

Through it all, Hope stood silently behind her own chosen tree, her hands gripping her bow and her nocked arrow, her heart thudding with anticipation and dread.

Her soul aching as it never had before.

She, Hope Preston, was about to shoot another human being.

Not accidentally, the way beginner hunters sometimes did. This wouldn't be any accident, a careless slip of the finger. It would be deliberate, direct, and premeditated.

It would be like murder.

They're not human, she tried to remind herself, as she'd been trying ever since Blair first suggested this plan. *Not anymore. They're machines. They're Terminators.*

But no matter how many times she said it, she knew it wasn't true. Not completely.

Because they *were* human. Real, living, thinking people. People Hope had lived with for three long months. She'd hunted with them, eaten with them, laughed with them. Once, six weeks ago when whooping cough had taken two of the town's children, she'd cried with them.

And now, she was going to shoot one of them. Maybe both of them.

Even worse, she was going to shoot them from behind.

And then, without warning, a sudden gunshot shattered the calm.

She jumped, her body twitching so hard that it jerked the arrow off the bowstring. Had Blair given up on her and decided to take matters into her own hands?

Hastily, Hope nocked the arrow into place again. Carefully, tensely, she looked around the side of her tree.

She was still trying to figure it out when a second shot hammered into her ears.

Only this time she spotted the flash from across the clearing and caught a glimpse of sparks as Blair's shot ricocheted off the helicopter's roof, beside the shaft that connected the helicopter to the big overhead rotor.

Blair wasn't even shooting at Lajard and Susan. Was she trying to wreck the helicopter?

And then, she got it. Blair was only pretending to shoot at the rotor, pretending that she'd given up hope of taking the aircraft back.

She was trying to lure the others into a counterattack. An attack that would turn Susan's attention toward Blair, and her back toward Hope.

With a conscious effort, Hope relaxed her clenched teeth. It had to be done. Drawing back the bowstring, she waited.

A third shot caromed off the roof... and with that, Susan finally rose from the pilot's seat and stepped past Lajard's half-concealed form to the far side of the cockpit. Taking hold of the door-mounted machine gun, she swung it toward Blair's position.

And as Hope's eyes blurred with sudden tears, she sent her arrow flying into the back of her friend's head.

She had expected a gasp, or a scream, or at the very least a violent spasm in response. But there was nothing. Susan's head snapped forward with the impact, but she made no sound. She regained her balance and again took hold of the machinegun.

Blinking back her tears, Hope drew another arrow from her quiver and set it into the bowstring. Maybe she'd missed the spot.

Or maybe Blair had been wrong about there being a vulnerable point there. In that case, Blair was already dead.

So, probably, was Hope.

And then, Susan froze.

Hope stared at the woman's back, her heart pounding even harder as she drew back the bowstring. Slowly, Susan turned around, and even in the fading light Hope could see the pain, confusion, and disbelief on her face.

And with a huffing gasp that Hope could hear all the way across the clearing, the woman stepped away from the gun and bent over, her hands jabbing into the space beneath the control board like a pair of striking rattlesnakes. There was a strangled gasp, and she straightened up, hauling Lajard up out of his hiding place by his upper arms.

"No!" Lajard gasped. His grabbed at her wrists, trying to pry her hands away.

But those were Terminator hands, and no mere human had a prayer of breaking their hold. Lajard tried to pull back, then tried to rock or squirm his way out of her grip. None of it worked.

"No," he snarled. "Valentine—listen to me. Attack Williams, not me. *Williams*, not me."

"No," Susan breathed, her voice dark and husky. "Traitor." Still holding onto his arm with her left hand, she let go with her right and shifted her grip to his throat. *"Traitor!"*

Through the far door, Hope saw Blair emerge from cover and run toward the helicopter, her gun ready in her hand.

"Traitor?" Lajard echoed. He jabbed his finger against Susan's chest. "Fool." He raised his voice. "You like kill switches, Williams? Try this one. *Dies irae.*"

Abruptly, Susan's shoulders sagged, her hands slipping from Lajard's arm and throat and dropping like broken tree branches to her sides. Her mouth dropped open and she gave a strangled gasp.

Contemptuously, Lajard turned away from her, swiveling toward Blair. His right hand darted under his jacket and emerged with a small pistol. Blair skidded to a halt, snapping up her gun toward him.

Frantically, Hope pulled back on the bowstring, knowing full well that her arrow would never make it to Lajard's back in time. The two guns were nearly homed in on their respective targets, and in less than a heartbeat Blair or Lajard—or both of them—would be dead.

And then, the thundercrack of a shot boomed across the clearing. Not from Lajard or Blair, but from somewhere to Hope's right.

The impact slammed Lajard into Susan, his head exploding with blood that sprayed across her face and onto the rear cockpit wall. He bounced off her immobile body even as Hope's arrow belatedly dug itself into his back. His knees gave way, and he fell to the deck.

Shaking like a windblown leaf, Hope stepped from her hiding place and peered across the clearing.

Halverson was limping toward them, his face rigid with pain, his shirt wet with perspiration, his rifle still pressed to his shoulder. His gaze flicked to Hope, then to Blair, then back to the helicopter.

"You two okay?" he called gruffly.

"Yes," Blair said for both of them as she climbed up into the cockpit. Crouching over Lajard, she twisted the pistol out of his hand.

She was peering down at the body when Susan gave a long, hissing sigh and collapsed.

Blair was saying something about staying back as Hope raced to the helicopter. Hope ignored her, brushing past and dropping onto her knees at Susan's side.

"Susan?" she called, wincing at her friend's blood-spattered face and her closed eyes. "Can you hear me? Susan, I'm sorry. I'm so sorry."

"Shh," Susan murmured, her eyes flicking half open. "I'm the one who's sorry, not you. I'm the one... I didn't want to hurt you, Hope. I never wanted to hurt you. But I couldn't... I couldn't."

"But you did," Hope assured her, her throat aching. "You broke Skynet's programming. You stopped him."

Susan shook her head wearily.

"*You* stopped him, Hope. Not me. You stopped him with this." She started to reach for the broken arrow shaft still embedded in the back of her head.

Her hand never got there. It flopped weakly back down onto the deck and lay still.

She was gone.

For a long minute Hope just knelt there, gripping the woman's hand, memories swirling through her mind like the bittersweet smoke from a cooking fire. Behind her, she could hear Blair and Halverson murmuring together, but she had no attention to spare for whatever they were talking about. Hope's friend was dead.

She had killed her.

"Hope?" Blair murmured quietly. "We have to go."

Hope tried to blink away her tears. She couldn't.

"Can we—we can bury them, can't we?" she asked, her voice shaking. "We have to bury them."

"We will," Blair promised. "But not now. Your father's in danger."

And with that, all the pain and sorrow abruptly flowed back into the far corners of Hope's mind, still there but no longer overwhelming her. Her father was in trouble. The grief and guilt would have to wait.

"Where?" she said.

"Bear Commons," Halverson replied. He had hold of Lajard's arms and was dragging him out of the helicopter, his face contorted with pain and determination. "We think that's where Skynet's base is."

"Go over there," Blair ordered, pointing Hope across the cockpit toward the door-mounted gun on the helicopter's right-hand side. "There's a safety harness attached to the wall. Strap yourself in."

Hope stood up, forcing herself not to look back as Blair dealt with Susan's body. She hadn't noticed before just how big and fearsome the gun looked. Especially up close.

The gun that Susan had been preparing to use when Hope shot her in the back.

But she wouldn't think about that. Not right now.

Backing into the safety harness, she began fastening it around her.

CHAPTER
TWENTY-FIVE

The first T-700 had nearly made it through to the surface now, and for a brief moment Kyle allowed himself the hope that the rest of the machines might have been buried so deeply underground that they wouldn't be able to claw their way out. That would leave just a single T-700 for them to face. Surely Connor's guards could stop a single T-700?

But then the machine reached the surface and stepped to the side, and Kyle's heart sank as he saw a second skeletal metal hand reach up from underground.

There were more of them down there, ready to come up and kill. Maybe even the entire tunneling contingent.

He looked at the medical recovery tent behind them. One of Connor's guards had a whistle to his mouth, and through the ringing that the underground explosion had left in his ears Kyle could faintly hear the frantic screech of the emergency code signal. Two more seconds, he knew, and everyone within hearing range would come running.

But it was a useless gesture, because there wasn't anyone out there. Not at this hour. Not close and well-armed enough. The only thing that stood between Connor and the Terminators were Connor's guards and their weapons, and Kyle and his shotgun.

And in that frozen second, as Kyle turned back to the Terminator standing in the fading daylight, he knew what he had to do.

He took off in a dead run, his shotgun gripped across his chest. The weapon still had three shots, and he would make sure he used those shots to their best advantage.

Something brushed his sleeve. He turned, and found Callahan and Zac running alongside him. Callahan's mouth moved, and even though Kyle's ears were still too paralyzed to hear the other's words, his lip movements were easy enough to read: *What are you doing?*

"Blocking that hole," Kyle shouted back. He waved his shotgun. "Get back!"

Callahan's gaze turned to the Terminators, and out of the corner of his eye Kyle saw his face harden.

He'd figured it out. Kyle couldn't hope to stop even one Terminator with his shotgun, not with its remaining three shells, not even at point-blank range. The one, single chance any of them had of slowing down the deadly invasion—

"Go on, get back!" Kyle shouted.

Callahan didn't bother to answer. He turned and said something to Zac, and Kyle saw the younger teen shake his head.

"Zac!" Kyle shouted. "Get back."

And then, to Kyle's chagrin, Callahan put on a burst of speed, pulling ahead as he charged the Terminators.

"Callahan!" Kyle shouted.

But it was no use. Callahan was bigger, older, and faster… and as he'd been willing to sacrifice himself earlier, he was now determined to take this mission on himself.

Kyle clenched his teeth. *Fine.* If Callahan wanted to get himself killed, Kyle couldn't stop him.

But even if Callahan managed to jump on the half-emerged Terminator, any hope of pinning it down would last only as long as it took the first T-700 to pick him up and toss him off.

Maybe Kyle could do something about that.

He would use two of his remaining shells on the Terminator's arms. Then he would throw himself at full speed against the machine's torso, with luck knocking it over onto its back. If he was still alive at that point, he would fire his final shell up under the Terminator's chin, in the direction of its braincase. Maybe a pellet or two would get through the metal and damage one or more of the motor control lines leading to the machine's limbs.

Callahan was a good five paces out in front now, and flicking his eyes to the side Kyle saw that Zac was also starting to pull ahead.

And, to his surprise, Kyle felt a grim smile crease his lips.

There had been times, back in Los Angeles, when he'd wondered about this far-away Resistance he'd heard so much about. He'd wondered whether he and Star would ever link up with it, and if they did if it would be worth his allegiance.

Now he knew. If Connor and the others could inspire men like Callahan and Zac to make the ultimate sacrifice, this Resistance was indeed worth Kyle's allegiance.

His allegiance, and his life.

The T-700's red eyes glittered as it contemplated the three reckless humans bearing down on it. At least it wasn't armed, Kyle thought with an odd sort of emotional detachment. That was something, anyway. His thoughts flicked to Star, and he wished briefly that he'd had a chance to say good-bye to her. But the others would take care of her, he knew now. The Resistance took care of its own.

And then, five meters in front of him, Callahan suddenly slowed, his head turning up and sideways.

He snapped his arms out to both sides.

Kyle was just starting to wonder if Callahan's courage and determination had somehow failed him when the T-700 standing in front of them abruptly disintegrated in a burst of dimly heard automatic gunfire.

Kyle twisted his head around. There, swooping in on them like an avenging angel, was a Resistance helicopter, its door-mounted machineguns blazing away as it spat destruction at the two Terminators.

A second later, Kyle stumbled into Callahan's outstretched arm. A second after that, he found that same arm wrapped around his shoulders as Callahan gripped the two of them, Kyle on one side, Zac on the other, with the released tension of a man who has just faced certain death and then had that doom snatched from him.

Kyle had cheated death too many times, him and Star, to go all sentimental that way. Still, his knees were suddenly feeling a little weak. Probably because he hadn't had anything much to eat since breakfast.

The chopper set down near the demolished Terminators. A half-dozen men armed with heavy weapons jumped out and headed to the machines' rat hole to see what else might be lurking down there.

And waiting behind them in the chopper, her face bright with relief, was Star. She raised her hand toward Kyle and the others and waved.

Kyle waved back… and as he did so, the tension of the day started to fade away, leaving only fatigue, hunger and thirst.

But that was all right. Because they'd made it through, and John Connor was safe.

And all was finally right with the world.

***

The area around Bear Commons wasn't the best battlefield position Barnes had ever seen. Even so, there were a good half-dozen places in and around the clearing's rim that should work well enough as defensible positions.

Skynet had other ideas. Barnes and Preston had just reached a big rock outcropping right at the edge of the clearing, when Preston spotted the broken T-700 dragging itself determinedly through the grass toward them. They stumbled from behind the rock to a wide tree trunk, only to have the Terminator change direction and again launch itself into a slow-motion charge.

Three moves later, the damn thing was still chasing them.

It would be easy enough to simply blow the machine back into its component parts and be done with it. Barnes had no doubt that Skynet was hoping he would do exactly that.

But Barnes knew better than to give in to that temptation. They had Barnes's rifle and the Terminator G11, with only around forty-five rounds left between the two weapons. Barnes had no intention of spending any more of them on a T-700 that was already half broken and of no serious threat. Not with Jik still skulking around somewhere out there in the woods.

Barnes frowned into the gathering darkness. Back when they were by the wrecked cabin and had been distracted by the T-700's attempted sneak attack, Jik had tried one of his own, running toward them across the clearing. He'd backed off when his ploy failed, but the fact remained that Skynet had sent him into enemy fire without hesitation.

And why not? He was a Theta, very tough, very hard to kill. He'd already taken on Halverson's hunting force, after all, and killed all of them.

So why was he still hanging back instead of going on

the offensive? Had Skynet actually calculated that Barnes could take him out with forty-five rounds before he could kill the two of them?

Or could something have happened that had suddenly made Jik's survival more important than it had been earlier?

That question was obviously on Preston's mind, too.

"You think he went back to where he killed everyone to look for a better weapon?" he murmured.

Barnes shook his head. "If there'd been any working guns back there, he would already have them."

"What about bows?" Preston countered. "Maybe he went back to get one of those."

Barnes grimaced. That one hadn't even occurred to him.

"Yeah, good point," Barnes grunted. "Well, whatever he's got, my guess is that he's waiting for full dark. You're the expert hunter—how close could he get to us without us hearing him?"

"Probably not too close," Preston said. "But if he's got a bow and some arrows, he can probably get close enough."

And then, faintly in the distance, Barnes heard a familiar sound.

"We may not have to find out the hard way," he said. "Hear that?"

"Hear what?"

"That," Barnes said, nodding his head to the southeast and the sound of a Blackhawk's rotors. "That's Williams in our chopper."

"It may be your chopper," Preston said ominously. "But that doesn't necessarily mean Williams is the one flying it."

Barnes scowled, a flicker of doubt darkening his new confidence. Could Preston be right? Could that be Lajard and Valentine in there, coming in to pick up Jik and head off on whatever new killing spree Skynet had planned?

The moment passed. Williams had gone to get the chopper, and she was better than that.

"Don't worry, it's her," he assured Preston, looking upward at the camouflage canopy. It had been starting to open before the H-K wrecked the cabin, but it was still mostly in place above the clearing. "The big question is whether she's going to be able to find us."

"Yes," Preston said thoughtfully. "You suppose that thing's flammable?"

"No idea."

"Let's find out. You still have any of that aviation fuel on your boots?"

Barnes reached down and touched his boot.

"Maybe a little."

"Give me a piece," Preston ordered, slipping the bow he'd taken from Halverson off his shoulder.

Barnes pulled out his knife.

"How big?"

"The biggest you can get without cutting off any toes."

Barnes nodded and set to work. A few seconds later, he had freed most of the upper toe section.

"Got it."

"Stick it on here." Preston handed Barnes one of his arrows and dug into his pocket. "Run it down to just below the arrowhead."

Barnes did so. Preston took the arrow back and handed him a small object.

"My lighter," he identified it as he set the arrow into the bowstring and drew it back until the wet leather was almost touching the fingers of his bow hand. "Gasoline fueled, so watch out for your fingers."

Barnes wasn't expecting much of the aviation fuel to still be left in the leather. He was wrong. At the first touch of the lighter's fire the piece of leather blazed into bright blue-yellow flame.

Preston angled the bow upward.

"I've always wanted to do this," he murmured, and let it fly.

The arrow shot up, tracing a flaming arc up toward the camo netting. It hit, jamming itself into the mesh.

For a long moment nothing happened. The fire smoldered and faltered, looking on the verge of going out. Then the fire began to gain new life. It caught, brightened—

And abruptly roared back to life, burning and spreading across the net. A minute later, the whole circle was ablaze, the flickering flames lighting up the clearing below.

"Perfect," Barnes said, picking up the G11 and returning his attention to the forest around them. "If she doesn't see that, she's gone blind *and* stupid."

"Now what?" Preston asked.

"We wait for her to get here," Barnes said grimly. "And we expect Skynet to make one last shot at taking us down before she does."

Blair had the Blackhawk in the air when she spotted the first glimmer of light amid the forest gloom. Frowning, she started to turn to Halverson, strapped in at the portside M240, to ask what it might be.

And then, abruptly, the glow flared and spread out. By the time the Blackhawk reached the river, it had become a complete circle of blazing fire.

"That's the place!" she heard Halverson shout over the wind buffeting her through the broken windshield. "That's Bear Commons."

Mentally, Blair threw Barnes a salute. "Get ready!" she shouted. "Hope?"

"I'm ready," the girl at the starboard gun called.

Blair pitched the Blackhawk forward, sending the aircraft racing toward the circle of flame. Hope might say she was ready, but Blair knew better. She'd seen the look on the girl's face after what had happened with Valentine and Lajard, and she was anything but ready to do that again.

Blair could hardly blame her. Shooting red-eyed metal Terminators was one thing. Shooting Terminators with human faces looking back at you was something else entirely.

They were nearly to the fiery circle now. Barnes and Preston were somewhere down there, Blair knew, hopefully still alive. Jik, another Terminator with a human face, would also be down there.

Blair would have to make sure that, when the time came to open fire, Jik was on Halverson's side of the Blackhawk.

The fire was fading as Blair eased them into a hover directly above it. Much of the camo mesh itself had already burned away, revealing a network of slender cables anchoring the mesh to the treetops around the edge of the clearing.

"What now?" Halverson called.

Blair settled her hands on the controls.

"Hang on," she advised.

Shoving the throttle forward, she sent the helo into a stomach-lurching drop straight onto the mesh.

Open-area camouflage nets were designed to support their own weight, the additional pressure of an occasional curious bird, and very little else. The mesh held the helo's weight for maybe half a second before collapsing in a flurry of displaced sparks and snapped treetops. Blair was ready, hauling back on the throttle to kill the Blackhawk's drop and bring it back up to treetop height again.

"Look sharp," she shouted as she set the helo into a slow clockwise rotation around its vertical axis. "They're down there somewhere. So's Jik."

"There!" Halverson snapped. "That clump of birch trees. I can see someone."

Blair craned her neck, angling the helo a bit so that she could look past Halverson out the portside door. But the fading fire wasn't bright enough to give any clear light to the edges of the clearing.

Paradoxically, it *was* bright enough to throw flickering shadows across the ground, adding that much more visual confusion to the gloom already filling the forest.

"I don't see anyone," she called.

"He's there," Halverson insisted. "Crouching behind those birches."

"Was it my father?" Hope called from the other side of the Blackhawk.

"I couldn't tell," Halverson said with an edge of impatience. "I need to get closer."

Unfortunately, that was exactly what they couldn't do right now. Like all Resistance helos tasked with hunting ground-based Terminators, the Blackhawk had a heavily armored underside. Hovering here at treetop height, they were reasonably safe from anything Jik could be waiting to shoot at them.

But once they headed down, all bets would be off. The main cockpit skin was much thinner and more susceptible to weapons fire, and Blair didn't have even the modest protection of a windshield anymore. A single shot into her head, and all three of them would die.

"We can't get closer," she told Halverson. "Not until we know who that is."

"How the hell do you expect me to figure that out from way up here?"

And then, almost as if on cue, there was a fresh flicker of

fire from below them. Not from the birch trees Halverson had indicated, but from halfway across the clearing. The flame faltered a little, shifted position slightly—

And then flashed across the clearing to impale itself chest-high against the trunk of a big tree a couple of meters away from the birches.

"That's a fire arrow!" Halverson shouted, a note of triumph in his voice. "That's Preston—he's marked Jik for us!"

"Can you see him?" Blair called. "Can you *see* that it's Jik?"

"He's there—he's right there," Halverson confirmed excitedly. "But I can't—damn it, I can't swing this thing far enough around."

"Hang on," Blair ordered, slowing the helo's clockwise rotation and starting it turning back the other direction. "And don't lose him."

Suddenly, without warning, a burst of fire from the forest on the other side of the clearing shot across toward them. Reflexively, Barnes ducked—

And with a sharp *thunk* a flaming arrow buried its tip in a big tree two meters to Barnes's right.

Preston gasped, dropping lower as a shower of sparks rained down.

"What the—? Barnes?"

For a fraction of a second Barnes just stared at the burning arrow. What the *hell* was Jik up to?

Tearing his eyes away from the fire, he looked upward.

The chopper, which had been slowly turning as Williams searched for a target, had come to a stop. He watched, with a surge of horror, as it started turning the other direction.

Moving around to bring its portside M240 into range.

"He's suckering them," he growled. "Jik saw you light the camo net with a fire arrow, figured we might be smart enough to try marking his position with another one, and decided to get there first."

"How could we mark him?" Preston said, his voice bewildered. "We don't even know where he is."

"We do now," Barnes said, looking across the clearing to where the arrow had come from. In the fading light from the smoldering camo net, he could just make out a figure standing motionless beside one of the bigger trees.

"Shoot him," Preston urged. "Come on, *shoot*. That'll show Blair who we are."

Barnes sighed. Only it wouldn't show Williams anything of the sort. If things had been reversed, if it had been Preston who marked Jik's position with a flaming arrow, the Theta would certainly respond by opening fire toward his attackers with whatever weapons he had.

Williams would know that. Rather than getting her to hold her fire, an attack on Jik now would simply get her shooting at him and Preston that much faster.

He looked up again, his mind whirring as he tried to figure out a plan. The chopper was too high for Williams to be able to distinguish either of their faces well enough for a positive ID. Ditto for their clothing, Preston's bow, or anything else they had with them.

Their only hope was to find cover.

Only there wasn't any. Not from a machinegun firing from above.

"Barnes," Preston said, the name a sigh of resignation.

Barnes squeezed his hand around the grip of the G11. The chopper was nearly to firing position now. Five more seconds, maybe six, and they would be dead.

He had exactly that long to come up with some way to stop Williams. Any way that he could.

"Almost there," Halverson called tensely. "Come on, come on."

"Easy," Blair said, frowning out the side door as the Blackhawk continued to turn back toward firing position. She could see the figure down there now, just visible in the flickering light from Preston's fire arrow. He was standing still, possibly hoping the hunters wouldn't spot him. There was a flicker of movement a meter to his side—

"Hold it," Blair said, leaning toward the door. Was that a second figure hunkered down in the bushes? "I see someone else."

"Oh, *damn*," Halverson snarled. "I *knew* it. He got one of the T-700s working. Come on, come *on*—we're almost there."

Blair bit hard at her lip. Yes, that could indeed be a T-700 down there. It could also be a T-600, or even another Theta they hadn't yet accounted for.

It could also be a human being.

But it *had* to have been Preston who had fired that arrow. Preston had a bow, and there was no reason she could think of why Jik would have bothered to pick one up.

And if that was Jik down there, he had every reason to position his reconstructed T-700 under just enough cover to masquerade as another person in hopes of throwing Blair off track.

She huffed out a breath. It wasn't perfect, but it made more sense than any other theory.

And until and unless she got some solid reason to think otherwise, she would just have to go with it.

* * *

"We're going to die, aren't we?" Preston murmured. "They're going to shoot us down, and we're going to die."

And then, with the chopper nearly to firing position, Barnes suddenly had the answer.

Maybe. Maybe the whole thing was complete insanity that would do nothing but get them killed a little faster.

But it was all he had.

"Here," he said, shoving the G11 into Preston's hands. Taking a deep breath, he left his partial concealment and stepped directly in front of the burning arrow.

And standing straight and tall, he threw his arms out to both sides.

"You want to stop me?" he murmured toward the sky, the way he'd snarled at Blair last night from outside the chopper. "Shoot me."

And as Halverson swung the M240 onto his target, the vague figure down there stepped directly into the light and threw his arms out to both sides.

And suddenly that image, and the accompanying words, flashed up from Blair's memory.

You want to stop me? Shoot me.

"Stop!" she snapped at Halverson, twitching the Blackhawk's nose to throw off his aim. "Don't shoot!"

"What are you doing?" Halverson snarled. "That's Jik."

"That's Barnes and Preston," Blair snarled back, resettling the helo's nose and looking past Hope out the starboard door. The flaming arrow had come from somewhere over there...

And there he was. Another figure, standing beside a tree.

Waiting to enjoy the show as Blair cut down her own people.

"*That's* Jik, over there," she called back to Halverson.

"Hang on—I'll bring the helo around."

But she didn't. There was no need. Even before the words were completely out of her mouth, the starboard M240 unexpectedly roared to life, sending a long, violent stream of machinegun fire down at the shadowy figure below. Even as Blair caught her breath she saw the body jerk and spasm, then duck behind a tree and stumble out the other side. Another long burst of fire, and it crumpled to the ground.

The roar of the machinegun ended, and Blair raised her eyes from the motionless Theta to the girl hunched over the weapon.

And in the dim light she saw the tension lines in Hope's young face. The grim set to the jaw, and the dark unyielding resolve in her eyes.

Hope Preston was no longer a girl. Not even a girl hardened by a tough forest life.

Hope Preston was a warrior.

And even amid all the death and misery of the post-Judgment Day world, Blair found a distant part of herself mourning the girl's loss.

And suddenly, the perfect plan fell apart. Without warning, without reason, the sky opened up and began to rain death on him.

"No!" Jik shouted in fury and disbelief. He ducked sideways, trying to get to the shelter of the tree beside him.

But it was too late. The heavy machinegun rounds had already hammered across his side, shredding skin and bursting blood vessels and shattering bone. His left leg collapsed beneath him, pitching him back out from behind the tree and into range of the guns again. For a moment the fire faltered, and then the stream of killing lead once again opened up full fury.

No! he tried to shout again. But his voice was gone, as was most of his throat. *No! You can't do this! I'm John Connor! I'm John Connor!*

He was still trying vainly to scream that message to the distant traitors when his vision faded into eternal darkness.

CHAPTER TWENTY-SIX

"It isn't often," Connor said from the middle of the organized tangle of tubes and wires that encircled his bed, "that I get the chance to commend and chew out the same group of people for the same actions."

Kyle carefully avoided looking at Callahan and Zac. With the tension of yesterday's events behind them, and with a little catch-up on food and sleep, he could see things more clearly.

Clearly enough to see that Connor was right. On both counts.

"Let's start with the chewing out," Connor went on. "Any of you want to take a stab at that one and save me the trouble?"

Callahan cleared his throat self-consciously.

"We should never have gone down into the tunnel, sir," he said. "Not without first reporting our find."

"You shouldn't *all* have gone down anyway," Connor said, a little less severely. "Obviously, I wouldn't have wanted you to abandon an injured teammate, either. But two of you could have gone down to help Yarrow while the third came back for help."

"Yes, sir," Callahan said.

"And not just for your own sakes, either," Connor added. "If it hadn't been for Star figuring out that something was wrong and pestering everyone until we pulled a hunting team and chopper back to look for you, we could have lost many more people to those T-700s. Including all of you."

Out of the corner of his eye, Kyle saw Callahan wince.

"Yes, sir," he said in a low voice. "We understand."

"Actually, I don't think you do," Connor said, his voice still stern. "You have no idea what you wandered into down there. In fact, *we're* still figuring it out. The search teams have already found one hangar-sized chamber at the far end of the tunnel, and they think there may be more."

"Something that big survived the explosion?" Zac asked incredulously.

"Yes, and I suspect it was deliberately designed to do so," Connor said. "Skynet had an impressive array of repair and refurbishment equipment down there, plus weapons, ammunition, and explosives. And, just for good measure, we also found the radio jammer that's been making such a mess of our local communications."

"And Terminators," Kyle murmured.

"A *lot* of Terminators," Connor confirmed grimly. "We've destroyed at least a hundred T-600s and T-700s already. And as I said, we haven't even finished going through the whole place yet."

"And you said it was *designed* to survive the attack?" Callahan asked.

"So it would seem," Connor said. "Some kind of contingency redoubt, set up on the chance that the Resistance ever managed to launch a successful attack." He gestured in the direction of the tunnel. "Interestingly enough, we nearly set up camp three kilometers that way, which would have put us almost directly above the main chamber. Luckily for us, we decided we liked this spot better."

Kyle shuddered. All that equipment, all those weapons, all those Terminators... and once again Skynet had chosen to turn those resources directly against John Connor.

"That's the other lesson you should take away from this," Connor continued. "One of the two things in this world that you can depend on is Skynet's single-minded determination. Short-term and long-term both."

He gestured toward the three of them; and as he did so, the sternness faded from his face.

"Which brings me to the commendation part of this meeting," he said. "I could give you a long speech about your bravery and resourcefulness, and what your own determination did for me and everyone else in the group. But since you already know those details, it would be pretty much a waste of time. So instead, I'll just say thank you. And well done."

Kyle swallowed hard, his last memory of Yarrow hovering in front of his eyes. He'd given his life for the others, just as Marcus Wright had died saving Kyle and Connor and all of Skynet's other prisoners.

Kyle had nearly had to make that same sacrifice. Someday, he knew, he would have to do it for real. He could only hope he would meet his death as bravely as they had.

"Thank you, sir," Callahan said for all of them "We're glad we could be of service."

"As I'm sure you'll continue to be," Connor said, eyeing each of them in turn. It seemed to Kyle that his gaze lingered a bit longer on him than on the other two, but that might have been his imagination. "And to that end, effective immediately, the three of you are being transferred to Barnes's shock force. You'll be trained as a fireteam, with the goal of eventually being integrated into Echo platoon."

Kyle felt his eyes widen. A *fireteam* assignment? Already?

"I—yes, sir," Callahan said, sounding as surprised as Kyle felt. "But I thought..." He stopped.

"You thought there was a longer evaluation period," Connor finished for him. "Normally, there is. But yesterday the three of you went through the fire together. Some people don't survive that kind of challenge. Those who do come out stronger."

Connor gestured toward them. "I said a minute ago that Skynet's determination was one of the two things you could count on in this world. The other is the courage and trustworthiness of your teammates. You've already become that kind of team. All we're going to do is make it better."

"Thank you, sir," Callahan said. "We won't let you down."

"I know you won't." Connor smiled. "Now, go get some more rest. Barnes could be back at any time. And as I'm sure Reese will tell you, he can be a *very* demanding man to work for."

It had been a long day, with a short and tense night before it, and by the time Blair finally woke up she found she'd slept for nearly nine hours.

Barnes hadn't slept as long, she discovered as she emerged from Preston's house. Neither, apparently, had anyone else in town. Aside from Preston and Hope, the rest of Baker's Hollow had already gathered their most vital belongings and disappeared, melting into the woods, heading God only knew where as quickly as they could.

Preston and Hope had stayed behind to say good-bye. So, to Blair's surprise, had Halverson.

And as they all said their farewells, Blair noted the subtle but real change had taken place in the three of them and their relationships.

Preston had gained an edge of quiet steel, his leadership no longer based solely on compromise and cooperation but now with a dose of confidence and gut-level belief in himself and his decisions. Halverson, in contrast, had toned down some of his brashness, with perhaps a grudging new respect for Preston.

And both men were just a little bit afraid of Hope.

The walk back to the Blackhawk was very quiet. Barnes never said a word along the way, and for her part Blair was still too tired and drained to feel like talking.

Certainly not with a man who still hated her.

They were in the air, heading over the mountains toward San Francisco, when Barnes finally spoke.

"You figure they blame us for what happened?" he asked.

Blair nodded. "Probably."

"Yeah," Barnes said. "'Course, there wouldn't be anyone left to do any blaming if we hadn't showed up. Sooner or later, Jik and the others would have killed them."

"I know," Blair said. "I think Preston and the others do too, down deep."

"Maybe."

For a moment Barnes was silent.

"You made a fool of me, you know."

Blair frowned at the sudden change of subject. "What?"

"Back at the camp, before the San Francisco attack," he said. "When you gave me that phony order from Connor so that you could help Wright escape."

"That wasn't my intention," Blair replied carefully. Even to her own ears it sounded pretty weak.

It obviously did to Barnes, too.

"Doesn't matter whether you meant it or not," he said. "You still made me look like a fool." He paused again. "But you were right."

Blair threw a frown at him.

"About what?"

"Wright," he said. "I've been thinking about it, and about the Thetas here. Valentine didn't want to do what Skynet wanted, but she still did it. Oxley seemed to really like the power he had. Jik—I don't know what the hell Jik was thinking."

"I think he really believed he was John Connor," Blair said.

"Could be," Barnes said. "You see what I'm saying. None of them, not even Valentine, could break the programming. Not without an arrow in the back of the head."

"They couldn't break from Skynet," Blair murmured as she saw where Barnes was going with this. "But Marcus did."

"Marcus did," Barnes acknowledged. "He broke his programming, saved Connor's life, and helped us get all those prisoners out so we could blow the place."

"Yes, he did all that," Blair said, a fresh lump forming in her throat. "But that was all him. What did you mean that I was right?"

Barnes snorted. "You were right about *him*," he growled. "You saw something—damned if I know what—that told you he could be trusted. If you hadn't seen that and done something about it—" He shook his head. "I don't know how it would have turned out. But probably a hell of a lot worse."

He waved a hand. "So anyway, there it is," he went on. "You wanted to know why I was mad at you. Now you do." He shrugged. "And I guess if he was worth your trust, he was worth mine. I guess."

"Yes, he was," Blair agreed. "As it turned out. And I *am* sorry about making you look... you know."

"Forget it," Barnes said. "I asked Preston why he put up with Halverson. He said keeping his town running was worth a little wounded pride. I figure if he can do it, so can I."

"I think sometimes we forget what's really important," Blair said. "Right now, the important thing is that taking out all three of the Baker's Hollow Thetas may persuade Skynet to abandon the project."

"Just in time, too," Barnes muttered.

"What do you mean?"

He hissed out a sigh. "I mean we were wrong," he said heavily. "You and me, when we were trying to figure out the test sequence for the Thetas. We got the part about Lajard and the others infiltrating a bunch of humans, and the part about Jik coming in with a whole set of false memories. But we missed something."

"What?"

"The bit where Skynet snatches someone from town—someone everyone already knows—and puts in a replacement," Barnes said. "You didn't see it, but there was a brand-new Theta half buried inside the cabin that the H-K wrecked. I don't think it was ready to go yet, but it looked damn close. The body they were using wasn't perfect, but they'd done a lot of work on the face."

"Who was it supposed to be?" Blair asked. "Could you tell?"

"Oh, yeah," Barnes said, an edge of cold darkness to his voice. "It was going to be Hope Preston."

A hard knot settled into Blair's stomach.

"We've got to win this thing, Barnes," she said quietly. "We've got to beat Skynet back, and we've got to break it and every single one of its Terminators into scrap metal."

"No argument here," Barnes agreed. "I wonder what it'll come up with next."

Blair took a deep breath. She and Barnes would probably never be friends, she knew.

But now that the barrier she'd unwittingly built between them was gone, they could once again be comrades in arms.

And she could settle for that. In the midst of the fires of war, she could settle for that.

"I don't know," she said. "But I'm sure we'll find out."

The End

ABOUT THE AUTHOR

TIMOTHY ZAHN has been writing science fiction for over thirty years. In that time he has published thirty-nine novels, nearly ninety short stories and novelettes, and four collections of short fiction. Best known for his eight *Star Wars* novels, he is also the author of the *Quadrail* series, the *Cobra* series, and the young-adult *Dragonback* series. He is currently working on the third book of the *Cobra War* series and a ninth *Star Wars* novel.

The Zahn family lives on the Oregon coast, where only a tsunami can ruin a perfect day.

ALSO AVAILABLE FROM TITAN BOOKS:

TERMINATOR SALVATION
THE OFFICIAL MOVIE NOVELIZATION

ALAN DEAN FOSTER

Judgment Day has come to pass and Skynet has destroyed much of the world's population. In this post-apocalyptic world, Resistance fighter John Connor and teenager Kyle Reese continue their brutal fight for survival.

The incredible story of the hit movie!

ISBN: 9781848560857